*The Blue Notebook*

*The Blue Notebook*

Michel Tremblay

translated by Sheila Fischman

Talonbooks

Talonbooks
P.O. Box 2076, Vancouver, British Columbia, Canada V6B 3S3
www.talonbooks.com

Typeset in Adobe Garamond and Tribute and printed and bound in Canada.

First Printing: 2009

The publisher gratefully acknowledges the financial support of the Canada
Council for the Arts; the Government of Canada through the Book Publishing
Industry Development Program; and the Province of British Columbia through
the British Columbia Arts Council for our publishing activities.

*Le cahier bleu* by Michel Tremblay was first published in French in 2005 by
Leméac éditeur in Montreal. We acknowledge the financial support of the
Government of Canada through the National Translation Program for Book
Publishing, for our publishing activities.

**Library and Archives Canada Cataloguing in Publication**

Tremblay, Michel, 1942–
[Cahier bleu. English]
   The blue notebook / Michel Tremblay ; translated by Sheila Fischman.

Translation of: Le cahier bleu.
ISBN 978-0-88922-619-7

   I. Fischman, Sheila II. Title. III. Title: Cahier bleu. English.

PS8539.R47C3213 2009          C843'.54          C2009-902844-1

*I know the answer, it's the question that I'm looking for.*

Rohinton Mistry
*A Fine Balance*

*Nothing is more harmful than untimely wisdom.*

Rita Monaldi and Francesco Sorti
*Secretum*

*To my artist, writer, composer, performer, director and designer friends whose contributions made the spring and summer of 1968 such a fascinating and exciting time.*

*Special thanks to Louise Latraverse who told me about the expression* folie circulaire.

*Prologue*

Hesitantly, she goes over to what she likes to call her "writing nook." A simple wooden table pushed in front of the window that looks out onto Place Jacques-Cartier. She found it at the Salvation Army at the corner of Guy and Notre-Dame the previous summer when she was looking for a bed. It's an old pine table that must have been used as a dresser or as a stand that held the doll collection of a little girl who is now an old woman or, who knows, maybe has been dead for ages. The chair was a little rickety; Jean-le-Décollé had glued a piece of wood to one leg. She can't see outside when she is working because the table is too low, but in the morning the sun caresses her hands and if the rest of the day is cloudy, the light falls onto her notebook in shifting sheets. She says it's better that way. That she's not so distracted by what's going on in the street. That she is better able to concentrate on what she has to say. It's where she wrote her red notebook; it's where she will start the blue one. This very morning. With pounding heart and trembling hands.

She places her felt pens on her left and takes the brand new notebook out of the glazed brown paper bag on which you can read in Gothic letters, Dupuis Frères Limitée. She folds the bag in four, an old habit of her mother's who can't stand waste and who ended up during spring or fall cleaning with drawers full of wrapping paper, ribbons, bows of every colour, useless and cumbersome, that eventually, reluctantly, she would throw out.

She goes out of her way not to be like her mother, but she still has that weird and rather silly habit that makes her roommates howl with laughter: it's a thriftiness they aren't familiar with and they laugh at her shamelessly. She grumbles that it's in her genes, that she can't open the garbage can to dump a bag that might be useful some day. And when the opportunity arises, when one of the three drag queens with whom she shares the big apartment on Place Jacques-Cartier needs *some tissue paper and swishes into her room with a gift to wrap or an object to camouflage, with her lips curved in a victorious little smile she opens her bottom drawer, plunges into the bric-à-brac and scoops up armfuls of colourful streamers and shimmering crepe paper.*

*She runs her right hand over the notebook. The cover is a beautiful bright blue with a lot of red in it, not one of those washed-out lapis-lazuli shades that she calls Blessed Virgin blue because of the robe on the statues of her childhood. She didn't pick it, it jumped out at her. As if it were meant for her. She was rummaging in a rack of notebooks of every colour on the mezzanine of Dupuis Frères where the stationery supplies are, she didn't like any of them, thought they were all ugly, then all a sudden, just as she was starting to lose hope, she found it, the last one in its pile, the blue she loves, the blue she was looking for. Immediately she thought about the biscuits in* Alice in Wonderland *that were marked: Eat me! If she had seen: Take me! on the notebook she wouldn't have been surprised. It was her notebook, it was waiting for her, she knew that right away, and now she is stroking it before she opens it because she realized a few minutes ago when she was eating breakfast that it was time to start writing the third installment of her confessions. The one about love, its trials and tribulations, its surprises and doubts.*

*Especially its doubts.*

*For the first time, she doesn't know how it will end, because she's still living it. Sometimes she even feels she's getting lost, drowning in it. The other two notebooks she wrote after the fact, when everything was over, dealt with, to explain to herself what had happened. This time, what she has to record isn't finished, is still ongoing, still alive in her, it's gnawing away at her and as she attacks the first page she doesn't know what will be on the last.*

*She opens the notebook. She likes to hear the spine crack. Runs her hand over the fold to make sure that it will stay open. Uncaps her first felt pen. Before, she'd always used a ballpoint, but she'd seen Janine, at the Sélect, write her bills with one, which the waitress claimed never made smudges and didn't need a lot of pressure. She bought one, liked its fluidity, the soft rustling sound it made on the paper, its dark black ink, its soft plastic tube, and she decided to use it for starting her blue notebook. She bought two more because she hates running out of ink in the middle of a page and now here she is, ready to begin.*

*But is she sure that she's ready to write about it? She feels familiar butterflies somewhere in the region of her stomach. Certain recent memories come back to her, tangled, confused, scraps of painful conversations, beautiful fragrant images, some nights spent sobbing, other nights of nearly unbearable pleasure. Will she be able to separate what's important from anecdotes not worth dwelling on? Most importantly, will she be able to present a portrait of Gilbert, to express who he is, everything he has given her, everything he's taken from her, his gentle roughness in bed and his nonchalance everywhere else?*

*Gilbert Forget and his fingertips worn down by his guitar strings, his shaggy hair, his elephant jeans, his mauve or lemon yellow T-shirts, the scent of patchouli that follows him everywhere and the peppery smell of his pale, pale skin … Yes, that, everything physical about him, she knows she'll get that down because there's something of a caricature about him that will be fairly easy to capture with a few good sharp strokes of a pen, but what it hides, the soul of Gilbert Forget, his essence, the depth of his wounds and the vastness of his love for her—so he claims: will she be able to put all that into words? She was able to express the shame of the first part of her life in her black notebook, her adventures the year before with the creatures from the Boudoir in her red notebook, but to execute a complete portrait of one man, the one moreover who has introduced her to physical pleasure and the boundless joy of feeling that she mattered to someone—does she have the talent? Will the blue notebook be the frontier that she'll never be able to cross? She feels at once excited at the thought of trying and worried about not being able to realize this project that is now beginning, that is so close to her heart.*

*A crazed flock of birds flies over Place Jacques-Cartier, singing their little hearts out. Her paternal grandmother would have called it the birds' wedding. It's funny, usually a birds' wedding happens in the*

13

*evening, around sunset. What's wrong with them this morning, criss-crossing the sky as if it were evening? Is it a good omen? Or a bad one? She really doesn't want to burden herself with superstitions, get lost in conjecture before she even starts, so she bends her head over the blue notebook and starts to write.*

# Part One

## *L'amour est un enfant de bohème ...*

The fall of the Boudoir was spectacular, the debacle shocking.

We were expecting it, of course, we knew that once Expo 67 was over, the city empty of tourists, the party of the century enjoying its final excesses, Fine Dumas's bar couldn't survive: too chic for the neighbourhood, too expensive for the locals, too pretentious for what's generally offered by the Main, that paradise for the poor and for lost souls briefly elevated, thanks to the mere presence of the Boudoir and perhaps for its greater misfortune, to the status of absolute must and meeting place for the well-to-do of the entire world. For us, Expo was a wonderful diversion from which we all profited, it's true, a golden gift from the gods, an opportunity, as the boss herself put it so well, to "enrich ourselves," at least for a while, and permission to live openly for six months with no fear of the authorities who for once, it seemed, were protecting, not persecuting us. Six months that sped by too quickly in a mind-blowing swirl of endless parties, of indescribable binges and avalanches of dollars that seemed as if they'd never stop.

But when the hour rang, when the time came to accept the fact that overnight the Boudoir had become obsolete, it was a shock for us all, though we'd been talking about it during the whole month of September because the city was more and more deserted by foreigners and the Boudoir was emptying out before our eyes. Around the time when Expo closed, even the weekends were depressing. There was less money, less fun too. Yes, we talked about it, but it was as if we were refusing to understand what we were saying or to see the true consequences for each of us of the Boudoir's closing and the implications for the life of the Main: poverty that once again was lying in wait for us, the return to the street for the drag queens, who'd got used to working inside, sheltered from bad weather and non-believers, the restaurant for me, though waitressing didn't interest me any more.

As for Fine Dumas, who may have been the biggest dreamer of us all, the most unrealistic at any rate, she spent her evenings sucking on her cigarette holder while pretending not to hear what was being said in the bar and not to see the collapse of her establishment. We all suspected that she was hiding piles of money somewhere, under her mattress or in some big suitcase because she didn't trust banks, that she must have made arrangements for her immediate future; but we also knew that she couldn't stand to be all alone in her apartment after reigning as absolute monarch over Montreal-by-night for more than a year. Like Gloria, the South American music specialist who'd ended up in a tiny apartment above a garage on Fullum Street after experiencing the beginnings of glory during the fifties, and as a result nearly went crazy.

It's impossible to picture Fine Dumas slumped in front of her TV set with a bag of chips in one hand and a Pepsi in the other. Fine Dumas is a creature of the night just like Babalu or big Paula-de-Joliette; she needs neon lights and the smell of alcohol to survive, and shutting her away at home would be condemning her to a slow and cruel death—even with the small fortune she'd no doubt made from the sale of her business.

And so between a boss who listened to no one and employees who managed not to understand the real implications of what they said, the final weeks of Expo languished in shared boredom until one night we were facing the inevitable: an empty bar and an abandoned brothel. It was a gorgeous Saturday in October, the air was soft as silk, autumn had not yet brought out its grand symphony of loud colours, the city was experiencing one last thrill of pleasure before the endless months of winter. And we'd all come up against a brick wall.

When the boss asked us to meet in the bar, we realized at once that something irreversible was about to happen, that the cataclysm was going to be set off, and a few handkerchiefs were extricated from see-through plastic purses and decrepit makeup kits that had lived too long. Babalu in particular seemed devastated already.

"What's going to happen to us without the Boudoir, everybody? I'm sure as hell not going to peddle my ass at the corner of the Main and St. Catherine! No way! Can the rest of you do that? Not me!"

She blew her nose, wiped away the tears that were drawing black lines on her chubby, fake Brigitte Bardot cheeks, she ran her fingers over her goose-pimply arms. I understood her. I understood all of them. The life that awaited them, the life they'd all known before the opening of the Boudoir, was shot through with many and various dangers, humiliating medical problems, over-long nights, excessively cold or hot, interrupted by pitiful and infinitely sad affairs that would profit some minor mobsters who were unscrupulous and heartless, deaf, mute and blind, ready for anything, especially the worst, all for the love of one measley dollar. For the six drag queens who'd taken up so much space in my life, the Boudoir had represented an unhoped-for salvation and they'd clung to it, hoping it would never end, though they knew perfectly well that it would only be around as long as Expo. And now the end was there, inevitable. We were walking straight to the gallows, heads high but with rage in our hearts.

Moored to the end of her bar like a ship in distress to its wharf in a storm, Fine Dumas had assumed the expression of a tragic actress, reserved for disastrous evenings when we passed through the bead curtains, maybe for the last time, as we all knew perfectly well, leaving the back room of the Boudoir where we'd spent such a wonderful summer. I had in any case, I who'd never dreamed of making so much money by having so much fun. I was surrounded by the brothel's six "girls": Babalu, Greta-la-Vieille, Greta-la-Jeune, Jean-le-Décollé, Nicole Odeon and Mae East. Wearing what I called my maître d' outfit—my green sequined dress and my red pumps—I was the one who looked like the madam. But gazing down from my four feet and a couple of inches, I was not reassured. Mimi-de-Montmartre and Greluche, the two waitresses, were already sitting close to Madame, over a beer they were allowing to get warm because the urge to drink, to get drunk in fact, wouldn't come until later, after the farewell speech we were all dreading. Fat Sophie, the Boudoir's musician, was still bent over the piano, her vast back nearly as wide as the keyboard as she tinkled a sad song. The Duchess didn't witness this distressing scene because the boss had told her some weeks earlier that she no longer needed her, not even on Saturday night. So the Duchess was the first victim of the wreck of the Boudoir. I wished she'd been there that night, because only she would have been able to ease the tense atmosphere, but Madame had forgotten or hadn't thought it was a good idea to advise her.

For once, the boss removed her cigarette holder from her mouth to speak to us. She even went so far as to stub the cigarette in an ashtray near her elbow. Several butts were still smoking there, proof positive that Fine Dumas was very nervous when you knew how much she hated dirty ashtrays.

"Sophie, leave that damn piano for once and come have a drink with the rest of us."

Fat Sophie did as she was told, after she'd closed the cover of her piano—something she never did. In her gesture there was a finality that devastated me.

Once the pianist was sitting at the bar, Fine Dumas regarded each of us in turn, and this time no one looked down.

I can't repeat precisely what she told us because I don't remember. I had to choose to forget it or I wouldn't have felt like coming back to it. But the fact is that I won't be hanging around here. It's too sad. And the reason for the existence of this blue notebook is not the fate of the Boudoir; the bulk of what I have to say is elsewhere, in what happened afterwards, and I don't want to linger over that sad, disastrous evening.

I will only quote the beginning of her speech to indicate the tone in which she spoke to us. After she'd lit another cigarette and released into the air-conditioned bar a curl of grey smoke, the one we'll remember most because it marked a major turning point in our existence, she looked at her watch, then declared as if she had to leave right away, or even that she had an important meeting, "The Boudoir has been sold."

Instead of looking at Fine Dumas while she was speaking, I studied the reactions of the nine individuals who'd been my fellow-workers for a year and a half, whom I would now have to abandon. I'd left everything behind to launch myself along with them into the only truly great adventure in my brief life; with them I'd built a world of illusion that had been somewhat ridiculous as an attempt to create something big with inadequate means; I had been handed the money they'd earned by selling a quick trip to paradise to passing strangers they would forget as soon as they were out the door; I had laughed—champagne glass in hand—with people I didn't understand a word of; I'd been at the centre of a perpetual party that had lasted a year, in the company of a merry gang of lunatics, outrageous fake women I'd been surprised to discover I adored; and now it would all be undone and disappear because the person in charge of the premises was too proud to bring her prices into line with those charged elsewhere on the Main.

Ever since she'd opened the Boudoir, Fine Dumas had claimed that she would rather shut it down than give a discount to nobodies from the Main, *noblesse oblige*; that her Boudoir, her lifelong dream, was and would remain an *exquisite* and *exclusive* place, even if that meant tearing it down post-Expo, which was what she was getting ready to do, with no remorse—I was sure of it—for the bodies that she'd leave on the pavement of St. Lawrence Boulevard. Had she thought about us even once when she'd made that important decision? Maybe. But not as individuals whose lives would be turned upside down by her decision, she was too self-centered for that. She must have thought of us as some vague and shifting entity that had existed before her and would continue to exist afterwards, and told herself, sure she was acting in good faith,

"Let them go back where they came from! I pulled them out of the gutter for a while, now it's somebody else's turn!"

Even me, a humble waitress she'd rescued from the Sélect when I hadn't asked anyone for anything? Very likely. Nothing is safe from a selfish person who'll use any means to shed her guilty feelings, to get out of an awkward situation. And selfish was Fine Dumas's middle name, of that we'd had plenty of proof.

My companions, all of them, were in tears. I was the only one whose eyes were dry. The boss had noticed that right away and she looked at me now and then, frowning, as if to say, "How come you aren't bawling? How come I can't get to you?"

I defied her one last time. I too had my pride.

We didn't shut down that night of course, but it was as if we had. The week-long reprieve we'd been given stretched out into a heavy atmosphere like the end of a vacation: six jobless drag queens putting on shows in a deserted bar; two idle waitresses killing time by slicing lemons that would never be used and would dry up on their plastic plates; the boss, predictably, had gone back to drinking; but the midget hostess, instead of twiddling her thumbs, and out of bravado, had bought a pile of paperbacks and had taken on Zola's Rougon-Macquart. The first volume, *La fortune des Rougon*, she'd thought was very complicated but she stuck with it and kept on reading; it gave her something to concentrate on besides what was in store for her the following week. And for the rest of her life. The tangled destiny of the Rougon and Macquart families helped take her mind off that of the little Poulin girl who at that moment had nothing ahead of her, especially not a desire to start her life over again. For the third time in four years.

There weren't really any farewells because we'd decided that I would go on sharing the apartment on Place Jacques-Cartier with three of the Boudoir's drag queens, for the time being anyway, and that through them I would hear about the others. I would hardly ever see them, but I'd always know what they were up to, what had become of them. Mimi-de-Montmartre and Greluche had got jobs at the Coconut Inn, Maurice-la-Piasse being only too happy to recycle some former employees of his old rival, Fine Dumas, who'd come to him for help (we mustn't forget that since the street belonged to him, Fine Dumas's six girls would henceforth ply the sidewalks of the Main to his profit and under his "protection").

Fat Sophie dropped out of circulation overnight; the only thing I know for sure is that she didn't go back to the Auberge du Canada where she'd worked for so long: I dropped in several times to check, but no one in the place knew where she was. People claimed that she had not even paid them a visit after the Boudoir closed. Eventually I believed them. She melted into the landscape and nothing was ever heard of her again. It was music that lost out because Sophie was extremely talented. But perhaps she plays for herself in an apartment somewhere that is huge and generous like her. Or so I hope.

As for Fine Dumas, the story going around was that she'd bought a house on Melrose Street in Notre-Dame-de-Grâce and was enjoying life in the shadow of a never-empty bottle of Scotch. But my three roommates were circulating a very different version. What they said was that no sooner had the Boudoir closed than she'd gone to see Betty Bird, who also ran a brothel but a more "traditional" one, and that she hadn't been greeted with open arms: no association possible, she'd blown it, in the past year she'd pissed off too many people in the red light district. No one in the neighbourhood wanted anything to do with her. She'd laughed at them long enough. Never again. Ever. Fine Dumas took it without flinching, head high and cigarette-holder erect. And of course she'd sworn to get revenge. But I doubt that Fine Dumas would enjoy playing the Count of Monte Cristo. Because booze will probably wipe out any vague desire for a counter-attack or reprisals. Will we hear about her some day, will she resurface like the genuine survivor she claims to be? I have no idea. But I hope that if revenge is what she wants, she'll come back in triumph!

It's funny, I sometimes have a dream that may sound ludicrous but that reassures and consoles me. I imagine Fat Sophie sitting at her instrument in a vast, brightly-lit, white room. An enormous grand piano, black and impressive, with a German name printed in gold Gothic letters above the keyboard. She is playing South American music, joyous, rhythmical, spirited, something ravishing from a 1940s musical comedy—picture Ima Sumac or Carmen Miranda hiding nearby, getting ready to make her entrance—then all at once the mood changes, the music becomes slow and sensual, the lights are low and Fine Dumas, more regal than ever, appears in one of her most stunning monochrome outfits, white perhaps, because it's the most luminous colour. She stands in the curve of the piano, bows with fake humility, like a great star, rests her right hand on the edge of the instrument as if she were taking possession of it, and sings. I know that this dream is for me, to meet my need for harmony, and that I'd be prepared to perpetuate this idyllic vision forever, simply to persuade myself that all is well for those two people I love. But I'm never taken in for very long by my own subterfuge, and visions much less wonderful quickly come to mind. Poverty for Sophie. Alcoholism for Fine. Loneliness for both.

As for me, I decided to take some time for reflection before I dragged myself to the feet of Nick, chief cook and manager of the Sélect, to see if he'll take me back. If he still wants anything to do with me. And so I spent the winter holed up in the apartment, reading the Rougon-Macquart, waiting on my three roommates, preparing tasty little dishes that they wolfed down at impossible times because now that the Main had gone back to what it had been before Expo, Maurice worked his "protégées" to the bone because he wanted to make up for the money he'd lost. That was how I learned that Babalu had nearly died from bronchitis in November and that big Paula-de-Joliette had been laid low by a double pleurisy in January. Maurice had put them back on the street as soon as they were better and the winter had ended in recriminations by my three friends who, several times a week and in increasingly morbid detail, planned the death of the dictator of the Main.

It was at the end of that winter spent vegging out, or rather the beginning of the next spring, because I remember that the snow was gone and that I was wearing for the first time a pair of lemon-yellow shoes, that Gilbert Forget entered my life officially, after a brief appearance during Expo.

My relationship with drugs has always been tinged with indifference. Not that they were lacking in the apartment! My three roommates often brought home from the Boudoir, or later on from the street, half-smoked joints or tiny cubes of hashish wrapped in aluminum foil they left lying around for days, and that I would eventually put in the garbage when it seemed that they'd forgotten them. They didn't overdo it, the proof being that they sometimes didn't remember if they had any, but Jean-le-Décollé often said that it relaxed him and helped him get the kind of sleep he needed after a rough night on the job. Today, I suspect that Jean indulges in things stronger than grass or hash because the Main is getting tougher before our very eyes, and a prostitute's life is more and more perilous, but that's another story ...

Still, after a few inconclusive attempts—grass made me laugh too much and hash affected me like a sleeping pill—I'd decided to stay away and to stick to good old booze, cause of my family disasters, of which I was nearly as suspicious and had as little to do with as possible. Besides, I hate losing control over what I say or do and my three friends were undeniable proof that artificial paradises, while agreeable for those who visit them, make them totally ridiculous in the eyes of their fellow-humans, so I chose to pretend indifference and abstained. I was often accused of being *square* but I replied that I'd would rather be *square* in my own parlour and alive, than in my grave with a rosary wrapped around my wrists and wads of cotton batting in my cheeks.

When Nicole, Jean and Mae were so stoned that they rambled on about their unhappy childhoods or the piggishness of men and didn't know what they were saying and you couldn't make sense of it, I would retire to my room and try not to hear their pissing and moaning or their laughter, which was too forced to be genuine.

I had adored sharing the apartment with the drag queens from the Boudoir, maybe because I worked there, too, because in a sense they were my fellow workers, but ever since I'd practically become their maid—in fact since they'd gone back to the street—they were tougher and nastier, the life imposed on them made them harder to get along with, less fun to be with. The abject nature of their relations with the johns on the street after the near-opulence of the Boudoir—especially, the quality of its clientele—the dangers that had multiplied, the hours they'd spent in the cold in January or downpours in March made them more cynical. Now that they'd known both sides of their profession they understandably didn't want to go back to the life they'd thought was behind them and that now was being imposed on them for a second time without their consent. I sensed that it might be a good idea to think about leaving before things between us became toxic and we reached the point of no return, because I hoped with all my heart that I would continue to love my three roommates.

But where would I go?

I didn't want to dwell on that either, not right away at any rate. I would ride it out and try to be more understanding, more patient with my friends. I concentrated on their funny side, which got me every time, on their wit that was still so distinctive and compelling, I tried to see life from their point of view, I asked about the Duchess—I missed her so much—I avoided talking about Tooth Pick, their unofficial pimp, for fear of seeing them explode in curses, I talked about how many tricks they turned, about money, about meals skipped, I turned up the heat when I went to bed so that they'd come home at dawn to a cozy apartment, I overdid it and they finally realized it and maybe started to question the implications of my presence among them.

My first meeting with Gilbert verged on the absurd.

It was during the Boudoir's boom-time last July. That morning, I woke up early and couldn't get back to sleep so I'd decided to go to Morgan's on St. Catherine Street West to buy the fishnet stockings I needed badly but had put off buying from week to week because I didn't have time. I hadn't been downtown for months and I didn't know if the festive atmosphere of Expo had spread to the heart of the city.

I was delighted to see, strolling along St. Catherine Street, a motley crowd decked out in clothes of every colour—including the inevitable families of overly cautious American families I mentioned earlier in my red notebook, all dressed in identical outfits of the same colour so they wouldn't get lost in the crowd. I saw some very beautiful human specimens, too, types I'd only seen in books: magnificent, regal-looking African women in shimmering robes; Asians with serious expressions and supple gaits; extremely elegant men wearing something other than the inevitable jeans or the cheap suit that seemed to form the basis of the average North American wardrobe. I heard all sorts of languages being spoken, from the most guttural to the most melodious, and even the perfumes given off by this crowd were different, not as sugary as the ones worn by men and women here.

So I was strolling along and looking all around me, delighted to breathe in air saturated with odours from all over the world, when I saw approaching me a wacky individual—I tried to come up with another word to describe my first impression of Gilbert Forget, but wacky is the right one—a perfect model of the new man of the 1960s, shaggy-haired, sloppy, scarily thin, with a beard like Captain Haddock and way too much self-confidence for me. A perfume that was new to me preceded him from quite a distance (later, I'd learn that it was patchouli), it smelled of damp, crumbly soil in which something is rotting.

And he was accompanied by two enormous black dogs that drooled while they inspected me, as if they were considering me for their next meal. They could have polished me off in no time and I had no desire to end my days lying on the sidewalk in Phillips Square, devoured by two mad dogs belonging to an American beatnik who'd come here for Expo and a good time.

I don't know why, but he thought I was Anglophone. And because I assumed he was American, it's not surprising that our first conversation took place in broken English. Around a misunderstanding.

Why did he choose to ask me? Later he claimed that right away he'd thought I was cute, thought it was the best approach, but I didn't believe him. Actually, I didn't want to believe him, I assumed he'd thought I was a pot-head like him.

So he approached me, holding back his dogs because they seemed a little too interested in me. They'd have gladly chased me down the alleys of Phillips Square, and it was obvious that they'd have rather fought than share my remains. The combined odours of patchouli and unwashed dog turned my stomach, but I told myself that I had to be polite with strangers and I smiled at the face that was bending down towards me, quite handsome when seen up close, very handsome in fact. Intelligent. Open. With two irresistible dimples like parentheses on either side of his spectacularly gorgeous mouth.

When he spoke I thought that he had an odd accent. I was too much under his spell though to realize that it was the same as mine when I speak English.

*"Good morning, ma'am! What a glorious day!"*

I looked him straight in the eyes. Big. Blue. Irresistible.

*"Glorious, I don't know, but it is a nice one ..."*

Idiot! Keep that up and he'll go away sooner! He's dangerous. No small talk with him!

He ran his hand over his beard and I saw a few toast crumbs fly into the morning air. Then, without further ado, he jumped to the heart of the matter.

*"Would you happen to know where I could find some good grass?"*

And yes, I blush as I admit it, I thought he was looking for a lawn where his dogs could run! A lost tourist who's tired of watching his animals relieve themselves within sight of everybody in downtown Montreal and is now looking for a big lawn where they can also stretch their legs.

I stepped back to avoid the suspect breath of the dogs and answered as politely as I could, *"Yes! There's a big mountain right in the middle of the city! It's called Mount Royal. Just go up Park Avenue, you can't miss it! Plenty of grass there for them to run around!"*

He gave me a funny look, I saw something dawn on him that I didn't get and he chortled in a way that I should have found insulting—he was laughing at me, after all!—but it made its way inside me like myriad little cries of joy that tickled me. He was having fun, but not at my expense. Or yes, it was, but not in a nasty way. The dogs, used to his laughter I imagine, had started to wag their tails at their master's happiness and suddenly they didn't seem so nasty.

"You aren't Anglo, are you?"

I smiled in spite of myself.

"No. And you aren't either … "

He laughed harder, bending down to be even closer.

"And you don't know what *grass* means in English, right?"

I only knew one meaning and I told him so without thinking.

"It's *gazon,* isn't it?"

What a gorgeous smile! What spectacular eyes!

He tugged on the two leashes.

"Don't change. I love it that there are still people like you … "

And that was what infuriated me! I thought I heard in his words a hint of condescension, a streak of contempt that I couldn't imagine the cause of, and as I've often said, I hate not understanding what's happening to me. So I gave him a piece of my mind even if—and maybe because—I thought he was such a dish.

"First of all, what gives you the right to talk to me like that? And second of all, what do you mean, people like me? Midgets? I'm too short to understand what you have to say from your summit that's so high above me, is that it? So I'm small, stupid, awkward and contemptible?"

I was laying it on a little thick, I knew that, but I also felt that I'd have to be aggressive with this man whose face was way too beautiful, who'd just had to show up to make me lose control. It had never happened before and it enraged me.

"Do you treat every woman like that?"

His winning smile disappeared. He straightened up as if I'd slapped him and put on a contrite expression that I assumed, wrongly, was phony.

"No, no, absolutely not! That isn't what I meant ... I wasn't talking about your intelligence ... "

I turned around as fast as my shaky little legs allowed.

He tried to stop me.

"Mademoiselle! Mademoiselle, let me explain ... This is all a misunderstanding!"

But I was too furious to let myself be convinced. What a pig! What arrogance! Who did he think he was?

At least he didn't run after me. Later, he confessed that he was sorry he'd let me get away. He'd been afraid I would make a scene, scream, call the police, and with what he had in his pockets, he really didn't want to be searched.

So why had he asked me about finding *grass*, in English, if he already had some on him?

To approach me, apparently. Because he thought I was pretty. To see if I came from the same "world" as him. But he'd seen right away that mine was too remote from his and reluctantly, he'd let me get away.

Meanwhile, I was furious, he'd ruined my nice day of shopping and I came home in a foul mood.

But still, I thought about that handsome face for a while before forgetting it in the swirl of events at the Boudoir every night.

*She sets her felt pen down beside the notebook.*

*Her fingers are numb. She didn't see the day go by. She barely heard her three roommates get up, walk aimlessly around the house, sing, squabble, laugh. Pop songs polluted the apartment air for a while, showers were taken, kisses dropped onto the top of her head, she heard herself say that all was well, she'd started writing again and needed peace and quiet. But she didn't answer when they asked if she was writing about Gilbert in her new notebook.*

*Jean-le-Décollé scribbled something on a scrap of paper and put it next to her without adding anything, "Do it! Spit it all out, you can do it!"*

*She's glad that she's finally been able to talk about Gilbert: first as a hazy portrait, a passing shadow, a first impression, the rest—the most important—will come later. Tomorrow in fact, because she wants to deal as soon as possible with the nub of the intrigue that propelled her into the arms of the much-too-handsome guy who'd turned her life into a nightmare as much as he had into ... into what? Into nirvana, to use one of his favourite words? Yes, she'd experienced nirvana, but in small pieces, by fits and starts, between waves of anxiety and questioning. A nirvana whose existence she'd never had a hint of before, that now she fears will never come back. Where is Gilbert right now? Crying over her, as he claims, a prisoner of his strange illness, or consoling himself in some artificial paradise or other, one that is more or less dangerous? She smiles in spite of herself. A year ago, who would have said that she would be thinking that way about a man she had abandoned and that she would make him suffer?*

*She shuts the notebook, runs her hand over the blue cover.*

*Tomorrow she'll go back to waitressing at the Sélect and the beautiful and terrible events it had set off. In the meantime, she has some chicken fried rice to prepare from the previous day's leftovers. The three drag queens eat as if they're still stoned before they leave for work and, for her, it is very important to feed them well. They work themselves to death in an impasse they'll never escape and the least she can do is make sure they eat properly.*

*She glances out the window. The sky has long since been empty. No birds' wedding, maybe it will come back at sunset.*

The waitress who replaced me at the Sélect at the end of 1966 was called Marguerite and she didn't last long. After her came a whole string of girls with a little or a lot of experience, all of them pleasant and full of good will, but none exactly right for the job. Not according to the customers, who thought they were too slow or not polite enough, or the employees—in particular Janine, the other night waitress—who thought they were sloppy and clumsy. From day one the poor girls didn't have a chance and they left seething with anger because it was a job that paid well, especially during the six months of Expo.

Then there was Nick. Every time I dropped in to the restaurant, he took my hand in his big hairy paw and told me how much he missed me. He would blow his nose, wipe his eyes with his dirty apron. He'd sputter a little while he spoke. I didn't altogether believe him, no one is irreplaceable, I know that, and Nick has the gift of the gab, but still, it was nice to be told that I was. Especially by the person who a few years ago had been so reluctant to try me out as a waitress, to whom I'd had to prove that I could wait on tables despite my peculiar physique. I may have been the first midget waitress in Montreal and he was as proud of that as I was. To make him happy then I told him that I missed his cooking— which was far from true, the mere thought of his spaghetti with smoked meat turned my stomach—but it brought tears to his eyes because it made him happy when people liked his food.

"If you ever want to come back, Céline, just say the word. Give me a call and you'll be back here in your cute little outfit. I've held onto it for you, it's in your locker … "

I went to check, once, to see if he was bluffing. My waitress outfit was there all right, folded carefully in what Nick called my locker—actually just a shelf in one corner of the kitchen—the little cap sitting on top like a crown, the apron rolled up tight so it wouldn't crease. With time it had got greasy but there was no permanent damage, the uniform was still wearable. It had warmed my heart and I'd thought to myself that if I ever felt the need, if life tricked me into going back where I had no desire to go, I wouldn't hesitate to ask Nick to rescue me.

I was on top of things just then, money was pouring in, I would never have imagined that what I thought was just an attack of nostalgia would one day become reality.

Then the Boudoir was shut down and I decided to live on my savings.

My three roommates, because they spent their money as it came in, were forced to go back to the street to sell their "charms."

After spending six jobless months playing sympathetic den-mother to three adult men who weren't very rational or mature, I felt it was time to go back to earning my living. Or rather, to go to work. For something to do. Because I still had money. Lots. Enough to last a long time, but I was bored. The enjoyable side of spending long evenings alone, doing nothing or making progress with the Rougon-Macquart, had soon enough worn thin and I was looking out the window more often. My red notebook had been finished for a while, writing interested me less because nothing exciting had happened in my life since the Boudoir was shut down and I wasn't ready to tackle fiction yet. So I tried films, theatre— which I like a lot but I couldn't go every night, I'd even gone, though I hate it, I'd actually gone to a hockey game at the Forum!

Nothing worked; what I missed was human contact, direct ties with clients. Of the Sélect as much as the Boudoir. More, even, because for the most part the Boudoir's clients had been only passing shadows I couldn't understand a word of because they came from all over the world, while a good number of the Sélect's customers had become more than acquaintances, almost friends.

And I now realized that I'd been missing them all that time. But I couldn't go back to the Sélect just because I was bored!

Meanwhile, there was no end to the winter, the snow would melt, disappear, come back suddenly, soft and wet, so the apartment seemed bigger and bigger, life emptier and emptier.

And in the end I didn't have to call Nick to the rescue. It happened without my prodding. Once again, fate made the choice for me, I was manipulated by an irresistible force outside myself.

If the new night waitress at the Sélect hadn't left, throwing her apron at Janine who'd said one word too many to her, I probably wouldn't be here today, sitting in front of my blue notebook, dithering before I officially introduce the handsome Gilbert Forget, object of my woes.

Because I know that I've been vacillating since the beginning of this chapter, stalling for time, postponing Gilbert's arrival because I'm afraid. Of him. Of memories that sting too much. Of what they could do to me. When that's why I write, isn't it? To untangle, verify, understand and, in the end, choose.

Let's go then, plunge into my return to the Sélect, the anticipated happiness at being back with my old work-mates and my customers, especially the night owls I'd always liked because they'd chosen not to live their lives like everyone else and did it so casually! It's funny, my three roommates have become customers again and I feel as if I'm growing closer to them. I wasn't cut out to be their mother, they understood that as well as I did.

Tomorrow, I swear, I'm going to start!

First, I have to write a few words about my return to the Sélect or something will be missing from my story. Some of the most significant events in my affair with Gilbert happened there, so I have to set the scene before I tackle the most important part of what I want to say.

I was greeted like a queen home from exile. But I had a strange reaction to the expressions of affection and the uncertainties of my return to my old job. At first I saw everything with a kind of sense of déjà vu that left me feeling uncomfortable and slightly dazed. I was living inside a dream that came back all too often and that I'd tried to forget; everything was familiar as if I'd only left the day before—the restaurant that had stayed the same, the employees who seemed to have been there forever, customers on whom I recognized certain clothes and even the scent of the perfumes they wore—though I'd been away for nearly two years and had changed a lot during that interlude. I must have seemed less familiar to the Sélect than it seemed to me, even if my appearance was the same— as was my way of working for that matter—and it bothered me. I realized soon enough that one doesn't forget the art of waitressing and that the amount of work it took was exhausting; I kept my nose to the grindstone much more at the Sélect than I ever had at the Boudoir. The Boudoir had been a picnic; the Sélect was a job. I switched from champagne to beer with no transition and the shock was a big one. Besides, going back to square one was not my favourite activity.

The Sélect, an unchanging institution if ever there was one, was the same as it had been two years before, in every detail, from the colour of the walls to the shape of the sugar containers, while I had experienced things that had made me totally different, if not someone else. Actually our roads had never been parallel; the Sélect was in decline, like something that is old and nearly finished because its development is complete and everything must die, while I had spent those years in search of adventure, hoping for something new, something exciting, enriching, that had taken me away from the restaurant's straight and uneventful existence. I had some trouble going back to it. I was seeing things through different eyes, understanding them differently too. I was more critical and I was afraid of lapsing into condescension or even contempt, two feelings that I most condemn.

But my routine was re-established, the purring motor that had marked my actions as well as my schedule for two years had a reassuring aspect that I must have needed, before I got down to thinking about what I'd do for the rest of my life, and eventually I calmed down. Went numb would be more like it; I'd come back to the Sélect to be busy, and busy I certainly was!

As I was no longer fixing the evening meal for my three roommates, they came to the restaurant around seven or eight o'clock before taking up their posts on the Main. This gave us a semblance of family life and added a lot of excitement to rush hour: Jean-le-Décollé, Nicole Odeon and Mae East knew most of the clients and went from table to table, clinking glasses, talking loudly, flirting shamelessly. As for me, I played the tearful mother, I called them to order, pretended I was ashamed of them, and as my role of mother hen was no longer serious, everyone was happy.

Winter passed. Spring, the real spring, announced itself in skies that were not so blue but more luminous, April smelled of wind from the south, and I was beginning to wonder if I'd made the right choice—I couldn't see myself spending the summer, my favourite season, serving never-ending hamburger platters when I could afford to take a vacation—when along came the event that I've been hesitating to bring up since I started this notebook for fear of getting it wrong.

I was wearing brand-new yellow shoes that night. I'd seen them in the window of a boutique on St. Catherine Street that I don't usually go to because they never have anything in my size, neither clothes nor shoes. I was looking for something flamboyant to celebrate the return of spring, something fun and bright, heels that I would hear tapping along the pavement finally free of its coating of ice, like the Easter Sundays of my childhood, when I spotted them in the middle of all the boring new styles for the season.

You would have thought they were shoes for little girls playing grown-up because it's very rare to see such high stilettos in such a small size. Though no little girl would dare to wear those shoes where her mother could see them! They had a touch of the hooker, too, which was quite amusing. I thought to myself that they'd be the last shoes I would buy as a creature of the Main, my farewell to the world of Fine Dumas, and I stepped inside the boutique. They fit. And made me a good two inches taller! I left the store wearing them. They tapped along the cement of St. Catherine Street the way I'd hoped, promising long, hot, idle days when I would wear light summer dresses as I strolled across Montreal, which like all northern cities is only beautiful in summer. Wonderful yellow shoes for summer to scare off the last April chill.

At the Sélect they were a real hit. Jealous Janine wanted to know where I'd found them; Madeleine, after she'd sniffed them like a hunting dog, decreed that they were genuine patent leather and that they were a great bargain, lucky me; Nick and his assistant whistled their approval because they're no good at compliments, specializing instead in non-verbal communication whenever a pretty woman comes into their field of vision. All the customers talked about them, too, both the regulars and those who'd dropped in by chance.

Around ten o'clock, the first rush long since over and the late-night one still far away, I was peacefully sipping a weak cup of tea with Janine, who was complaining again about her knees which were causing her more and more pain, when the door opened to laughter and the voice of a girl belting at the top of her lungs some song about airplane propellers and airline names.

Janine rolled her eyes.

"Not them again! You look after them, I'm not up to it tonight!"

It was the merry gang who were working on a show at the Quat'Sous, a theatre on Pine Avenue, who came several times a week after rehearsal—famished, noisy, uproarious and absolutely wild. They would sweep into the Sélect, eat a lot and drink more, and usually end up bellowing in chorus some of the songs from their show, quite good from what I could hear.

Janine couldn't stand them. She claimed that they smelled of sour beer and rebellion, that they'd never accomplish a thing in their lives, just make noise along with all the other hairy lunatics like them, and that they were rude. Actually, she was the one who was disrespectful of them, who rushed them and wasn't liked. She thought they were stingy while I thought they were generous; Janine found them tiresome, while they entertained me with their nerve and their freedom, like spoiled children who were unacquainted with censorship. Actually, they treated Janine the way she treated them; she didn't accept it and suffered the consequences. She would have liked them to go elsewhere, preen themselves across the street at Chez Géracimo, but their hearts were set on the Sélect and it was obvious they had no intention of changing. Even just to tease her.

So I was the one who'd inherited them a few days earlier, regardless of whether they were in my section or Janine's. I was efficient, I served them quickly and well, they appreciated it. They had adopted me just as I'd adopted them, they asked for me as soon as they arrived, ostentatiously turning up their noses at Janine. They even called me the Pearl of the Sélect and generally presented me with tips that would have turned Janine green with envy if I'd told her. But I didn't want to make things worse kept it to myself.

Anyway, hairy they were. The guys at least, the girls looked a little more conventional. The musicians made me think of the race of new men who were being called *beatniks*, who decked themselves out as we'd never seen humans do before.

We were around the same age, but the resemblance ended there. I had just spent a year and a half in a drag queen brothel in Montreal's red light district, while they, some at any rate, had taken a three-year course at the National Theatre School, working on Molière and Shakespeare. The oldest of them, Yvon, had been working as an actor for several years and seemed to play the role of *paterfamilias*. Though our life experiences couldn't have been more different, something had clicked between us, some inexplicable affinity had settled in around the little ceremony of the evening meal, maybe because I laughed at their jokes, didn't yell at them like a prudish auntie if their stories were off-colour, and I understood their excitement at the prospect of going onstage to proclaim what they had to say rather than performing other people's ideas. They seemed to be putting together something that was vital for them, and I liked their unshakeable enthusiasm.

They spent the time talking about creativity, about the importance of expressing oneself, about culture which had to be repatriated, they reinvented the world and I was a little envious, wondering where I would be today if I'd agreed to act in *The Trojan Women* in 1966, an event that now seemed so far in the past. There would have been a different Céline Poulin I imagine, she would have developed in a direction that I can't imagine, become a Céline Poulin profoundly different from the one who for two years has been writing in notebooks of various colours about her demons and worries, a person I would have been curious to know, even for just an hour, to gauge the differences, good or bad.

What connected me to them was similar to the relationships I'd developed two years earlier with the students at the Institut des arts appliqués, when I'd replaced Madeleine, one of the waitresses on the day shift, who was sick.

I put down my cup of tea while they were shedding their coats. Janine hid in the kitchen. I'd have liked to tell her she was going too far, that surely she didn't hate them so much that she couldn't stand being around them, but I kept my mouth shut.

Robert, the curly-headed one who if I understand correctly had composed the songs for the show, seemed to be in brilliant form, roaring with laughter when I got to their table. Their tables, rather, because there were more of them than usual and they'd taken over the three large booths at the back, tossing their coats wherever and sprawling as if they were at home. The whole cast, I supposed. Louise, the singer in the group and Mouffe, Robert's girlfriend, were talking about costumes when I arrived with my order pad.

When he saw me Robert shouted, "My favourite waitress! The Pearl of the Sélect!"

And then, noticing my shoes, "The sun of St. Catherine Street!"

Everyone looked down at my shoes and I blushed at the appreciative applause.

And then I heard the remark that would turn my life upside down.

*"Good evening, ma'am! What a glorious night!"*

I recognized his voice at once, of course. And replied straightforwardly, *"Glorious, I don't know, but it's a nice night!"*

It was him all right. More handsome than ever because he'd shaved his beard and now his hairless face was even more gorgeous, his dimples more pronounced, his smile more devastating, his eyes if possible more blue, brighter anyway. I didn't know how to interpret that brightness and, later on, I regretted it ... I would have spared myself a lot of trouble ... Anyway.

He stepped over the person sitting next to him and came over to say hello. When he was standing in front of me all unfolded, I remembered how tall he was. He had to bend down to talk to me and I had to break my neck to listen.

"Together at last."

I opened my order pad, pretending to be busy.

"At last?"

He rested one buttock on the Arborite table.

"I didn't know that my grass supplier worked at the Sélect! If I had, I'd have come here before."

"I wasn't working here last summer ... And about that grass, I got it a few minutes later and I was very embarrassed ... I can be naïve but that was ridiculous ... And by the way, how are your dogs?"

"They weren't mine, they're my neighbour's. I look after them now and then ... "

There were frowns around the table, quizzical looks passed from one booth to another, knowing smiles exchanged.

Mouffe fiddled with her straight black hair, which gave her a very interesting Indian look.

"You know each other? You never told us that, Gilbert Forget!"

Gilbert. I liked his name right away. I'd never met a Gilbert before and I thought it sounded romantic. If his name had been Wilfrid, my immediate future might have been less complicated.

Louise straightened her little round glasses as she made a show of opening her menu.

"Gilbert is an unfathomable mystery. Watch out, Céline. You never know if he's coming or going … He's always full of surprises."

At these rather sibylline remarks—should I suspect a love affair gone sour?—Gilbert's smile got wider. A charmer who knows his strength and how to use it.

"I'm sure what I eat will taste better if you serve it, lovely Céline."

I gave him a shove to send him back to his place at the end of the bench.

"Meanwhile, you're in my way."

Everybody laughed. Including him.

We must have already formed a very odd pair because people were giving us very curious looks.

Robert, sitting at the next table, coughed into his fist, then said, "Meanwhile, I'm hungry!"

The fine thread of the first sign of complicity between Gilbert and me was immediately broken. He became a client again and me, the waitress. He went back to his seat and plunged into his menu.

"What's good here, man?"

The answer came from nearly ten mouths at once, "Hamburger platter!"

He closed his menu, put it on the table.

"Hamburger platter it is. With a beer … and a smile from Céline!"

I know it's easy to say after all this time, to claim that I suspected everything or at least caught a glimpse of it before it began, but I think it's true: I see myself again standing next to the long bench, holding my order pad, I'm looking at Gilbert after taking his order.

And I think to myself, Don't touch, he's not for you, you'll pay dearly …

But he had the last word.

When I'd finished taking all the orders he held up one finger as if he wanted to add something to his.

"I just wanted to say, Céline, those yellow shoes are far out!"

That face made me melt. My back and around my waist were hot, sweat was running down between my shoulder blades. I felt as if I were liquefying and that when they'd finished eating all that would be left of me would be a puddle around two yellow shoes.

But they finished their meal without incident because that was what I wanted. During that hour I didn't look in Gilbert's direction, I served him exactly the same way as the others, concentrating on what I had to do, which was considerable given the number of plates, glasses and cups that I had to transport for the hungry crowd. I didn't want to leave myself open to any comments and I knew that they all had an eye on me, especially the two girls, so I was imperturbable, efficient, I even had the impression that for once, I'd become chilly, like Janine. I mustn't delude myself though, because I sensed that the remarks were proceeding at a good pace anyway: they were all waiting for me to go away so they could talk about what had just happened. When I came back to their tables, a heavy silence fell and I even thought I'd caught some quiet laughter a couple of times when I was bringing their desserts. I acted as if I didn't notice anything, of course, ever the busy waitress, but I was beginning to look forward to their departure so I could catch my breath and try to understand what had just gone on.

Had he been flirting with me or was he just a guy who was nice to everyone so they'd like him, ready to do anything to make people appreciate him? Besides, what could a man his size want to do with a midget like me? Aside from an affair that he could brag about to his buddies. Above all, I didn't want to become the subject of his

45

showing off, the victim of some boorish behaviour among males whose testosterone was out of control!

Too handsome, he was too handsome, that was the problem, and I would have to be very cautious with Gilbert Forget.

As I was writing up the bills for the table with Louise, Mouffe, Robert and a few others, I heard someone, Yvon, I think, saying to Gilbert two booths away, "Go on, ask! The worst that can happen is she says no!"

Had he told his friends that he intended to ask me out? Was he at that point already?

My ears turned red all at once and I wasn't the only one who noticed. Robert gave a kind of nervous laugh as he reached out for his bill and Mouffe's.

"My God, Céline, what's going on? Your ears are as red as a beet! Are they ringing too? Is somebody, somewhere, talking about you? I wonder who that could be ... "

Everyone laughed. I had to smile. While I tried to think of something intelligent to reply. Which, to my great shame, I didn't. I'm not used to letting people step on my toes and there was no way I was going to leave those three booths without making someone shut up, I didn't know exactly who—Robert? Gilbert?—or why, and I decided that I'd stay there until I'd given them a piece of my mind. Which made no sense, I knew that, because nothing serious had happened. On the contrary. I should have been flattered, should have bragged about it to Janine or Nick, shown off my trophy, handsome Gilbert, with a superior look ... It's what Janine did, after all, when someone came on to her!

But I've suffered for too long from other people's nastiness to let a big slacker, no matter how handsome, think he could use me without my reacting. But was that all he wanted, to use me? There's nothing I hate more than my own waffling over something silly. With time I've become too suspicious. Part of me told myself to let it go, I could always put a stop to it before it was too late, but ... How can I put it ... Did I really have a sense, in between the booths

46

at the Sélect, of what Gilbert could make me suffer, as I wrote earlier? No. If I think about it, I don't believe I did. It was too soon. No, it was pride that was making me try to find a retort, some lapidary phrase that would settle scores with them. Those artists wouldn't leave the restaurant before I gave them a reason to … to what? To admire me? Surely not. To not look down on me? They'd never done that, and that night, they'd just used a trivial anecdote to have a good laugh. But as the time approached to go to the cashier and pay their bill, the more I felt a need to prove to them that I wasn't just some little idiot they could laugh at without suffering the consequences.

But they hadn't made fun of me! Where did I get that idea? I'd become nothing more than wounded pride and I hated when that happened!

They all walked past me, one by one, on their way to the cash with their bills, smiling strangely. I was in their way. I saw my tips in the midst of the remains of a far from gourmet meal. Several dollar bills. Some twos.

They were about to get away from me when, maybe from lack of imagination or simply out of irritation because I couldn't think of something personal to say, I dipped into the Duchess's repertoire of snappy cracks, which was huge and had nourished the past two years of my life.

I tried to copy in every respect what she, queen of the dauntless and master of the well-placed insult, would have done. I rested my arm on the booth closest to me, no easy matter in view of my height, I raised my head the way great Hollywood stars—Joan Crawford or Rosalind Russell—used to do. And I said, with a French accent that wasn't nearly as successful as the Duchess's, "Kindly take note: my dance card is full for the next twelve years!"

From their stupefied looks I realized how pathetic I'd just been. I had brought on ridicule instead of nipping it in the bud as I should have done, with a certain dignity, by pretending to ignore what had just happened. I'd given credence to an event that didn't have the slightest importance.

I was off, nearly at a run. I must have looked like a little dog that skitters away at top speed because he's been caught doing something he's not supposed to. A punished pet that goes and hides behind a piece of furniture.

Janine, Nick and Lucien, his Haitian assistant, were waiting impatiently for me in the kitchen. And of course they wanted all the details. I don't know if Françoise, the cashier, had told them but they already knew that something worthy of interest had happened between a client and me, and it was obvious that they wanted juicy details. They could barely hide their excitement, with smiles that they hoped were candid but that contained a hint of mockery. Gossip after all is one of the great commodities that restaurants revel in, so I didn't really take offence.

I played along because it stopped me from launching into my usual negative analysis of what had happened, when I should have been flattered. Which I was, but I wouldn't admit it, to keep from deluding myself. For a while I played the innocent with my friends before giving in and, even then, I tried, in conclusion, to minimize the incident.

"He was nice to me, that's all. He's a womanizer and he probably lays the same trip on any girl he meets; we see it every night and they're such fools it's pathetic ... The only difference this time is that he did it to a midget ... I'm probably his first midget and he decided to do his act in front of everybody to get people's attention, that's all ... Just you wait, he'll never come here again, he'll avoid the Sélect like the plague as of tomorrow so he won't have to face me ... The last thing that guy wants is to be seen with a small person!"

I knew that bringing up that subject meant there was less danger of the discussion's dragging on. My work-mates are careful about my dwarfism, and when I want peace, I bring it out as my ultimate argument. It works nearly every time.

I added, pretending I was on my way to the ladies' room to change, "Anyway, I can't stand braggarts like him."

Which was only partly true. No, I don't like braggarts, but I liked him a lot, I couldn't deny it, and I'd been afraid it would show if I started going into detail. I always blush too easily when I tell a story and it's easy to guess what's on my mind. My visit to the ladies' room was well-timed: I'd raced through my story and I was sure that everyone could see how distraught I was, so I had to leave to cook up a new attitude.

I thought the matter was closed, but predictably, Janine wanted more.

"So? Did he ask you out? You aren't telling us things. Did you say yes? When's the wedding, lucky you?"

I turned around to look her straight in the eyes before I left the kitchen. I leaned on the partly open door to give an impression of composure.

"Exactly, let's talk about weddings. Can you see us walking down the aisle? Wouldn't we be a sight! He'd practically have to carry me on his shoulders so people could see me! They'd have to put me on a ladder so I'd show in the wedding photos!"

The vision I'd just suggested must have struck their imagination because no one dared say a word as I walked away. I myself was stupefied at the thought of the picture Gilbert and I would make if we ever went out together (which was far from likely since he hadn't asked). How would we go about it? If we held hands he'd look as if he were taking his little girl for a walk ... Or going arm-in-arm— just about impossible, I'd have to stand on tiptoe and even then ... Walk side by side, hands in our pockets, like buddies who'd run into each other on the street and are strolling along, catching up? Lovely evening in store! And so romantic!

I'd pulled the little stool over to the bathroom sink as I always do and was splashing cold water on my face.

I thought I'd long since dealt with all those questions that had haunted my teenage years. My relations with boys had always been spoiled by the overly critical notions that made me, inevitably, a subject of ridicule in my own eyes. I had rejected energetically the few pitiful attempts at seduction by pimply-faced teenagers nobody wanted, the physical difference between us being too great, or so I thought. My sexual experiences had been inconclusive because I held myself back. I'd always rejected the theories of some of my childhood friends who claimed that people with a peculiar physique, no matter how extreme, could have an amazing sex life for the simple reason that they were different, that what they had to offer was rare, but time had passed and the earth hadn't moved. I refused to gamble on it, even at the Boudoir—though I'd often sensed that my appearance could have been an advantage. Magnificent men of every colour and a variety of sizes had tried their luck—in vain—with the hostess who looked down on them despite her tiny size, and I may have missed out on some incredible nights! Or so I was told by the "girls" of the establishment, poking fun at me.

And now a small-town ladies' man, a hairy pot-head, maybe not too clean and reeking of patchouli, had just called all that into question.

I even went so far as to ask myself how long it had been since I'd slept with a man. And I censured myself before I started to count, for fear that I'd start to howl. So why not let things develop, why be stubborn and make it impossible to get together. My goddamn pride again?

My goddamn pride again.

That's right, fear of rejection, even by someone who was coming on to me. This was practically paranoia and I was ashamed. Why would someone come on to me just to reject me later? It made no sense! I wasn't so important that someone would go to the trouble of humiliating me in such a gratuitous way! Maybe something about me really did attract that handsome guy! Why not check it out? I who like to verify everything.

No. Impossible. I wasn't worthy of the interest of such a handsome man, I'd have to stop dreaming right now or I'd suffer. As usual.

I quickly finished putting on my face, gave my hair a vigorous brushing—twenty-two strokes as my mother had taught me—and left the ladies' room.

To find myself nose-to-nose with Gilbert Forget.

Nose-to-nose, well, maybe not quite. Let's say it was nose-to-an interesting part of his anatomy.

Without waiting till I got over my surprise, he said, "Are you finished work?"

I didn't give him a chance. I told him with a superior little look, walking around him on my way to the kitchen, "I'm not in the habit of changing my clothes till I've finished my shift! And I don't clean up the restaurant in my regular clothes."

He was shifting from one foot to the other like a shy little boy who's not yet comfortable in his body. A little boy over six feet tall! I thought he was touching. Instead of telling him off as I'd intended. That gave him the courage to try pursuing a conversation that had started off so badly.

"Are you going straight home?"

I shut the door behind me, thinking that surely he wouldn't follow me into the kitchen.

He pushed it open and stuck his head in. And saw Nick sweeping the floor while Lucien scoured the last saucepans.

"No customers in here!"

It didn't seem to bother him too much because he went on talking to me as if nothing had been said.

"I was just wondering if you'd have one last drink with me before you go home ... "

Nick pushed the door shut with the flat of his hand.

"Wait till she leaves to ask her ... But I don't think you've got much chance, cowboy."

Cowboy? Gilbert Forget was nothing like a cowboy, aside from the fact that he was wearing jeans. Even so, there's nothing western about elephant pants! Everything about him said beatnik, flippant, dope, over-strong espresso and over-long nights, and absolutely not the open air and chasing cattle and singing country! A guitar, yes, but no Hawaiian sobs!

Feeling a little sorry for my tall suitor, I shouted through the door, "Wait outside, I'll be there in two minutes!"

Janine, who was leaning against the huge refrigerator smoking a cigarette, came out with a laugh that startled me.

"Nobody but you, Céline, would tell a hunk like that to wait out in the cold for you in the middle of the night! You'll get what you deserve if he finds himself a hot babe on St. Catherine Street and leaves you behind cooling your heels … "

I smiled as I put on my coat.

"I don't think there's much danger of that."

Shrugging, she mashed her cigarette.

"You're pretty sure of yourself all of a sudden!"

"Actually I'm not, but I've got a feeling I can be sure of him— for tonight anyway."

"On top of it all you're pretentious!"

I blew her an insincere kiss as I was leaving the kitchen.

"I'm not pretentious. But if he came all the way to the ladies' room to look for me, I don't think he's going to leave me for the first female he sees."

She followed me into the restaurant. Now she was the one who looked like a puppy trotting along behind me.

"He followed you into the ladies room?"

"I didn't say that, Janine, I said *to* the ladies' room! He didn't come in to help me change!"

"What did he say, what did he say?"

I slowed down at the cash register where Françoise was very carefully counting the night's take.

"Look, Janine, is it all that surprising for a guy to ask me out for a drink?"

She came to a sudden halt in front of the first booth, unable to come up with an answer.

"Umm ... no ... that's not what I meant ... Come on, Céline, you know that's not what I meant ... "

"I'm going to start feeling sorry for you and not ask what you did mean because, if you ask me, you can look till tomorrow morning but you won't come up with an answer that makes any sense ... See you tomorrow night, Janine ... And if you ask me one question about what's going to happen, you'll regret it! Wait till I say something before you give me the third degree, okay? Besides, I might not even feel like talking!"

She and Françoise, looking stunned, stood frozen in the restaurant doorway, the cashier with a wad of bills, the waitress nervously lighting one last cigarette before leaving. The prospect of not knowing a juicy piece of gossip the next night must have incensed Janine and she must have been wondering how she'd be able to restrain herself.

Gilbert was leaning nonchalantly against the streetlamp at the corner of St. Catherine and St. Denis. Immediately I thought about my roommates doing the same thing at the corner of the Main, but for other reasons, and I had a kind thought for them, poor dears, who were freezing their butts for hours for next to nothing now that the Golden Age of the Boudoir was in the past. How would they react to the existence of Gilbert Forget, should I ever decide to talk about him? With sympathetic smiles? Words of warning because they didn't want me to be hurt?

Gilbert tossed his cigarette butt in the gutter—I knew from the smell that it wasn't regular tobacco—and smiled as he walked up to me.

"Does this mean it's yes?"

"To a drink? It's no. But we can walk together if you want ... I live nearby ... "

"Where?"

"Place Jacques-Cartier."

"That's not next door ... "

"With legs like yours you shouldn't complain."

He sensed right away that he was on slippery ground—this wasn't the moment to talk about the difference in the length of our legs—and he didn't push it. We stood rooted there at the corner of the street, not sure what to do. He stuffed his hands in his pockets and heaved a sigh whose meaning I couldn't grasp.

"So. Shall we go?"

I took advantage of a green light to cross St. Catherine heading south.

A heavy silence settled in. I took four steps to each one of his, that was the first thing I noticed. The tall lanky guy and the wobbly little girl. One question was burning my lips but I knew I mustn't ask it: Why? Why had he asked me to go for a drink, why were we there not talking when his certainly more interesting friends were waiting for him, I was sure, in some hip café in the neighbourhood, to smoke pot, drink, or talk about the show they were working on with such passion? Our worlds were so unlike that a topic of conversation was practically non-existent, that was obvious; after all I couldn't talk about my waitressing job and he knew that I didn't know a thing about the music world. So? Simple sexual attraction? I was attracted to him, that was undeniable, but him ... He could probably get it on with any girl he wanted, so what was he doing with someone like me?

The same damn problem! When we're starting our first walk!

It was a chilly night, one last jolt of cold wind was cruelly shaking Montreal to remind us that the real spring hadn't arrived yet and that knowing nature's undeniable hypocrisy, a nasty surprise was always possible. Especially in April, the most treacherous month of the year. Cars drove by on our left, sending up sprays of icy water because it had rained earlier that evening.

Gilbert looked at my yellow shoes.

"You know you're wrecking those pretty shoes of yours ... "

It's true that they were all wet and sticking to my skin, already starting to stretch out of shape. After just one night.

"It's true, I am, but they've already served their purpose. I wanted to feel like spring was here and they made me feel it ... Once they're dry, tomorrow, I'll know whether I can wear them again ... If I can, that's good, but if not ... I'll put them on a shelf in my closet as a souvenir ... "

"Of our meeting?"

"So far, Gilbert, there's been nothing memorable about it."

Right away I wished I hadn't said that. It was uncalled for. And cruel. I nearly expected him to drop me on the spot, I deserved it. But all he did was give me a long look and say nothing. Was he more perceptive than I thought? Did he understand why I was worried, and was he trying to find a way to let me know? To reassure me? To convince me of his integrity, his candour? Was the braggart finally going to appear in all the splendour of his bad faith?

If he was trying to think of something to say he hadn't found it because we said nothing for a good while. Finally I broke the silence. One of us had to say something before we got to the apartment on Place Jacques-Cartier.

"You must've thought I was really brainless last summer ... "

He couldn't help laughing at the memory of our first meeting, no more successful than this one as far as that's concerned.

"At first I thought you were a ... a ... "

"A junkie?"

"Maybe not, but someone who knew where to find grass ... "

"If you'd said *pot*, sure ... That, at least, I knew what it was ... But *grass* ... that's too specialized for me ... How come you didn't know? That's hard to believe."

He hesitated briefly then went on, "Actually I had some on me ... "

"*Pot?*"

"Yes."

"So why ask me?"

"Can't you guess?"

My cheeks turned red but I knew he couldn't see it in the dark. What was I getting into? I could guess what he was going to say and I didn't want him to because I wouldn't believe it and maybe that would hurt him.

He asked again, "Can't you guess?"

I stopped walking, I crossed my arms. He turned around and I saw his handsome face in the streetlamps of Bonsecours Street.

"I know what you're going to say, Gilbert, and I want to ask you just one thing. If it's not true don't say it."

He crouched down in front of me to talk. He didn't know that was the last thing he should do. There's nothing I hate more than when people bend down to talk to me, when they feel that they have to huddle down to be at my height. It's a lack of respect, especially when it's unconscious, and I can't stand it. I'm not a child, my ears are fine and I have no trouble hearing and understanding without people bending in two because I'm small.

I should have got in his face, insulted him, hit him, sent him back where he came from with cruel words and the order never to get in touch with me again ... In fact I nearly did. I froze in the middle of the sidewalk when he started to bend down, I straightened up as much as I could, which is what I do whenever I feel offended, I pulled back a little, even opened my mouth to let out the first insult that came to mind, anything as long as it was hurtful, when a hint of something in his big blue eyes, true innocence perhaps, sincerity without a hint of contempt or condescension, stopped me. I realized right away that he was bending down so that our eyes would be at the same level, that was all, there was no judgment in his behaviour, it was most likely a sign of genuine interest, of the beginning of affection. What he was about to say was important for him and he wanted to look in my eyes to see if his message had got through. So I let him talk, even if it meant telling him at the end of his presentation never to start again: a man as a little guy is ridiculous, a man as a little guy courting a midget is grotesque!

He'd taken my gloved hands in his and in his nervousness, was squeezing them a little too hard. Up close, he smelled of patchouli, cigarettes, pot and something indefinable—later I learned that it was the smell of his body—that excited me. After just a few words I could have jumped on him, so strong was the attraction. The summer before when he'd talked to me under false pretences, I'd thought he was handsome, but now, standing on the sidewalk, his face half-hidden in the dim lighting on Bonsecours Street, I thought he was absolutely stunning! If I can remember everything he said to me, it's not so much because I listened carefully but because of the simplicity of his words, their obvious sincerity that went straight to my heart.

His compliments were new for me; no one so far had ever said that he'd thought I was beautiful as soon as he saw me, that he'd grabbed the first pretext to talk to me, that he'd been glad to see me again after letting me get away ... I realized he could have been the biggest liar of all time. I knew enough about that kind of trouble-maker though—I was brought up by an alcoholic mother who always lied—to boast that I could recognize a braggart when I saw one, so I was sure that I wouldn't let myself be dazzled by what Gilbert had to say. I looked him straight in the eyes, thinking to myself that he was an actor and an incredibly good one because he seemed totally sincere.

When he'd finished his little homily he straightened up and stuffed his hands in his pockets again, never taking his eyes off me.

"So, anyway ... Will you give me a chance or are you going to reject me again?"

Twice before I'd found myself at a crossroads with a decision to make that would change the course of my existence—the first when I'd agreed to try out for *The Trojan Women* two years before, the other a few months later when I'd decided to go along with Fine Dumas in the adventure of the Boudoir. When I looked at Gilbert Forget on this sneaky early spring night, I had the impression that I'd now come to a third: what I would say in the next few seconds to this stunning specimen of a man of whom I felt so unworthy would without a doubt determine my immediate future. Or at least the state of mind in which I would live through the days, the weeks and maybe even the months to come. This man seemed too extraordinary for me to let him get away but if I did give in to him I still didn't know what I was getting into.

Though I told myself that I had to stop analyzing everything like that, that I had to tell him quickly yes or no, that it was unfair of me to leave him hanging out to dry there on the sidewalk, I was aware of the seconds passing and I was doing nothing to encourage him or let him down. Reject him a second time and he might walk away with no hope of return, leaving me with my loneliness. But now I was sentencing myself to loneliness once again, wasn't I?

I gave a hint of a benevolent smile, the one that I use only rarely and reserve for people I love.

"We'll start by going to my door, it's not far, after that we'll see … "

The rest of the walk was a kind of hesitation waltz of meaningless words exchanged to mask the uncertainty of both of us. I couldn't help thinking that despite his sincerity and simply because he was a man, Gilbert was hoping for a guarantee of good luck and already saw himself spending a rapturous night with a passionate midget who'd be grateful to him till the end of her days. Though I wanted to be more positive, taking the events as they occurred without searching for a meaning they probably didn't have, I couldn't help believing that he was hiding something. I'd burned my fingers too often in physical relationships with men not to feel a nearly pathological wariness that had me paralyzed at the prospect of what was liable to happen in the next few hours. I wanted above all to avoid another letdown. Especially in the arms of this gorgeous hunk.

After all, if I was so concerned, if I was so afraid of being let down and suffering as a result, I just had to kiss his cheek at the door of the apartment on Place Jacques-Cartier, tell him goodnight and leave him on the sidewalk high and dry, then go upstairs and wait for my three roommates to tell them about my misadventure ... The comfort of friendship out of fear of love—as usual ... I thought I was being ridiculous, a voice was shouting at me, "Make up your mind, say something, out with it!" I wished a thousand deaths for these overly gloomy—and useless—thoughts of mine. Why complicate something that's simple?

I was exasperated by my inability to make a decision and I wanted to slap myself when we got to my door.

He put his hand on my shoulder.

"If you haven't decided, there's nothing we can do about it, right ... You seem like sometimes you want to say yes, sometimes you don't ... But we're at your house now, Céline, you have to decide, I can't do it for you!"

Without giving it another thought I jumped into my destiny with both feet, reciting to myself all the clichés I knew: come what may, *qué sera sera*, it's in God's hands, the future belongs to the bold, a bird in the hand is worth two in the bush, fucking shit ... All that to hide the one and only truth, the simple fact that I wanted this guy, I'd been celibate too long. Miguel the Mexican I'd met at Expo some eight months before seemed far away.

I tugged at the sleeve of his windbreaker, which was too short and too thin for the season.

"How about one last coffee? Or one last beer?"

Again, that smile like a knife in my heart.

"I ought to say no, you deserve it ... "

Turning the key in the lock I was positive that what I was doing was definitive.

The coffee, of course, I couldn't find.

The pretext was quickly forgotten; we got down to serious business the minute we were through the door, before we even got to my room, and in no time we were on the parlour floor, between the immense coffee table with the morning papers still strewn on it and the hideous 1940s-vintage sofa inherited from the parents of Nicole Odeon, one of my three roommates.

The preliminaries proved to be complicated because of the big difference between our bodies, his long, mine—to put it mildly— rather compact. I'd never before made love with a body that took up so much space and I'm sure that I was his first midget. It took us a good while to find the movements that pleased us both, a satisfying rhythm and, as far as I was concerned at any rate, to chase away the notion, a little disturbing under the circumstances, that to an outsider we would have looked funny, if not ridiculous.

Though I loved what he was doing and was excited by what I was trying to do for him, I felt in a way detached from the tangle of arms and legs that we created on the carpet. I couldn't help imagining what we must look like, especially me, so small in his arms, so busy between his limbs that were so far from each other, and his handsome face that I'd have liked to keep in my field of vision as long as possible. Our lovemaking, as I imagined it at least, must have looked more like a wrestling match between animals of different sizes than an exchange of intimate caresses by two consenting adults. I was afraid that I'd look like his victim and he like my torturer—a lion slitting the throat of a gazelle—and that bothered me.

In the middle of a kiss that was beginning to relax me, the acid taste of his mouth and the strong smell of his body, that mixture of patchouli and sweat that would soon affect me like a drug, gradually diminishing my ridiculous hesitations, Gilbert suddenly raised his head.

"We aren't comfortable here. Where's your room?"

He carried me across the apartment like a fireman saving a child from the flames—except that he was giving me a long, luscious kiss—and flung me onto the bed, saying, "Let yourself go, Céline, don't resist … I can hear you thinking and it bugs me! Don't think! You don't think when you do what we're doing!"

So I stopped resisting. Let him guide me. I cut away the part of my critical and above all, negative imagination that kept me from achieving orgasm and I opened the part of my mind whose floodgates had been closed for too long. Sensuality. I shed my analytical sense, gave myself over to the pure pleasure, stripped of any esthetic sense, that turns us back into the animals we were originally. I became an animal again—instinctive, active, energetic; I caressed, I bit, I growled, my fists pummelled a hairy chest where I could hear a heart beating in unison with mine. I was everywhere at once, acting, resourceful, or motionless, concentrating on the waves of my own pleasure, the cries emerging from my mouth so inhuman they'd have been scary had they not welled up from deep inside me, I explored parts of the human body I'd never seen up close, I devoured things that I didn't know could be put in my mouth, scratched a skin I'd have been happy just to stroke but that I wasn't capable of not bruising. In other words, with my mind turned off and my senses on the alert, I experienced a moment of violent and devastating grace that I'd have gladly prolonged until the end of time.

At dawn I found myself exhausted, breathless, in a ruined bed filled with spicy odours and the snores of a satiated man. He'd put his arm around me and, yes, now that I'd got my wits back I could allow myself to become critical again, I must have looked like a doll. But I didn't care. At the age of twenty-three, for the first time I had spent an unforgettable night in the arms of a person who might very well become essential to my survival, and the smile I was wearing probably looked like that of a cat bending over a bowl of cream.

You should have seen the look on my three roommates' faces the next day around noon when Gilbert emerged from my room! And his when he got a look at them!

I hadn't told my friends that I had company—I assumed that when they came home at daybreak after their night's work we'd finished making love and they'd thought I was alone—and when they got up I'd fixed them the kind of late breakfast they like: copious and greasy. As for Gilbert, I hadn't had time to explain my arrangements with three drag queens from the Main who'd been my work-mates, *in a whorehouse*, for more than a year and with whom I'd been sharing the huge apartment for even longer.

Nicole, Jean and Mae were waxing ecstatic over my perfectly cooked bacon and my scrambled eggs with cheese when the door to my room—the first on the left after the kitchen—opened on the stark-naked Gilbert who was trying to untangle his mop of blonde hair with my hairbrush. A priceless picture: my three friends gawking while Gilbert froze on the threshold, arms raised and blushing like a little boy. He didn't even think to cover himself. He stood there in the noonday sun as nature made him. He was more than handsome, he was glorious.

And all he could say was, "I thought I heard voices ... I figured it was the radio ... "

Then he closed the door to put his clothes on.

The silence that followed was eloquent. It was my turn to hear them thinking and what I could read in their minds made me want to howl with laughter. Needless to say, they were astonished, but went on buttering their toast as if everything was as usual. They were goggle-eyed though, and I knew they were trying to think of something not too compromising to say: after all, I had the right to get it on with whoever I wanted, but they mustn't look surprised at what a dish he was so they wouldn't insult me.

And as I should have expected, the silence didn't last, curiosity winning out over discretion, which I must admit is not a characteristic of drag queens.

Jean-le-Décollé dropped his knife onto his plate.

"My God!" he said in English. "I'm in love!"

Mae East patted my leg under the table.

"I don't know where you found it, dear, but make sure you don't lose that one! And when you're finished, hand him over to Auntie! Name your price! And more! The sky's the limit!"

Nicole Odeon, hilarious, had placed both hands over her heart.

"I'm not hungry anymore. I have to take off ten pounds! Or twenty!"

I replied, teasing, "More important, you have to take off a good foot and a half!"

We laughed, we howled, we clapped our hands, Nicole even threw herself against my bedroom door as if she wanted to smash it open, like in an old Italian neorealist melodrama, and eggs got cold while cup after cup of coffee was poured.

Fifteen minutes or so later, as Gilbert hadn't come out of the bedroom, I started to feel guilty about leaving him alone and I asked my three friends to excuse me while I went to see what was going on. Was he in the bathroom, had he showered, was he waiting for me to get him and make the introductions?

Mae East chewed on a limp slice of toast.

"If he didn't know we were there he must've had a shock, poor thing! We don't look like creatures of the night at breakfast, we look like we've escaped from a battlefield! Noon, the drag queen's Waterloo!"

Then, stopping and pointing to the two others, "Theirs, anyway. I'm gorgeous always!"

Nicole ran her hands through her blonde hair which needed a dye-job. Badly.

"If you aren't back in half an hour, Céline, I'll put out the fire with a kettle of cold water!"

I pushed open my bedroom door, laughing but a bit worried all the same.

Gilbert, fully dressed, was sitting on the bed and pretending to read *La Débâcle*, one of the final volumes of the Rougon-Macquart, which I'm finding rough going because descriptions of battles aren't my favourite reading

"Aren't you coming out for breakfast with us, Gilbert?"

He looked up from the book and what I could see in his incredibly blue eyes I didn't like.

"What are those *weird things* anyway?"

Just what I'd been afraid of.

So I sighed and sat down on the rumpled sheets beside him to explain.

He listened attentively, nodding now and then to let me know that he was following. He started a few times because he'd heard a lot about the Boudoir during Expo but had never set foot inside, his opinion being that a brothel featuring transvestites was grotesque. He had no idea that he was going to find out that I'd been its official hostess. He'd hit on a waitress at the Sélect and found himself with a former hostess in a brothel. I could understand his surprise, but I also sensed that his reluctance was due to something else, that his use of the term *weird things* earlier had come from something deeper than surprise, and for a while I was afraid I was with one of those intolerant, unbearable males, who always fear their virility is being questioned and are suspicious of anything that doesn't follow the unwavering line of what they want the world to be: irremediably straight.

Was he suspicious of transvestites? This longhaired beatnik, this guitar-strumming, pot-smoking gypsy?

He tried to reassure me, swore that he wasn't intolerant, explained that he'd been taken aback and it would take him a while to get used to my entourage, and I'm sorry to say that I was relieved because he was talking about the future, not worrying over problems that his prejudices towards my roommates might create. His brow was furrowed in worry while he spoke to me. I concentrated on the fact that he wanted to see me again, that I hadn't been a one-night stand, I ignored the rest—my concerns, my questions, his obvious discomfort—to persuade myself that all would be well, and I took his hand to lead him to the kitchen. He followed close behind as if he were walking to the gallows.

Everyone was polite, we shared a good laugh, Gilbert ate a hearty breakfast, yet something was missing around the table over the next half-hour. I couldn't put my finger on it, it was hard to pin down. I may have been the only one who had that impression, but it seemed to me that this whole display of cheerfulness was forced, self-conscious, stilted, that some indefinable discomfort hung over the breakfast. The jokes my three friends cracked weren't too dirty and they didn't simper and flounce as much as I would have expected, subtlety not being their strong point; after what they'd said about Gilbert a little earlier, I'd have expected them to eye him hungrily and, kidding around, make barely disguised advances or come out with the cracks drag queens specialize in. And Gilbert responded to the winks and the limp innuendoes with laughter that sounded hollow, with shrugs that he seemed unable to control and tried to disguise with hilarity.

I saw Jean-le-Décollé frown several times, which worried me. Did he think that Gilbert wasn't right for me? Did he foresee problems, crises, tears on account of the huge physical difference and for other reasons that I couldn't see? Jean is an excellent judge of character, he was quick to discern people's good points, their flaws, possibilities and shortcomings; that was how he'd become a kind of chief or in any case an important and respected advisor to the drag queens of the Main. Did he foresee in this handsome specimen I'd spent the night with some flaws that were invisible to me? Was he reconsidering his *I'm in love*? And, with the other two sensing it, was Gilbert's rating dropping in the kitchen of the apartment on Place Jacques-Cartier for some mysterious reason? I felt like getting up in mid-conversation to scream and pound my fist on the table and say, "Do you think I could have twenty-four hours of happiness without having to question everything?"

For a few hours I'd let myself go, done thrilling things that had transported me, and now I was back where I'd been the day before, worried and tense.

His coffee finished, Gilbert asked if he could take a shower and, to my amazement, no one offered to accompany him.

We heard him singing the same song Louise had sung the night before, about airlines and propellers. But no one around the table said a word, which was absolutely abnormal, and I started to panic. I got up from the table and went to make a fresh pot of coffee, set it on the burner, and turned to my three friends.

"Okay, I want to know what's going on."

Jean-le-Décollé sipped some cold coffee.

"Come and sit down, Céline."

Mae East got up to fill the butter dish.

"Something happened when you went back to your room with Gilbert ... "

Nicole Odeon put her hair in a pink elastic to make a ponytail.

"Jean-le-Décollé recognized him first."

Frowning, I looked at Jean-le-Décollé.

"Do you know him?"

He heaved a long sigh as if he didn't want to say what would come next. I felt my heart skip a beat and sink into my stomach. Okay, I was about to get some more bad news, better prepare myself. But what came out of Jean-le-Décollé's mouth was simply one more mystery that left me no further ahead.

"Yes, we know him. You don't, you haven't been around the Main long enough. Gilbert is the son of Madame Veuve."

*Sighing, she shuts the notebook, looks up at the window.*

*That's it, the first part of the story, her meeting with Gilbert, is finished. Everything has been put in place—location, characters, action, soon she'll start to develop it and take it not to its conclusion, because nothing is completely finished yet, but to the delicate situation she's in at the moment, the choice between two poles, each as unappealing as the other: to drag out an affair that would never stop providing highs and lows—the highs sometimes thrilling enough to be dangerous, the lows too intense to be bearable—or to put an end to it once and for all, regain the dismal peace of mind she'd had a scant few months earlier and drown in it forever. On one side, passion, on the other, peace. Either one impossible to live with.*

*Meanwhile, starting tomorrow, she'll have to write the story of Madame Veuve. It will take her away from her story, she knows that, but she could use a break, a diversion, before tackling the main part of what she has to say.*

*It's one of those sticky nights that she loves. She thinks about her bed, about the coolness of the sheets, which won't last long, about the hours she'll spend preparing the important piece, half-fiction, half-reality, that she's getting ready to start the next day. The background of Gilbert Forget. His crazy mother. His incredible childhood. His hell and artificial paradises. His first salvation, the guitar. His second salvation, her—or so he claims when he spends hours on the phone crying and pleading with her not to abandon him.*

*She yawns, sighs, cracks her knuckles.*

*A small piece of moon is reflected in a window on the top floor of a building across the street on Place Jacques-Cartier. She gets up to take a better look.*

*Céline switches off the lamp, a fake Tiffany she bought for the huge sum of ten dollars from an antiques dealer on Notre-Dame Street and turns towards her bed.*

*"À nous deux, Madame Veuve!"*

First Insert

*The Story of Madame Veuve*

Madame Veuve had confided in Jean-le-Décollé one night when, for once, instead of driving her crazy, alcohol had for some unknown reason restored her wits. She was a ravaged woman, something like a crow, all beak and claws—in the thirties she'd been plump and golden like fresh-baked bread, with a creamy complexion and masses of hair—but for years now, she'd been dragging along in the condition of the eternal widow that was responsible for her name. Everyone avoided her, claiming she was insufferable, mean, quarrelsome; she provoked battles wherever she went, insulted everyone she ran into, particularly anyone who tried to help her. She wore her reputation as a kind of Typhoid Mary, like a royal mantle, went to the most squalid dives and drank from bar to bar during her final years, stingy with serious or lasting human contacts, but generous with well-aimed insults and invective that most of the time was incomprehensible.

All because of love. All because of the war. All because of Gilbert, her son. Or so she claimed that night, one hand firmly clamped around the 40-ounce bottle of Bols gin that Jean-le-Décollé had brought to their table, the other hand on the wrist of the transvestite who dared not move for fear of making her lose the thread of her fascinating story. She talked on and on, eyes dry and wild, emotion forever buried in a corner of her heart that she'd long ago refused to acknowledge.

Jean-le-Décollé knew part of her story, the second, postwar part, but like nearly everyone he didn't know how her fall had begun, and had always been curious. So much malicious gossip was making the rounds regarding Madame Veuve that you didn't know what to believe. People chose to swallow everything, especially the most unlikely inventions, because it was easier than seeking the truth.

It was said that she'd given birth to twins, had killed the girl and kept the boy, allowing him to grow up without looking after him because she wasn't interested in children anyway. It was widely claimed that she was the official abortionist to the whores on the Main, a pitiless butcher though not one prostitute had died after an abortion, Doctor Mondor being very well paid by the pimps and madams of the Main to ply his trade. She was said to be a witch, a miscreant, ready and willing to do anything. In fact, she'd been merely a poor girl torn apart by tragedy. Every neighbourhood in the world has its pariahs; those in pariah neighbourhoods were even more to be pitied because their sins, genuine or false, are seen as more serious and darker by the God-fearing whose accusations are mainly expeditious and dictated solely by intolerance. That was how, strictly out of convenience, Madame Veuve had become guilty of the most disgraceful acts on the Main, where they abounded all year long.

In the mid-1930s, Madame Veuve had enjoyed quite a fine career as a stripper in Montreal's red light district, under the name Peach Blossom. It was the eldest Cotroni who'd dubbed her, impressed by her fresh complexion, more like that of a country girl than a sidewalk susie, and by the perverse pleasure she displayed at undressing in public, especially when she'd had a little nip. Very popular with the American jazz artists who came up to Montreal in the summer to perform in the clubs on Notre-Dame and Craig Streets, she'd ended up with a mistaken reputation for liking black men when they were the ones who travelled to see her strip with calculated slowness and exceptional sensuality on the stage of the Coconut Inn or the French Casino. Some of the big names in jazz had fallen madly in love with her and she was credited with a lot more affairs than she'd actually had. Her dressing room, not much bigger than a closet, was always full of flowers, and every evening handsome men, fashionably and beautifully dressed, invited her to their tables where she proved to be charming and even quite witty. But it stopped there; most nights she went home alone, while rumours did the rest.

In the early 1940s she met Fabien Forget, a soldier on leave who was about to depart for the front, one of the unskilled jobless men who signed up more to earn a living than to fight the wicked Hitler. She'd thought he was good-looking, had taken pity on him because he'd said that he might not come back, and had married him on a whim. Peach Blossom's woes had begun as a melodrama experienced by thousands of women all over the world: marry to give her little soldier a reason to survive and come home, slip a lipstick-smeared photo into his baggage, have a teary farewell that hopefully will be temporary, and a few weeks later realize that she's pregnant.

Peach Blossom had immediately trumpeted all over the Main that she was expecting the child of her hero who'd gone off to war. She'd enjoyed a happy pregnancy among half-naked girls, strippers or cigarette-girls of various kinds who'd pampered her because she was living a dream that they could never afford—a child to love. She had stopped showing herself in public after her third month but kept visiting the Main every night, bigger and bigger, more and more radiant, drinking less, smoking hardly at all. She even went so far as to act as advisor or critic to her colleagues, often improving their acts. The jazzmen watched her get bigger, paid her compliments even more flattering than before, which she accepted with elegance and restraint. She was a lady now, wanted it known and to be treated with respect.

Gilbert had been a wanted child and his first photo had taken off quickly for Europe. Like all the photos that his mother had taken during his first two years. He was cared for by his maternal grandmother, a fat woman of boundless goodness who let him do anything because she adored him, while his mother, who'd unashamedly gone back to work, brought home enough for the three of them to live on. Peach Blossom wrote to Fabien that she was depositing in the bank every cheque the government sent her each month as a mother married to a soldier. All that money would be used one day to turn their son into a doctor or a lawyer: no one would know that his mother had been a stripper and his father jobless. He would become an important man, recognized and praised, while they stayed in the wings admiring him, never angry if he happened to forget them a little because he was too busy. He would live on their behalf what they hadn't been lucky enough to experience or rich enough to buy for themselves.

Gilbert grew up brilliantly and, like all spoiled children, quickly became a little devil.

But Madame Veuve hadn't lingered over her son's childhood that night, sitting with Jean-le-Décollé in the smoky bar—a bottle in her hand and a tear in her eye. Instead, she'd taken a shortcut to arrive at the cursed morning in 1944 a few days after the landing when she'd received the same telegram as hundreds of other women in Quebec: the French-Canadian soldiers had been used as cannon fodder and hers was lying somewhere on the beaches of Normandy. It wasn't put that way of course, governments have always known how to disguise their words and shamelessly flatter the people they unscrupulously make use of, but the meaning was the same, the sacrifice too great, and the consequences devastating.

And on that morning, the legend of Madame Veuve was born.

It was said that she'd lost her mind as soon as she read the telegram but the truth is much sadder: Peach Blossom had first lived through a kind of debilitating denial that had lasted for several months. She denied the existence of the telegram, acted as though nothing had changed, and every night went to work at the Coconut Inn or the French Casino, undressing in front of clients whose exacerbated desires she was no longer even aware of. She claimed she'd got letters from her Fabien saying that he'd survived the horror of the landing and would soon come home, the war was ending with the retreat of the Germans who were totally surrounded. She read the news in *La Presse* and claimed that she'd received it in letters from Fabien.

Insanity took hold of her a little at a time and no one realized it until the night when a tearful widow dressed all in black turned up at the French Casino, holding a little blond boy by the hand. Peach Blossom was coming to work. That was when people understood, too late, that she was crazy and that nothing could be done for her. And that the widow lady's name, Madame Veuve, was born.

What had happened to make Peach Blossom drift into madness? What significant event or insignificant drop, what small setback or inconsequential disappointment had been the final straw that had cast the lovely stripper onto the streets of the Main veiled, gloved, dignified in her pain but totally out of place in a world from which black, the emblem of sorrow, was banned? No one ever knew. And it didn't interest the inhabitants of the neighbourhood as much as poor Peach Blossom's eccentricities.

She began to wander the neighbourhood at very odd hours—the bars with strip shows were only open at night but she walked up and down the streets in the middle of the afternoon, with her child in tow—demanding now at the bank and later at the clubs where she appeared that people call her Madame Veuve Forget. Malicious tongues, among them some nude dancers whom she'd guided when they were first starting out, claimed that it was the role of a lifetime and that she overacted it just to draw attention to herself. Her real friends took pity on her and offered help which she refused, maintaining that she didn't know what they were talking about; she was a widow and she wanted to be treated as a widow, that was all. She saw nothing exaggerated or ridiculous about her behaviour, she was convinced that she was acting quite normally under the circumstances. And that was how from Madame Veuve Forget, she'd become quite simply Madame Veuve in the minds of the denizens of the Main.

But matters began to go seriously wrong the day she expressed a wish to perform in her widow's weeds, to take onstage what she was living rather than go on doing the eternal Hindu princess or the Queen of Sheba. She had been clear and convincing when she went to see her boss: the men would definitely be turned on by the sight of a beautiful widow who stripped to show them a magnificent body that they could dream of possessing because she no longer had a husband and was quite obviously yearning for physical love. The owner of the French Casino—though he'd seen it all, from the most vulgar to the most amazing—was afraid that such a morbid act would empty the club, so he refused to give her permission. She slammed the door and stomped out, swearing that never again would she set foot in the club. He was sorry he hadn't held onto her, he even pleaded with her, in vain, to come back to the French Casino when her act, so innovative, started to bring in a lot of money ... She turned to the Coconut Inn then, the other place where she performed, that was a lot less selective, which is one way of putting it, and in her madness experienced her greatest success. Brief, but stunning.

The act acquired a following, a few drag queens still use it on Halloween or the third Thursday in Lent. Peach Blossom, now known as Madame Veuve even on the posters at the door of the Coconut Inn, three times a week performed a very sensual kind of dance of the seven veils, but the Salome who emerged stark naked at the end—after checking that no representative of the police was in the house—was not the little girl, barely nubile and spoiled rotten, who demanded the head of John the Baptist from a drunk and adoring Herod who couldn't say no to her, but a mature woman, obviously authoritarian, who promised the stunned spectators the fake submissiveness, active and expert, maybe even a little despotic, of a very capable woman who was tough and yearning for love. They remained the masters, but she would take them to heights that only an experienced widow, starving for dangerous caresses, could know and share. The men who came to the Main, including several students who would later become stars of Quebec theatre and variety shows, were baffled by this act, which made a fortune for the Coconut Inn for a while, at least until Madame Veuve proved to be insufferable. Which didn't take long, with the help of alcohol. And goofballs, of course, which kept her awake nights when she'd had too much to drink and would have preferred to go home and sleep rather than make all those men gasp, men who in any case she would push away without further ado when her show was finished and her last drink downed.

The jazzmen were home from the war, they'd gone back to work and were now pushing their way into the Coconut Inn again as they had during the 1930s when Madame Veuve was still known as Peach Blossom and Fabien Forget hadn't yet come into her life. If they were the same ones, they didn't recognize her in her new role of tearful widow and they allowed themselves to be aroused and seduced by her lascivious dance and her black veils. And so she had them for the second time. Flowers started to appear in her dressing room again, some jewels too, but Madame Veuve seemed to prize nothing but the presence of her son at her side and strong drink which blunted her pain.

Gilbert grew up any old way in the midst of pimps, dealers, hookers and drag queens, all of whom adored him. He was an unruly child, and charming, who knew how to make himself scarce when he sensed danger—his mother when she'd been drinking, who could explode at any time, with insults and well-aimed slaps; the other girls in the club, whom he liked to tease by hiding things in the big dressing room of the Coconut Inn, who got fed up with finding half-eaten all-day suckers stuck to their underwear and punished him but not if his mother, whose rebuffs they feared, could see them. And he took shelter where no child before him had ever been accepted, tolerated because they thought he was funny with his curious little face and his laughing eyes: the Main when it was sizzling hot.

Especially in summer, he would settle into the doorway of a shop that was closed for the night and observe the games played by hookers and johns spread onto St. Lawrence Boulevard like a show—the same every time but every time renewed—whose meaning he didn't grasp, but saw as an endless parade designed just for him. Part of the fascinating procession, women who sold their charms, specializing in trickery and pretence, was unchanging, but the other, those who paid for dreams that were doomed to bitter disappointment infinitely repeated, was constantly renewed, though some components, the regular clients, eternally willing victims, came back with comforting regularity, like bit players paid to prove that deep down nothing ever changes and that the world can be a reassuring place. Gilbert moved around in a non-stop party of which he didn't understand the stakes but drowned in it with delight—an unstable child searching in vain for a solid base on which to moor his existence. That was how this smart little boy, with the look of a resourceful devil, met Greta-la-Vieille, before Greta-la-Jeune arrived in Montreal. Greta's comical auntie side appealed to Gilbert right away and he thought of her as his godmother, not understanding what she was doing out on the street at such a late hour, or what the men who'd approached her wanted. At first she'd told him that she and her friends were waiting for the bus, but he found it odd that they never boarded it when it appeared. (Nor did he understand till much later that Greta-la-Vieille was not a real woman and the shock was devastating.) From Greta-la-Vieille he moved quickly on to the other drag queens and he often said with a cynical smile that he'd been brought up by a bunch of women with beards while his mother took off her clothes in front of a bunch of men without balls, but that's another story ... Jean-le-Décollé had actually got this information not from Madame Veuve herself but from Greta-la-Vieille, and much later.

Years passed, Madame Veuve was getting old. Alcohol was withering her, her insanity showed itself in more and more frequent bouts that ate away at her body as well as her mind. She had let pass any chance to get out of it—well-to-do men who would have liked to be with her for a while, the owner of the French Casino who'd offered her a fortune if she would come back to perform in his club, there were men who proposed marriage, sometimes shy, other times urgent, nearly vehement, who'd left her cold—and her act, never modified, was starting to bore those whom it used to excite.

The Coconut Inn gradually emptied out and she was blamed. Nights when she performed to a nearly empty house, she was actually obliged to pay for her drinks. The amount of alcohol was reduced, the price increased.

The rest, at least up to her spectacular death, is depressingly banal. Abandoned by students and suitors alike because she refused to try anything new, Madame Veuve stopped dancing overnight, without a word to anyone, and began to wander like a lost soul through the red-light district, her hand outstretched, her voice loud. She begged for her booze and her daily bread, reminding everyone who she'd been and what she'd represented to them. She insulted those who pretended not to know her and flattered excessively the unfortunates who deigned to give her the charity of one cheap drink or a few cents to pay for another. As soon as her back was turned, they would hear her cackling and howling curses each more unbelievable than the others and regretted they'd helped her. She now smelled not of peach blossoms but of unwashed underwear and dried urine and she dragged around with her through the red-light district, which wanted nothing to do with her, her threadbare costume and her widow's act. Madame Veuve was no longer an unusual stripper everyone was talking about, who *must* be seen, but a poor nut-case who didn't interest anyone. They didn't drive her away, though, strictly out of charity and perhaps a little because she gave the neighbourhood something it had always lacked: the lunatic who's a local legend, the outlaw everyone loves to hate, the deposed star who can be pointed out to visitors, with explanations of who she'd been and what could happen to poor strippers when their beauty was gone. That was how the most serious rumours sprang up and began to spread: witch, abortionist, murderer of her own child … It was easy, people took advantage of it.

Madame Veuve had become the foil that every society requires to meet its shameful need for the cruelty that relieves it of its frustrations and excuses in its own eyes, the sensual little injustices committed on others for no good reason, purely out of cruelty: she'd become the Main's whipping boy, for some reason it was the only way she'd found to hold onto some importance in the eyes of those who'd lionized her in the past. But was she less unaware than she seemed? Did she take pleasure deep down in the shame and contempt she could see on the faces of those she met outside the door of the nightclub where she'd enjoyed such success? Had masochism, nourished with alcohol and exacerbated by the early signs of madness, replaced the pleasure of taking off her clothes in public and seeing men gasp with desire in front of her? She couldn't have said, because she wasn't able to understand what was going on inside her head. It had been a long time since she'd been able to step back and see things clearly.

Every now and then, Madame Veuve went to see her mother, who was still bringing up her son in her home, to rest, warm up, bathe and drink whatever there was to drink. She would give all her attention to Gilbert, who had long since stopped following her on her peregrinations, covering him with kisses and cuddles, acting out endless scenes of regret and remorse, which left him cold. He went on, showing tremendous patience, playing his role of useless walk-on, of passive spectator who doesn't have the right to speak but whose pitiless judgment was becoming clearer with every scene. He had admired his mother and everything she represented, now he saw it all as disastrous and dangerous, and he hid himself in his grandmother's skirts. No more Main on hot summer nights, no more girls waiting for the bus, most important, no more Greta-la-Vieille, to whom he'd taken a sudden dislike, though he had loved her so much, once he'd understood what she was. He even developed a certain—and understandable—disgust for everything Montreal's red-light district and its denizens represented. Especially the transvestites, professional liars, sellers of degenerate illusions, though they'd taken such good care of him when his mother left him to cope on his own.

It was said that Gilbert's desertion had broken Greta-la-Vieille's heart. When she approached Madame Veuve at the corner of the Main and St. Catherine to ask about the boy, his mother told her disdainfully to mind her own business. If Greta dared to remind her that it was she who'd looked after Gilbert while she, the real mother, took off her clothes to make men hard, Madame Veuve replied, better a real mother who takes off her clothes to make men hard than a fake adoptive one who just bends over, fully clothed, and gives them quick blowjobs. Only the arrival of the boy who would later become Greta-la-Jeune, her adoptive daughter, her heir, her alter ego, could take Gretta-la-Vieille out of her apathy, but all that would happen years later.

When Madame Veuve had talked about suicide to Jean-le-Décollé after pouring out her heart over a bottle of Bols that she'd drained all alone or just about, he didn't believe her and he still regrets it today. He says that she'd never talked about killing herself before, that he should have at least found it strange, should have worried, questioned her, but when she finished she was so drunk that she was incoherent and he thought she'd brought up hanging herself to sound interesting, to make him stay with her for a while and order a second bottle of gin. A threat so the night wouldn't end there. So the party, pitiful though it was, would go on. He often blames himself for leaving her there in the smoky bar, bent over her empty glass, her cigarette burning away in the ashtray.

He never saw her again. His final image of her is that of a grey head nodding two inches away from a fake marble table on which damp circles left by glasses are drying.

It was a few days before Christmas. On the morning of the twenty-fifth, she was dead.

Stories about Madame Veuve's suicide are, of course, abundant. No one saw her do it, but everyone has their own idea about it. It must be said that its spectacular nature lends itself to various and preposterous interpretations and speculations. The one that's probably closest to the truth, Jean-le-Décollé heard from Madame Veuve's mother, a woman of limited imagination who found her daughter dead on Christmas morning, lying naked on a snowbank. Unlike the denizens of the red-light district, she had no reason to embellish her story. She didn't add a hidden meaning or distinctive signs, she merely told what happened.

On Christmas Eve that year, Madame Veuve had come down with a nasty flu and had spent most of the day in bed. She claimed that her bones and her head ached, said she felt more tired than she'd ever felt in her life, and swore that she was going to kill all those germs with glasses and glasses of strong, hot gin punch. Flavoured with cinnamon—it was Christmas, after all. At supper-time her wine had already made her maudlin but she'd insisted on sitting at the table with her son. Gilbert, exasperated by her rambling, had got up from the table after barely touching the meatball and pig's feet stew prepared specially for him by his grandmother who couldn't digest that kind of food and knew that Madame Veuve wouldn't taste it either: an enormous kettle of stew cooked just for him, which would congeal in the big cast-iron pot before it was thrown out. Just as he was about to leave the house, his mother told him that a wonderful present would be waiting for him when he woke up the next morning. No one believed her because they couldn't imagine what kind of present it might be.

According to Madame Veuve's mother, her daughter was more nostalgic than usual that evening and she'd talked a lot about the more or less recent past when she held in the palm of her hand all the real males and influential professionals who came to see her undress, all of them dreaming that she belonged to them when only Fabien Forget, her one great love, had mattered in her life. She mixed up everything, her marriage, her child, her work, dates and events, she was even starting to claim that her glory had spread beyond the limits of the Main, which was of course false, when her mother recommended that she go to bed.

Christmas Eve was sad and long, but calm.

At dawn, not finding her in her bed—she'd come in to ask her daughter if she'd had a good night—she had searched the house, thinking she would find her hunched over the toilet bowl or fast asleep in the tub. The apartment was empty. Worried, she went out on the balcony without even putting on a coat, and found Madame Veuve stretched out naked on a snowbank, stiffened by the cold, her skin already blue. Her widow's weeds were spread around her as if she had performed one last striptease before she died, slowly peeling her clothes off in the cold of the night for an audience of ghosts she'd chosen to join.

That at any rate is what her mother claims. She tells anyone who'll listen that her daughter got up in the middle of the night, dressed in her shabby widow's weeds, had one final drink to give herself courage and a little warmth, that she'd gone down the stairs, her bearing like a queen's, and that she'd undressed one last time on the only stage she could find. Accompanied by the music of the wind. She's certain that it was the most successful, the longest and most erotic striptease by the celebrated Madame Veuve and that only the stars could tell how beautiful it had been.

Other testimonies have been added since then: neighbour women who say they'd seen her climb onto the snowbank and undress, singing; others who swore that she'd jumped, stark naked, from the balcony, flinging her clothes in the air like a shower of confetti. The sickest claim is that she died with all her clothes on and that someone abused her after he'd removed her clothes, but those no one believes. Not now at any rate, since Madame Veuve has become venerable.

As for Gilbert, he never talks about his mother. And no one else should talk to him about her—or else.

*\*\**

The legend of Madame Veuve is one of the most enduring on the Main, which needs such memorable stories to survive and icons to glorify. The story has been transformed over time, it has grown, become more important, and the memory of Madame Veuve will never die, fed as it is by the popular imagination and the need for larger-than-life characters to admire.

It is even said that many girls of both sexes and a wide range of specialties virtually worship a certain Sainte-Veuve of the Snowbanks, who watches over them along with Gypsy Rose Lee and Lili Saint-Cyr, up there in the strippers' paradise.

# Part Two

*... il n'a jamais, jamais connu de loi ...*

*This morning she feels strong enough to get to the bottom of the problem. She will try to get straight to the point without beating about the bush too much and stay as close to the truth as possible as she tells about her second meeting with Gilbert Forget and about everything magnificent, everything painful that it set off.*

*She has a quick breakfast, excited at the prospect of getting back to the blue notebook, which she has neglected for more than a week, ever since she finished writing the story of Madame Veuve, in fact, from information gleaned here and there from drag queens and hookers she knows.*

*She enjoyed writing that part, but it had taken her away from her main narrative a little and for a few days she was afraid she wouldn't be able to pick up the thread of her ideas. She closed the notebook and put it on the small table she'd pushed to the bedroom window that she used as a work table. She often glanced at the notebook when she went by, opened it now and then to re-read parts. She adores breaking up the autobiographical part with some fiction, as she'd done in her red notebook, and she promises herself that she'll keep doing that but she's not sure if it will harm the unity of the whole. Is "The Story of Madame Veuve," interesting though it may be, helpful for understanding what will follow—the terribly complicated relationship between her and Gilbert? In a sense, yes, if she ever writes Gilbert's story ... Not now though, it's too soon ...*

*Too bad. She decides to stop asking herself such questions, which are no doubt pointless. That's how she works, quite simply. At any rate she likes the story too much to remove it. Tearing out pages from her notebook and throwing them into her wastebasket would demand an effort that's beyond her. And in the end, something would be missing from her blue notebook, of that she's sure.*

*She can't wait to get back to writing, but is afraid she might lack energy or objectivity, for the difficult task ahead. Several of the stories are painful, others fill her with shame, and she doesn't want to let herself erase the events or their effect on her merely so she won't upset herself too much so she won't suffer. She thinks she's been able to get around that trap in her first two notebooks and now she intends to continue in the same way.*

*It's a grey and rainy day and she's not unhappy. Nothing will distract her from what she has to put down, and the confession, so she hopes in any case, will be more muted, expressed in a minor and possibly a more personal key. She's beginning to recognize her tendency to wander all over when she writes, to make digressions that aren't always useful, to lose her way in overly long sentences that she then has trouble cutting, and in pointless details, but in the end she will think that she mustn't censor herself under the pretext of respecting a certain form of unity.*

*Where to begin? Yes, that's it, describe the separation, the less dramatic one, after her first night with Gilbert … what came next will no doubt follow on its own.*

*Her felt pen awaits. She takes off the cap, telling herself that she mustn't go for so long without writing, she misses it too much, and she dives with surprising ease back into the evocation of her first love.*

92

It was a long time before I saw Gilbert again.

We hadn't parted on bad terms that day, far from it, we'd even spent part of the afternoon walking around Old Montreal, laughing, with me muffled up in my winter coat because the severe cold, the real thing, the kind that you think will hang around for six months, had come back overnight, and with him clapping his hands together or putting them over his ears, his clothes inadequate for the cold, but he insisted he was too happy and excited to go home. I'd put my yellow shoes back on so I could hear them click along the sidewalk again, but my feet were so cold that I soon regretted it. We didn't mention the fantastic night that had just ended, but each of us must have been thinking about it nonstop. Something sexual, something very exciting was still passing between us whenever we touched, and his tight jeans let me confirm the effect I was having on him. I was amused and, even more, flattered.

He hadn't mentioned my three roommates and I, thrilled as I was to have him next to me, was afraid to broach a subject that might possibly come between us, so I took full advantage of these extra hours of bliss I'd been granted.

Just before he disappeared into the Place-d'Armes Metro, Gilbert kissed me in front of everybody, crouching down on the sidewalk as he'd done the night before on St. Denis Street. And again I wasn't brave enough to ask him not to. To my surprise I even felt a kind of pride at the thought that people could see us. Above all I didn't want to admit that I was starting to like it. But when I saw him from the back going down the stairs into the Metro station, I had an odd impression. The thought, fleeting yet precise, that I might never see him again went through my mind and somewhere deep inside me I think I actually bade him farewell. It was ridiculous, we'd spent a fantastic night, we'd exchanged phone numbers, we'd promised if not sworn that we'd see each other again—to "do it again" in his words—so why was this mild anxiety choking me? The fear of losing the first man who had introduced me to sexual pleasure, the fear of not finding another? Yes, without a doubt, but something else was bothering me, a hazy thought that I couldn't put into words, a still-vague risk of danger that I was afraid would become clearer.

What then? The fact that he was the son of Madame Veuve and was reputed to be horrified by transvestites? Because I was determined to stop thinking about that, I was trying hard to look elsewhere, but when that thought crossed my mind, I told myself that I might be very close to the heart of the problem. How could I reconcile all that? On one hand, people whose joys and sorrows I'd been sharing for nearly two years now, whom I'd come to adore; on the other hand, the arrival of a man I'd stopped waiting for, convinced as I was that I was unworthy of anybody's love, who was liable to change my life dramatically. It was too soon to talk about love though, I was well aware of that, I'd known Gilbert for less than twenty-four hours, but his obvious sincerity when he said that he wanted to see me again had filled me with hope—I who had always struggled to turn away any positive thoughts about the future because I'd been told too often that I didn't have one. Especially with men who, as my mother kept saying throughout my teenage years, would never be interested in a midget.

As for my roommates, without urging me never to see Gilbert again while he was taking his shower, they had nonetheless drawn a portrait of him dark enough to discourage me. I don't think it was lack of goodwill, jealousy or bitchiness that was coming out, no, at first they'd been too excited by the presence of a man in my bed to be malicious afterwards. But they knew Gilbert, by reputation in the case of Mae and Nicole, personally for Jean-le-Décollé, and they obviously wanted to protect me from the dangers he might represent. Jean-le-Décollé had been categorical: Gilbert was an unstable man with a changing nature and mood swings as spectacular as they were unexpected and frequent, and he often took refuge in drugs while passing himself off as a musician, no doubt to disguise his lack of composure when his talent for the guitar was average at best, an aging spoiled brat who was used to people being utterly devoted to his precious person—and charming, yes, but also, and inadvertently, a deadly poison as is often the case with men who are too good-looking and who always get what they want.

"Do as you please, Céline. It's your life. And I know I'm the last person to give you advice, I have scars on my heart to show what I've been through. But listen to what I have to say and believe me, please believe me: that guy is not for you. He's bad news ... "

Right away, I believed Jean-le-Décollé. And I'd almost decided to say goodbye to Gilbert before it was too late, before I grew too attached and did something stupid, but when he stepped out of the shower smelling of my lime blossom body cream, his smile broad, his movements affectionate, my negative thoughts all left me, I was thrilled again to be appreciated, complimented, and right away I forgot my friend's warnings.

Turning my key in the lock late that afternoon, after my enjoyable walk with Gilbert, I intended to ask my three pals for more precise information, but the apartment was empty, there was a smell of pot in the parlour and a note for me on the door of the fridge: "See you at the Sélect after your shift tonight, we've got a lot to tell you."

I of course had never met Madame Veuve, she died long before I arrived on the Main, but I'd heard about her, especially from the drag queens who for some reason kept her memory alive even more assiduously than the strippers of various beliefs and forms of worship who observed them almost fanatically. Every one of Fine Dumas's "girls" possessed some relic of the saint, no doubt as phony as the Blessed Foreskins that had crisscrossed the world during the Middle Ages—a black thread from the widow's veil, a lock of her peroxided hair or a scrap of fabric that may have been used in one of her acts. If asked what they did with them, they would reply that anything touched by the blessed Widow of the Snowbanks was sacred and that the curative properties of those venerated objects would prove to be many and priceless, for the soul as well as the body.

Babalu, for instance, the Boudoir's Brigitte Bardot, always had somewhere on her, even while plying her trade, an old wad of chewing gum—I swear I'm not making this up—which, legend has it, Madame Veuve had stuck to the underside of her makeup table at the Coconut Inn just before she left the club for good, and another stripper, a fetishist who was in love with her, had collected it reverently and put it inside a locket that she wore around her neck. If anyone made the mistake of pointing out to Babalu how absurd the story was, she'd glare at them as if to say that what mattered was the belief, not the object: it didn't matter if the gum was real or not, or if the story was sheer invention, if she, Babalu, had decided to believe. She knew then, or at least she suspected—like the Christians with their Blessed Foreskin, no doubt—that the relic was a fraud, but she preferred to swallow it hook, line and sinker simply because she needed to believe, as did most of the girls, even if the object of worship was ridiculous. She would show you the locket she claimed she'd inherited from another queen, but for which she must have paid a fortune, then recite with imperturbable seriousness all the wonderful things the Blessed Wad of Gum had done for her since she'd acquired it.

Finding out that my Gilbert was the son of the famous phony saint, the miracle worker of the red-light district whose miracles had yet to be proved, could not leave me totally indifferent. For two years I'd been hearing about the bright little boy who'd covered the neighbourhood long before I worked there, an adorable little blond imp who was passed from one to the next like a teddy bear and who grew up in a childless environment that was home to the most questionable elements of society, and there he was in my bed—a gorgeous adult, a little mysterious, true, just the slightest bit weird but so charming and so very expert at what I'd been missing till then that I was afraid I wouldn't be able to live without it.

That's what I was thinking about that afternoon as I got ready for work. I'd never pictured Gilbert as an adult and I had trouble seeing him as the child he'd been in the stories about his mother, which came close to fantasy, I knew that, but my curiosity—too often uncontrollable like my imagination for that matter—led me to ask a bunch of questions. What had Gilbert done between the time when he'd disappeared from the Main and the time when he'd ended up at the Sélect? Had he gone to elementary school, had he attended the National Theatre School like his friends—though he hadn't mentioned acting during the hours we'd spent together—did he earn his living as a musician, did he earn his living at all? I suspected that it was too early in our relationship to ask him something like that, but I did wonder if I'd be able to stop myself. If I ever saw him again. I couldn't get over the impression I'd had when I watched him go down the staircase in the Place-d'Armes Metro station. The possibility of a final farewell that for a moment had been imposed on me. Would Gilbert become in my memory a legend like the one surrounding his mother, that would serve to magnify an encounter that had no future?

I've never known how word had got around—probably a visit from one of my three roommates or by someone they'd spoken to, who'd rushed to the Sélect to repeat it all—but whatever it was, when I got to the restaurant just before the six o'clock rush, the whole staff plus a few regular clients who were already seated gave me a triumphant welcome.

I was so embarrassed I hid in the kitchen for a good fifteen minutes, waiting impatiently under the innocuous teasing of Nick and Lucien. What shocked me was not so much that they knew what had happened the night before, it was the way they were carrying on about it. When Janine or Madeleine met someone, we showed a little more restraint. Was what had happened to me surprising enough to provoke such a reaction? She's finally found someone who deigned to take an interest in her, poor girl, we should encourage her and let her know that we're as relieved as she is! I knew that I was showing bad faith, that there hadn't been a hint of condescension in their behaviour, that they were sincere in their awkward way, that it was my reaction, not theirs, that was excessive. No way, though, could I take it all with a grain of salt and play along. Actually, I refused to see Gilbert as a simple trophy. Especially because I was already afraid of losing him …

When Madeleine stuck her head in the door and said that everyone thought I was taking a very long time to change, I nearly told her to go to hell, though I adore her.

She frowned and looked me in the eyes.

"Where's your sense of humour, Céline, honestly!"

Then shrugged and walked away.

She was right, I was taking everything way too seriously, but I was still uncomfortable. How should I react? I had absolutely no experience with this kind of thing! Tell them everything? Or say nothing and stick to double-entendres and cheap insinuations? Use Gilbert to make a reputation for myself that I didn't deserve? I knew that things wouldn't sort themselves out—just the opposite!—if I stayed with the cook and his assistant when the rush was about to start, that I was just postponing the inevitable, so I decided to face the sarcasm and jump into the fray, regardless of the consequences. No matter what.

But when I went into the restaurant, neat and tidy in my waitress outfit, cap straight and notepad in hand, it was as if they'd realized their faux pas and had consulted one another during my absence, or maybe Madeleine had spoken to them, because they acted as if nothing had happened. Suddenly there'd been no triumphal entrance—Triumphal entrance? What triumphal entrance?—they were waiting, perfectly innocent, for me to go up and down the aisles and take their orders, nothing more. As usual. A respite because the busiest time of day was about to start, or had they really given up when they saw how uncomfortable I was? That, too, I would never know.

The place had been full since I'd got there. Heads were bent over menus, you could even sense some simmering discontent if the starting signal for the evening meal didn't come soon.

The clients who were already there when I arrived were red-eared as they gave me their orders. I could sense the curiosity in their voices, the wish to know everything in their eyes. I merely played the efficient waitress while I jotted in my order pad a little more diligently than usual, the side orders of fries or the extra barbecue sauce.

Aimée Langevin—who'd disappeared from the restaurant for a long time after her three years at the Institut des arts appliqués and had come back the week before, slimmer and calmer, along with some of the actors she'd performed with in *The Trojan Women* two years earlier and the young director who was starting to have a serious reputation—was the only one who alluded to the thing that mustn't be mentioned. Which saved me from a terrible evening.

I hadn't noticed them at first, most likely because they were quieter than usual. Eight of them were packed into a booth meant for six, elbow-to-elbow in the overheated restaurant, and they seemed impatient to eat. Were they rehearsing somewhere near the restaurant? Or going to the theatre at eight and in a hurry? Rita, who'd played Andromache in *The Trojan Women*, was chewing on the slice of lemon that came with her cup of tea. Someone had got there before me, since I hadn't been there to serve them.

I apologized for making them wait.

Aimée reached out to touch my forearm.

"We understand. In fact we'd all like to be in your shoes."

The aptness of that remark and the smiles that blossomed on those friendly faces washed away some of my remaining hostility and rancour. Indeed, why had I resisted what had been in the end simply understandable happiness for a girl who's just met a guy? Once again I had thought first about my distinctive physique and what I believed the others thought about it, when instead, besides being happy for me, they'd been jealous of this start of a relationship, of the possibilities and the problems it represented. Doesn't everyone, always, like to find themselves in the early days of a love affair? The others had been happy for me, couldn't I be happy for myself?

The rest of the evening rush went by in a rather pleasant kind of fog that I let myself slip into while letting my mind wander, in spite of the torrent of orders and the impatient clients, onto everything that had happened during my first real night of love. I even brought my fingers to my nose now and then to check whether Gilbert's private odour was still there. If the clients had known they'd have probably shuddered in horror.

Aimée Langevin and her group had left me a huge tip and she came to see me before she left, obviously curious to find out more.

"I'll drop in tomorrow night for a cup of tea."

I winked.

"If I give you all the details, we'll go through a whole box of teabags!"

As much as I can, I avoid the late-night conversations that Janine tries to start when the restaurant is empty, the customers gone, and we have another few hours of work. She gets on my nerves with her ready-made judgments and her way of interfering with everybody's life, of wanting to solve all their problems by herself. If she folds the paper napkins while she smokes those strong cigarettes of hers, I'll fill the salt shakers and sugar bowls; if she starts bustling about with a bottle of vinegar in one hand and a rag in the other to scrub off the tables and booths stains that are sometimes suspicious, left by certain customers who are bigger bastards than the rest, I stay at the employees' table next to the kitchen door with one last cup of tea. If I'm unlucky enough to be taken hostage by her endless prattling, too shy to tell her to shut up or to walk away in mid-sentence, I pretend to be listening, nodding now and then or making a sound that could pass for something resembling agreement. Actually she doesn't talk to me, she listens to herself talking. And it can go on for hours. In fact, I've been known to fall asleep in the middle of one of those lengthy orations, without her seeming to notice ... Lucien, Nick's Haitian assistant, calls her the chattering magpie and likes to enrage her when she goes on for too long by imitating obnoxious bird cries to cover her voice. She calls him a bad-mannered immigrant, he calls her a repulsive racist. She complains to Nick, he complains to me.

That night, though, I wasn't going to avoid the conversation; I knew that by listening to her, I would find out everything that had been said about me and Gilbert and of course I wanted to know what malicious gossip was being spread via bush telegraph. To my amazement, though, instead of her usual monologue, she asked me a number of serious questions. For once, Janine didn't want to judge, decree or decide (she'd do that afterwards, when I'd told her everything she wanted to know!) But each of her questions bounced off a wall of silence, or else the answer she got was monosyllabic like the ones that I generally give her but that, this time, she was obliged to listen to and maybe saw as unacceptable insults in view of the interest she'd deigned to show in my situation which until then had been seen as hopeless.

Then she decided to change tactics by using a tone of voice close to that of a friendly confession or a personal confidence. For a while, she'd been asking impertinent questions about Gilbert, questions about size, performance and staying power when, finally realizing that she'd get nowhere with this method, she stretched out her hand to touch mine, something she'd never dared to do before, even though she was lavish with hugs and kisses and cuddles of every variety with others. I'd always suspected, though, that I disgusted her and I was amused to see how hard she was struggling against her disgust. I could see her coming from a mile away, I laughed at her by showing an imperturbable face, but instead of bursting her balloon right away I let her carry on: for once I listened to the usual string of stale clichés that constituted her armchair psychology and it took a lot of control not to laugh in her face.

"Sometimes, Céline, there're things that are hard to let out but that have to get out anyway ... Things it's hard to admit. Things that hurt. If that's the case, if what happened to you last night is ... I don't know ... humiliating or shocking or sad, you have to let it out ... It's no good keeping it in, hiding them, it will only hurt you more ... You just need the right person to listen to you and you've found her ... Trust me, you'll feel better ... "

Besides not being very subtle, the way she tried to worm information out of me showed incredible naïveté, and I felt a little sorry for her. She didn't let my stubborn silence get her down though: she probably thought that she'd find a sensitive point and set off the avalanche of confidences she hoped for. And then, of course use it, not against me, she isn't mean, but to spice up her conversations with clients and the other employees and to perfect her reputation—already significant, especially with the drag queens—as a tremendous giver of advice and outstanding settler of conflicts of every kind. She was thinking not about me but herself. I was the last bastion of resistance to her wonderful generosity— along with Lucien, who also knew what she was up to—and she thought she'd found the way to crush it for good by making me her debtor.

"Let yourself go for once, stop holding back ... It'll do you good. The guy's already got a reputation so if he did something bad to you, everybody should know ... He has to be dealt with once and for all ... There's too many like him who get away with murder and it has to stop. When I saw you leave with him last night, I knew how it would end and I should've stopped you ... "

And when I finally understood—it was about time—that what she *really* wanted was for things to have gone badly between Gilbert and me so she could blab about it all over town, because she couldn't imagine that I might have spent a wonderful night because a midget couldn't have good and satisfying sex, the thought was inconceivable, I was so angry that I could see the moment coming when I'd have to hit her.

To make her drool then, I told her everything. Ev-ery-thing. She wanted details, she got them! But not the ones she was expecting. She thought she'd be hearing the heartrending outpourings of a whining, frustrated, frigid freak. Instead, she got a description of revels like she herself couldn't even imagine, so I hoped anyway: the smells, the sensations, the cries, the waves of pleasure, the silly giggles, the tears when it was just too good, the exhaustion after so many orgasms, the rest periods between sessions of sublime love-making and even the frustration at having to get out of bed and have breakfast in the morning, with promises to do it again—it was all there. I was lyrical, I was to the point, I found the *bon mot* and the right expression very easily, I practically mimed what I told her and I know for sure that the picture I painted was clear and possibly disturbing. For once, I parked my modesty at the door and had a fabulous time watching her blush to the roots of hair that was too blonde to be believed. She sat there, unmoving, spellbound, she didn't even think to close her mouth which hung open over her cup of coffee that had been cold for a while. She didn't try even once to interrupt me, something unheard-of, and as my story came to an end, she just murmured, as she swallowed her spit, "Well, how about that ... "

If I had described some endless horror, some unbounded pain, she'd have had millions of things to tell me, advice to lavish, words of consolation both hollow and empty to dish out, she'd have played guide, mentor, guru, she'd have tried to take control of my life the way she did, gladly and unscrupulously, with anyone so misguided as to confide in her, but before this brazen display, this triumphant explosion of delights shared in a vast explosion of excess people dream of but can't even hope to experience because they imagine that it can't exist, she was paralyzed, suspended, I think, between the most naïve amazement, (Why her and not me?) and the utmost incredulity, (It's impossible, she's saying whatever comes into her head to impress me!)

But she simply stacked the paper napkins she'd folded earlier and got up from the fake leather booth without adding a word. I honestly think I was the very first person who'd ever left her speechless: faced with someone else's misery she was very forthcoming, even chatty, but confronted with happiness, she realized that she was disarmed and useless. The vulture hadn't found the rotting food she'd been looking for and now, vanquished, was going back to her nest.

All of the evening's tension, my uncertainty, my doubts, had been cleared away by my gymnastics and the relief I felt made me sleepy. I could have stretched out my arms on the Arborite table, rested my head on them, and slept till morning, I was so exhausted.

But I'd forgotten the note that my three roommates had left before they went out ...

Just as Lucien, bent over until he was nearly on all fours, was getting ready to lock the restaurant door, they flounced in behind the Duchess, who was sporting her tragedienne's expression. With their usual sense of drama, they'd dressed for the occasion, all in black needless to say, and looking like a chorus of weeping women paid to lament over the tragic passing of an important member of the royal family. The Duchess—a black and pink whirlwind reeking of Tulipe noire by Chénard—came up next to me and hurled herself at the booth as if the fate of the world depended on it. She was sweating bullets, her jet-black wig had shifted and was hanging over one ear, like a beret on the young leading lady in a French film. Suzy Prim. Or Sophie Desmarets.

"Hands off, Céline! Don't touch! Don't even think about it! He'll turn into your own private Tooth Pick! He'll put you through what Tooth Pick put me through!"

After the memories I'd just poured out to Janine, I didn't want anyone to show me leniency, mainly because I didn't think I needed it. Nor was I in the mood to be given advice on the lines of, "I, who have suffered more than you, don't want to see you suffer the same trials and tribulations," as the numerous woes of the Duchess, especially the latest ones brought back from Acapulco in February, were the least of my worries just then. So I held up my hand to silence her. After that I stood up on the seat to be at the same height as the other three who were already crowding around the table. I made eye contact with all four, one after the other, very slowly, then said loud enough to be heard all the way into the kitchen, "Do you mind if I live my life without everybody I know thinking they have to butt in? Can I? Thanks. And good night!"

Then I left to change my clothes.

Having no word from Gilbert and too proud to call him myself, after four or five days I thought I'd never see him again. Or maybe every now and then if he ever came to the Sélect with his friends. Which wasn't likely to happen any time soon, as it seemed that he wanted to avoid me. Another smooth talker, I feared, very intense and very sincere in my presence but who forgets I exist as soon as he turns his back. I had put a brake on any regrets I might feel though, because I had no intention of suffering, especially not after being with him only once, no matter how wonderful it had been. And so I wrapped my pleasant memories in imaginary cotton batting on which I'd written the words *do not touch* and went on with my life as if nothing had happened. If by misfortune my thoughts turned to him, to his blue eyes, his devastating smile, his fantastic body, his smell, his humour, I tried to distract myself by keeping busy with whatever there was to do. Meaning that I was often hyperactive. Sometimes it worked, sometimes I felt like smashing everything around me—human beings included.

I'd seen my female co-workers at the Sélect suffer a thousand deaths, turn antsy and even mean when they were waiting to hear from someone who wasn't calling. The drag queens with whom I'd worked at the Boudoir were also different when they were abandoned and I refused that it be my fate to become one of those broken women who have just one focus in their lives—a man who isn't there, and it kills them.

My friends, the ones from the restaurant and the ones from the apartment on Place Jacques-Cartier, made themselves discreet—which was something of an accomplishment—and didn't mention his name even once during the two weeks when he disappeared. Not even the Duchess, though she could have said I told you so, he's not the man for you and he could drive you mad the way I'd been driven mad by Tooth Pick, right here in Montreal, and by the Peter in Acapulco she never shut up about. Because of course they all thought that I was suffering in silence. That I was hiding my anger and my moods from them by pretending that the night had never happened. I wasn't hiding them, I'd buried them, deep enough that I couldn't find them myself.

I had nearly reached my goal, total oblivion, I only thought about Gilbert every other night, when I imagined that his scent still hung in the air of my bedroom, when he landed back into my life, without a shred of guilt and happy as ever, one night when Nick had decided to close early because the restaurant was empty and I would be able to have an early night. I was coming down with a spring flu and I had a violent headache that was hammering at my brain. I would down a bottle of aspirin, then bury myself in blankets and hope I'd feel better tomorrow.

Janine, who'd already changed, was on her way to the door saying goodnight when they turned up. I heard their voices first, which I'd recognized of course, especially that of Louise, the singer, which was the most distinctive, and I thought to myself that even though they were all here, Gilbert probably wasn't. He would have preferred to finish the evening somewhere else … Then I heard his laugh and I froze right there between the tables, in front of the kitchen door.

The first thing that struck me when I finally turned around though was Janine, who was coming towards me, taking off her gloves which were too heavy for the season. She didn't want to miss one bit of what was going to happen, damn her, she wanted to see everything, hear everything, so that later she could repeat it to anyone who'd listen. Exaggerating, going over any parts that weren't juicy enough for her, even inventing details if she had to … I beckoned to her. She came over to me, probably assuming that she'd have a front-row seat when I blew up.

"If you don't mind working without your uniform, Janine, would you look after them ... I've got the flu, my head is splitting, I want to go home ... "

She looked disappointed—serving these grubby individuals was the last thing she wanted to do—but she didn't dare refuse, it was the only excuse for staying she could think of.

"Well ... I was leaving but as a favour to you, poor dear ... "

Her tone, concerned, anxious, was phony; the magnanimity she wanted to show, even more: she was hoping to seem concerned, even though she couldn't hide her excitement at the prospect of an imminent drama, and her expression—half-delighted, half-sad—was both grotesque and hilarious.

And it was then, I imagine, that Gilbert noticed me because all at once his voice was louder, clear and cheerful, "Céline! Love of my life!"

He threw himself at me, took me in his arms and started to waltz in the aisles of the restaurant. Why didn't I scream? Why didn't I slap his face? Why didn't I demand then and there that he put me down, leave, and never set foot here again? Why? His smell? His big eyes? His oh-so-sincere smile?

Because his smile and his joy at seeing me again were sincere, that was obvious. I've always been able to recognize hypocrisy and bad faith on people's faces, I grew up surrounded by their phony smiles and duplicity because they kept trying to protect me from other people's reactions to my physique, so I developed a keen sense of the feelings I provoke in other people. And what I read on Gilbert's face as he was waltzing me through the Sélect and singing my praises was beyond any doubt terribly sincere. He was glad to see me and he showed it quite innocently, with no ulterior motive.

As if we'd seen each other the night before.

He finally put me down at the employees' table and took a seat across from me, lighting a cigarette. Then he asked, moving the ashtray closer to his left elbow, "Mind if I smoke?"

I shrugged.

He slapped the table as if I'd just said something hilarious and I wondered if he was drunk. But he didn't smell of booze and his agitation was different from my mother's when she'd been drinking. His eyes didn't shine with the wet, dull light of a committed alcoholic. Was it pot? Or something stronger? Given the people he hung out with, it wouldn't have surprised me. No, he seemed in full possession of his faculties, just a little more excited than the last time I'd seen him. In any case, it was his thoughtlessness that held my attention. Had he forgotten the minute he was out the door that we were supposed to call each other?

He waved to Janine, who joined us, a little too eagerly for my liking. She'd shed her coat and was taking the orders of Gilbert's friends at one of the big tables next to the window that looks out on St. Catherine Street. It was the first time I'd seen a waitress at the Sélect working without the obligatory uniform and it was strange. I thought she looked like someone's aunt who, instead of fixing a meal for her guests, was asking them what they wanted before she cooked. She bent over Gilbert, obsequiously, as if she was going to drink in his every word, though she must have been thinking about everything I'd just told her and was going over parts of it, licking her lips greedily.

"Tell my buddies I'm eating with my darling. I'll see them after rehearsal tomorrow afternoon. I missed her so much I can't spend another hour without her."

He looked at me with eyes nearly as loving as on the night when he wanted to start again what we'd barely finished.

"Why didn't you call me, Céline? You didn't want to see me again?"

Surely he wasn't going to put the blame on me!

"Since when is it up to the girls to call the guys?"

He seemed as surprised as I was.

"Céline! What century is this! We aren't in the 1940s! It's the 1960s, the years of liberation, the years when things erupt, the years when everything's finally possible and everything's allowed! If you wanted to see me you could've called. I'd have been here in half an hour!"

"What about you, did you want to see me?"

"Did I! I was just waiting to hear from you!"

"So why didn't you call?"

"I didn't want to pressure you, Céline. I wanted you to be free to decide! I didn't want to push you! I didn't want to stick like a burr."

"Neither did I! Did you ever think of that?"

He took a long drag of his cigarette and blew the smoke out his nose.

"You wouldn't have, Céline. I didn't want anything in the world as much as I wanted to hear from you. I won't say I sat by the phone for two weeks, you wouldn't believe me and you'd be right, I had other things to do, rehearsals and all that, but often, several times a day, I'd wonder how come I hadn't heard from you ... In the end I figured I'd been a one night stand for you and I shouldn't push it ... "

I had the same reaction as before, when he'd started coming on to me: if it was an act it was a very good one, because it was all there—the frown, the eyes damp with emotion, his right hand covering my left one, the cigarette he'd forgotten in the ashtray. If it was all phony and calculated, Gilbert was without a shadow of a doubt the world's worst son-of-a-bitch.

"I didn't eat here so you wouldn't be uncomfortable. If I had to walk past the window, I crossed the street so you wouldn't see me ... "

He must have read the doubt in my eyes because he stopped in mid-sentence.

"I hope you believe me."

I didn't answer. Of course I *wanted* to believe him, I'd *prefer* to believe him, but I didn't intend to behave like an idiot.

"What will it take for you to believe me? I'm no liar, Céline, I've got plenty of faults but I'm not a liar. If there's been a misunderstanding it's both our faults, not just mine! I'm not some cold-blooded bastard who took advantage of you and dropped you right after, please don't think that … And the reason I worked up the nerve to come back here tonight was so I'd know, because in the past two weeks I've been asking myself plenty of questions too!"

It was at that moment, I think, that I became aware of the strange over-excitement I hadn't seen before, which caused a subtle change in him. He was both the same and different. When he looked at me it seemed as if the rest of the world didn't exist for him, but if, say, he was giving Janine his order, all that intensity was directed at her and it was me who no longer existed, or so it seemed. I told myself it was impossible, that I was being ridiculously jealous when he looked somewhere else now that I'd got him back, but something in my chest—a tiny hint of anxiety, my heart beating a little faster, butterflies fluttering in my stomach—was telling me that if I had to make a choice I had to make it then and there. That this new over-excitement, this strange feverish intensity there'd been no sign of two weeks earlier, were the key to a door it would be dangerous to open. Jean-le-Décollé had said something about it, but I couldn't remember what.

All at once Gilbert, whom I'd seen naked, with whom I'd shared the supreme pleasure, whom I'd caused to double up with laughter in my bed, was becoming an unfathomable mystery simply because of his undeniable sincerity despite the change that had come about in him. He was different, yes, his behaviour didn't quite correspond with my memory of him but I couldn't claim to know him well enough to have encountered all the facets of his personality. What was important for the moment was that he wasn't lying. If he'd been a liar, if he'd turned out to be a monster of male egotism, I'd have known right away and dropped him there in the middle of his act, with no scruples or remorse. But I believed him and it was a lot more complicated than if I'd sensed that he was trying to lie to me.

Besides, wasn't he right when he said that I could have called him? What had stopped me? Not concern about appropriate behaviour, of that I was positive. But fear of rejection. As usual.

Everything I did was always steeped in that. All my life I had preferred to go without rather than risk being turned down. And when I was unlucky enough to be refused something, my reaction was way out of proportion. My fear of rejection was too acute, too painful I suppose, and sometimes I was way too cautious. This time though a human being was involved! I'd got along without Gilbert's company for two weeks and now he'd just confessed he'd would have liked to see me again! I'd been brave enough to throw myself into his arms—but not to call him. Which explains the sense that I was saying goodbye to him forever when he started down the steps into the Place-d'Armes Metro station: I knew that I wouldn't call him and I thought that if he didn't call me I'd never see him again.

He plunked his elbows on either side of the plate that Janine had just brought him, simpering like a little girl. After the vamp act, which didn't seem to have worked, now it was the little girl who's decided it's high time she lost her virginity. It was indecent. In any other circumstances I'd have thought it was funny, but now I could have smacked her. She was too big an idiot to remember that we'd be working together the next night and that trying to seduce a man she'd been bad-mouthing was a true betrayal. But I suppose that for her it was the present moment that counted and she wasn't thinking about the consequences of her action. She was trying, in case reconciliation between Gilbert and me turned out to be impossible ... She too was ready to suffer in order to experience what I had. Or to check and see if I'd lied. Nonetheless, I was savouring a little victory: which of us when all was said and done would seem more frustrated, her or me?

In any event, if Gilbert was aware of her little game he didn't show it.

He wiped his lips after chewing his first mouthful for a long time. A remnant of what he'd been taught was good manners? Had his grandmother, Madame Veuve's mother, taught him that he must chew his meat twenty-two times before he swallowed—like my mother with her strokes of the hairbrush—if he wanted to take full advantage of the benefits of his food and did he still obey automatically after all these years? While I practically swallow whole whatever food I put in my mouth to ignore my mother's advice … Across from me then was the very image of a beatnik—the clothes, the appearance, the posture proved it—but well-educated, which was also surprising! The thought of it amused me and I was weak enough to forget what I'd learned about him earlier, the inexplicable agitation that had worried me, and I smiled. He slapped the table.

"At last, a smile!"

He knew he'd won and didn't hide his satisfaction. Which was quite adorable actually. Is any gift more gratifying than giving someone a second chance? It makes you feel at once relieved and generous.

He poured salt onto his fries—too much—and opened the bottle of ketchup.

"Anyway, I'm kidnapping you tonight! No Place Jacques-Cartier! I'm taking you to the heart of the next in-place, right near the future towers of Radio-Canada and the CBC! St. Rose Street awaits you, my dear. It isn't renovated, it looks pathetic, the floors aren't level and the walls are barely standing, but they say that the artists who want to get closer to Radio-Canada and Channel 10 will be moving in before long … Some day, anyway … Meanwhile, I've found a pad that costs practically nothing … It's tiny, you couldn't call it pretty, but it suits me … "

Did he want to avoid my apartment so he wouldn't run into my roommates again?

Somewhere in my head a voice was shouting at me to stop analyzing everything and let myself go—for the sheer pleasure of letting myself go.

"You haven't answered. Still mad? That's not what your face says … "

The answer that emerged from my mouth was one of the most pitiful things I've ever said.

"All my things are at home … "

He broke into the wonderful loud laughter that I'd liked so much when I heard it explode from my pillows, the burst of unalloyed joy that transported you to a world without questions from where anything serious was banned for as long as it lasted, which you wanted to stretch out until the end of eternity because it was made up of the very essence of happiness. Never had laughter delighted me like that. And I didn't want to lose it. At the risk of … My inner voice broke into my thinking.

"At the risk of nothing. Leave it alone. Just enjoy it!"

Gilbert had put his hand on my arm when he was laughing and a lovely warmth was flooding me all the way to the elbows.

"Don't think you'll need a nightgown! And we can buy a toothbrush at the Pharmacie Montréal on the way if that'll put your mind at rest for tomorrow morning … "

"I need more than a toothbrush. I need aspirin, I'm coming down with the flu … "

He frowned.

"Are you saying that to get rid of me?"

"Of course not. I've been feeling lousy all day."

In the face of my hesitation he leaned across the table. His shirt rubbed against his fries, I saw a little ketchup stain form, and I thought that it was going to change his odour, that I'd have to wait till he was undressed to smell it again. So I was intending to see him naked before the night was over, I couldn't hide it, and my reluctance fell away all at once.

Why fight it?

I decided to make him wait a while though, like last time.

"Let's go for a walk first, then we'll see … "

I didn't suspect that the road I was agreeing to travel at that moment would lead me, as early as tomorrow morning, into the darkest corner of the soul of Gilbert Forget.

While I was changing in the ladies' room, Gilbert explained to his friends, who were paying their bills, that contrary to plans he wouldn't be going with them to Michèle Sandry's show at the Cochon Borgne, a few doors west on St. Catherine Street. After that he went to the employees' table to wait for me over one last coffee. When I came out, the restaurant was empty, with Janine hanging around at the cash register while she put on her gloves. Holding his keys, Lucien was waiting till everyone had left before locking the door. The same small ceremony was repeated at the Sélect every night, I was used to it and didn't even notice it, but now there was something rare in this place where even when there aren't any customers, you can always hear the sound of conversation because the staff is talkative: a weighty silence tinged with an uneasiness that was hard to define spreading through the restaurant. It was as though the three individuals squeezed into the entrance—Janine, Lucien and Françoise—were expecting something important to happen, as if some part of the evening that would make it genuinely successful were missing.

Were they waiting for Gilbert and me to leave to see if we were going in the same direction? Did they think that Gilbert was trying too hard and that maybe I should put him in his place? With their help? When Gilbert bent down to help me on with my coat, all three turned their heads in our direction, ready to intervene. I even spotted Nick's face in the little square window in the kitchen door. So I was right. They were waiting to see my reaction before deciding if they'd come to my rescue. They'd seen Gilbert debating, gesticulating, negotiating, but they didn't know the outcome of our conversation and were all set to protect me if the need arose. I was both touched and annoyed. It was very kind of them to want to defend me, but they knew I could manage perfectly well on my own. After all, Gilbert wouldn't be the first man I'd put in his place with a well-chosen insult, should it be necessary. Our evenings were filled with every variety of drunk and to gain respect we had to learn quickly how to bring them under control, and they knew that so far no one had got the better of Céline Poulin!

Gilbert was all excited, hopping like an over-excited puppy as we made our way to the exit.

"When I think that I was on my way to the Cochon Borgne to laugh at Michèle Sandry! Another evening wasted … "

Françoise frowned when we walked past the cash and Janine gawked.

"Weren't you supposed to have the flu?"

I gave a smile that was intended to look reassuring.

"See you tomorrow, girls."

Lucien hesitated for a second or two before pushing open the door to let us out. It was so touching that I wanted to throw my arms around his neck and kiss him on both of his beautiful gleaming black cheeks.

"Everything okay, Céline?"

I patted his hand as I passed him.

"Everything's fine, Lucien. Go to bed. Go to bed, everybody, see you all tomorrow night."

Outside, it smelled of spring. Of hops, too, because the wind was from the east and the stench from Molson's brewery was coming all the way up from the Old Port to St. Catherine Street. Gilbert took a deep breath.

"When the wind is more from the southeast than the northwest you know that spring's arrived. Did you ever think, Céline, the first thing you smell here in Montreal in the spring is beer? Maybe that's why we drink so much."

I shrugged while I unbuttoned my coat because the air, saturated with that pervasive smell, was slightly sickening. And clinging.

"But the northwest wind doesn't stop Montrealers from drinking beer all winter ... "

He laughed, clapping his hands. As if he were applauding a good bit of dialogue.

"You're right ... because this winter I drank beer, it's true, I can't hide it ... And it's never in short supply at our rehearsals!"

Small talk between two people who don't know what will be decided in the next few seconds.

The two of us stood planted there in front of the Sélect, Gilbert hopeful, me hesitant. Like the first time. It's not that I didn't want to go home with Gilbert, the prospect of experiencing again what I'd discovered in his arms two weeks before was incredibly exciting, but without really admitting it, I wanted to let myself be desired. That was new for me, and thrilling.

The sky was red, as it has been in every big city in the world for the past few years, apparently. Because of the electric lighting that's reflected in the sky or something like that ... It wasn't very pretty and I'd have preferred an enormous blue vault dotted with stars or pierced by a full moon to celebrate this brand new joy in my life: a man who desired me. I would have liked a perfect night like the ones in novels and films, and music too, a great orchestra that would describe my feelings in long melodies too easy to hold on to and hard to erase. The object of all this excitement was, however, a long lazy individual whose eyes were too blue and who was incapable, I knew it, of bringing me genuine happiness ... but after all, maybe genuine happiness wasn't what I was looking for ...

I stuffed my hands in my pockets when the time came to move, for fear that he would grab hold of one—the same image came back to me: a daddy helping his little girl to cross the street. We would never look like a pair of lovers in public and we had to accept it, even if it was mortifying.

Gilbert was dragging his feet a little as we headed south across St. Catherine. He was downcast, like a little boy who's been punished.

"Did you decide?"

The light had turned red and we had to get a move on.

"You mentioned the Pharmacie Montréal ... Actually I have to go there ... Because of this flu I'm coming down with... I'll walk with you for a while as I said ... Along the way I'll decide what I'll do after that ... "

He seemed so disappointed, so downcast all at once that I told myself it was cruel to keep teasing him.

"Okay, dummy, I've decided, I'll go home with you ... But there're a few things we have to get clear ... "

His triumphant cry startled the few passers-by. They wouldn't have imagined that it was this wobbly midget who'd made the handsome blond guy so happy and I wished I could turn to them and say, "What can I say, I have that effect on men!"

On our way to St. Rose Street we paid a quick visit to the pharmacy, where I bought aspirin as well as what I needed "for a sleep-over," those little things that men find useless and silly, but that women, me anyway, hate going without. He laughed at the sight of my paper bag which he thought was unwieldy and I told him he'd be very happy tomorrow morning to have me in his bed smelling of lime blossom and fresh breath, as well as being over my incipient flu.

St. Catherine Street east of Amherst was empty and I thought to myself that I would probably never set foot there alone, it felt so abandoned, sad and dangerous in a way that I couldn't describe but that was all-pervasive. A woman alone in this part of town at such a late hour would not be safe, of that I was certain, even though we were just a few blocks from where I worked. People would assume she was a prostitute or a willing victim. For all our claims that Montreal isn't a dangerous city, the atmosphere permeating this part of the street refuted it, and I couldn't help looking over my shoulder frequently to see if some sleazy, malicious individual was following us with a butcher knife.

Gilbert noticed it.

"Why do you keep looking back like that, as if you're scared?"

"I confess, I don't feel very brave … "

He gave me a wink, set my bag on the ground, and started to hop and skip like a boxer practising for a big fight.

"I'm here to defend you."

I stopped in the middle of the sidewalk.

"That's what I'm afraid of … "

That wonderful loud laughter again. So candid. A drug I was afraid that I could never do without.

The smell of hops had been getting stronger after Wolfe Street and I wasn't sure that it was coming just from the Molson brewery: every time we walked past one of the many taverns—it was closing time—our nostrils were assailed by the combined odours of undigested beer and rancid sweat that were being blasted to the sidewalk in great bubbles of dry air through noisy ventilators. If ever I had to come back to Gilbert's place, especially if I were alone, I'd take a taxi. To avoid danger ... and the smells. If it was already so strong in April, imagine the July heatwave!

Guessing at my hesitation in this neighbourhood which he obviously loved, Gilbert chose to defend it, serving up for the second time his theory that this part of the city would become the heart of Montreal's cultural life because of the two Radio-Canada towers, though work on one of them had stopped more than a year and a half before, and the proximity of the studios of Channel 10. I'd been hearing that ever since starting work at the Sélect four years earlier, but I couldn't see any striking difference. An entire Montreal neighbourhood had been demolished to put up those two towers and it was said that once they were finished, in a year or two if work resumed, they would already be too small and probably obsolete. Meanwhile, tens of thousands of some of the most destitute Montrealers had been driven towards the north of the city where everything cost more and they were liable to starve to death, quite unscrupulously one of the most colourful neighbourhoods in town had been wiped out, but "the development of the nerve centre of the city's artistic life" hadn't started yet, the section of St. Catherine Street where Gilbert and I were walking, which was abandoned, dirty and foul-smelling, proved it.

I left him to his rambling, telling myself that surely he would wake up one day and realize that his poor St. Rose Street was never going to change. The cultural revolution hadn't happened yet, those in charge had been content with simply killing part of Montreal, then abandoning it to an unenviable fate.

"You look so sad, Céline. Don't you feel like coming to my place?"

A real guy question. Everything had to revolve around him, simply because he was there. It was almost reassuring, actually, to see that he wasn't all that different from the others ... My reply skirted his question.

"I wouldn't want to give you my flu ... "

"I wouldn't mind catching your flu ... If it means you'll be spending the night."

We walked down Champlain Street, dark and cheerless with its old houses so decrepit that they seemed uninhabited. He started to sing the song that talks about propellers and airlines that was part of the show he was taking part in.

I took advantage of it to change the subject.

"What exactly is this show you're rehearsing?"

He started hopping and skipping again, I suppose because my question had sent his adrenalin level up a notch. He was agitated again as he'd been earlier that evening, as if he couldn't control himself, as if he were skidding out of control without wanting to and couldn't get a grip on himself. He was talking fast, getting carried away, not finishing his sentences.

"Ah! It's going to be amazing! Amazing! You can't imagine ... Montreal's never seen anything like it ... There's songs ... sketches ... monologues ... but it's not a variety show. Not really. Not the kind we know anyway ... It's so different we haven't even come up with a name yet, if you can imagine ... For now we're just calling it *the show* because it's the only thing we can come up with ... I'm incredibly lucky to be part of it."

"Have you known them long?"

"No. Well ... See, it's not me who was supposed to do what I'm doing. It's Chubby, a buddy of mine that got sick ... Mono ... They had to find somebody in a hurry."

"Is that how you ended up playing guitar in the band?"

"Oh, I do all kinds of things ... I'm not just a guitarist ... I'm in a sketch with Mouffe and Yvon ... I've never done that before but I do my best ... They get impatient sometimes because I'm slower than the rest of them ... But Mouffe is more patient with me ... "

"Is Mouffe the one with the straight black hair?"

"Yes. And she's with Charlebois ... Do you know him?"

"I don't think so."

"His songs are amazing, Céline! We aren't in the woods any more with our *ceinture fléchée* and our step-dancing, those songs are so modern ... So new ... The rehearsals are incredible ... but scary."

"When do you start?"

"Next month ... if all goes well."

"Are you ready?"

"No. Sometimes I think we never will be. I mean we haven't even got a title!"

We'd turned left onto St. Rose. A row of two-storey houses, without balconies and seedy looking, that opened directly onto the street. You went up two steps and right away you were at the front door. In the summer, when they're crushed by the heat, the population of St. Rose Street must put their chairs on the sidewalk and gossip over their soft drinks, keeping an eye on the children so they won't run between the cars. But now, in the spring, and in the middle of the night, you could think it was a ghost town in an American movie: no one in sight, a few shattered windows, a little draft because the street was so narrow.

"Here we are. It isn't a palace but it doesn't cost much and I like that a lot."

I who boast so often about having no prejudices, I confess that I was expecting an indescribable mess, the smell of stale cigarettes, dirty plates sitting on empty pizza boxes, a bed unmade for months giving off a sickening funky smell—in a word, the pad of a bohemian who lives alone. What I found was totally different. It was attractive, it was clean, everything was neat and tidy, the dishes were done and the floor was gleaming. The living room, furnished with taste though without a big budget, bathed in diffuse indirect light from an assortment of old lamps that Gilbert had disguised with coloured scarves. As for the bedroom, it would have shamed a soldier's barracks: you could have bounced a coin on the bed, the spread was so taut, nothing was lying on the floor and it smelled of patchouli and incense, not, as I'd expected, of dirty sheets and unwashed underwear.

I was a little ashamed of myself and my surprise, which I tried to conceal with a series of compliments that maybe went too far, did not escape Gilbert, who was smiling proudly.

"You can't get over it, can you, that it's clean and neat? Everyone who comes here has the same reaction. I'm obsessive. Not about myself, sometimes I let myself go, but the environment I live in has to be perfect. When I come here and see everything in its place it's reassuring. I don't know why. The only thing that doesn't fit is me, the rest is organized. I don't try to explain it … I've always been like this."

I accepted the beer he offered me, even though I'm not crazy about it and wanted to move on to other things, and we settled on the living-room sofa.

I told him again how much I liked his apartment, I even confessed to surprise about his taste in interior decoration. What I did not admit though was that it worried me a little: the lanky beatnik who lives in a house so unlike him, where you'd expect to see a hooker or a drag queen, not a guitarist from an avant-garde show, didn't reassure me and I was beginning to wonder what kind of world I'd landed in, with what kind of weirdo. Was Gilbert even more unusual than he'd seemed at first? He wasn't homosexual—oh no, not another prejudice!—he'd proven that, but I was worried about what turn the surprises might take.

Our second night of love was, if possible, even more phenomenal than the first. From the start of our lovemaking, just as we were launching into the preliminaries, I put aside my critical sense, I didn't think even once about how we must have looked—him, the tall, blond Viking with arms and legs that went on forever and me, the busy little creature who had to make a huge effort to be able to follow the action—and, totally free of inhibition, I took off into the sheer delight of sensations and odours. I read in his eyes and I heard in his voice the pleasure mounting, exploding in incoherent cries, I felt him going soft after each orgasm, then come back to life after some silly laughter and inconsequential caresses. He watched, he followed, he stoked my own pleasure with grunts of encouragement, his body long accustomed to what was new for me, his hands everywhere at once, his mouth burrowing and skillful. We rolled out of bed and continued on the floor what we'd started between the sheets; he smoked a cigarette lying on a carpet that smelled of disinfectant while I curled his pubic hair around my sticky fingers. The smells that filled the room drove me wild with excitement and I imagined myself steeping in it until the end of my days. Like the first time, I wanted it never to stop. But, as my mother would say with an exasperated sigh as she set her empty glass on her bedside table, "All good things must come to an end," and I saw with apprehension the time when we'd have to go back to our ordinary lives: for him, rehearsals for the show without a name, for me the Sélect, hamburger platters and revolting coffee. And Janine. With, at the end of the tunnel, the hope of getting back to it as often as possible, as long as possible.

Towards the end of our fun and games, though, at the darkest moment of the night, just before the approach of dawn, I sensed a change taking place in him that I couldn't account for. An absence appeared in his eyes, not suddenly or abruptly but uncoordinated, jerky; his body was less present and his mind, which I'd felt was in unison with mine for several hours, had started to wander strangely outside what was happening between us. At first I thought it was exhaustion, then I told myself that probably the fatigue came from repetition, that we'd taken advantage of and even somewhat abused the night which was ending and that it might be better to keep our interest in one another intact for future sessions by waiting to dull this all-consuming passion when the time came to make love ... He gradually stopped laughing, barely hinting at a smile when he pushed aside—but nicely—my attempted caresses, and I was a little worried when I finally fell asleep. Not in his arms either, but curled up in a ball at the edge of the bed.

A few minutes later—it was still dark—he woke me up with a slight push. His voice was strangely altered: it was deeper, nearly broken, he didn't finish his sentences, a little like the night before, but drained of any excitement, and what remained was the uncontrolled agitation that had so surprised me.

"Sorry, Céline ... I didn't want to wake you up but ... sorry to ask you this, Céline, but you have to go now ... "

At first I thought I was dreaming, that I was transporting my worry into my sleep, which I was using to get rid of it, but everything was real, his hand that was shaking a little, his body that didn't smell the same now, his barely recognizable voice. I rubbed my eyes, yawning. He had put his burning hand on my hip.

"Gilbert, have you any idea what time it is ... It's still dark! We just got to sleep ... "

He moved away from me; I heard him get out of bed, extricate himself rather, because he dragged himself to the other end before he got up, as if his body were all at once too heavy, though a few minutes earlier he'd got into bed with such agility.

"I know ... But ... You have to go ... "

"Why, what's going on, what's so different now?"

"Me, Céline, me. I'm not the same as I was … "

I know it's idiotic but in the middle of this very serious scene I started thinking about *Dr. Jekyll and Mr. Hyde*, one of my father's favourite movies, and I smiled in the dark. Was Spencer Tracy about to turn into a bloodthirsty monster and murder Ingrid Bergman or Lana Turner, with jerky movements and ridiculous grimaces? But the next thing he said cut short the nervous laughter I could feel rising in my chest, "There are things about me that you mustn't know about, Céline, that I don't want you to know about … Not right away … Please, do as I say … Or you may regret it."

Suddenly, I don't know why, I thought it all sounded like a pretext, that it was probably hiding something more important than a simple glitch in Gilbert's personality, another woman maybe, an official girlfriend who was too much in love to be understanding, who was waiting in the wings for me to leave so she could take back what she thought of as her place. Had he dared to be so untruthful to me? I wanted to get to the bottom of it. Right away.

"My God, Gilbert, is another woman going to come and enjoy the bed I warmed up for her without knowing?"

He let out what could have been taken for a snicker but that was just an ugly kind of grunt tinged with irony, "Of course not. If only that was it … it'd be more bearable. What I don't want you to see, Céline, can't be fixed; maybe I'll explain it all to you some day but now … What we've just done is too wonderful, I don't want to ruin it, Céline, so go away now … Please … "

I had no intention of leaving St. Rose Street as an undesirable, a favourite who'd tumbled into disgrace. Even in a taxi. I refused outright to leave his bed at this, to say the least, ungodly hour.

"I'm strong, Gilbert, I can take it. If you have some shameful secret, keep it to yourself; if you've got something to tell me, tell me now, but I'm not walking into this strange neighbourhood at five a.m. like a banished mistress who doesn't know why she's being kicked out!"

I turned my back to him and went back to sleep despite his protests, which were weaker and weaker.

When I woke up, Gilbert's place beside me was empty. And cold. I thought he might have gone to rehearse as it was nearly noon. But I heard a sound coming from the kitchen, then I realized I was smelling pot, not toast and coffee. I threw my clothes on, deciding to shower at home. Especially because Gilbert had started smoking so early in the day. Was that what he couldn't admit? Was he doing more drugs than I thought? As early as breakfast? What he didn't know was that I'd been living for some time with drag queens who didn't sneer at a quick toke when they got up ... I managed to avoid them when they were excessively hilarious or when what they had to say seemed confused, and that was what I wanted to do with Gilbert if he turned out to be too far gone for my liking. I had no intention of having a muddled, hard-to-follow conversation while I was making my coffee, not even with him. I would tell him I wasn't angry, I understood, then I'd leave him to his solitary pleasure and his rambling. I was disappointed but I thought it wasn't as terrible as finding him drunk at dawn as my mother so often was ...

In the kitchen, nothing had been moved. Everything was gleaming and clean. So Gilbert hadn't eaten yet. He was at the table in front of what I thought at first was the classic paraphernalia of the addict that we were used to seeing in American movies—the rubber garotte, the syringe, the small spoon, the matches—but which to my relief turned out to be just a baggie of pot, papers and a rolling machine. As I approached the table, I noticed that Gilbert was more prostrate than sitting and that his head was hanging dangerously over his lighted cigarette—a real one, not a joint. Was he so stoned that he was unconscious? His back was hunched though he usually holds himself so erect, his left leg was trembling and his shoulders shaking from what seemed to be irrepressible sobs.

And when he heard me come in, he showed me a face that was unrecognizable—red and puffy, a Medusa head from which all charm had disappeared and where now there was only suffering and fear. His hair was plastered to his forehead and sweat was pouring down his neck. I was no longer looking at the person with whom I'd shared so much pleasure just a few hours earlier, but at someone so different that I didn't want to know him. Or even to find out if he existed.

He wiped his tears before he spoke to me.

"I told you not to stay."

I laid my hand on his damp arm.

"What's wrong? Are you sick? Is it food poisoning from your bad eating habits? I hope it wasn't the meat at the Sélect ... "

Too pragmatic, as usual. The man before me was obviously shattered and I was carrying on about food poisoning!

He pushed away my hand with surprising brusqueness and his laughter, cynical, frightened me.

"I'm not poisoned—not like that anyway! I told you to go ... I didn't want you to see me like this!"

He picked up the baggie and practically waved it under my nose.

"I even tried to smoke so it wouldn't show, but it's made it worse, I'm more down than when I woke up. I'm suffocating, Céline, I wish I could die, right here, right now!"

I put my arms around his head. His odour was different now. Unpleasant. It was no longer the kind of man's smell that makes you want to kiss him and caress him but a musty smell like sickness, an unhealthy exhalation that turned my stomach. Still I stayed there, with my arms around his neck, his nose against my chest because I knew he needed it.

"I didn't want you to see me like this! I didn't want you to know this about me! You'll go away, you won't want to see me again! Ever! Just like the others!"

And for the time it took for a heartbeat of mine and a long sob from him, I had a vision. I don't know if you can talk about a vision when hearing, not sight, is involved, nor do I know if I have the words to express what I felt, or rather heard, so quickly, so fleetingly, but so clearly. Was it because my hope of happiness with Gilbert was collapsing in this obsessively clean kitchen or because my future, once again, was, with no warning, taking a turn that I wasn't expecting? In the end, wasn't I hearing my own sense of helplessness? I have no idea, but the fact remains that for a fraction of a second I had the impression that every cry of distress in creation was echoing in my head. All the howls of despair sent out around the world along with Gilbert's exploded in a single universal note of suffering that struck me like a dagger. A bouquet of intolerable sorrows from the four corners of the world that brought tears to my eyes. Revelation or warning? It only lasted a brief moment but to me it was like an indelible burn, like another sudden stroke of fate that once again and in spite of myself was taking on the task of changing the course of my life. But it may just have been my own implosion that was being revealed in a great and manifold cry. I wanted to run away, to leave Gilbert there in his kitchen, holding the baggie, his left knee shaking, and at the same time to stay there and console him as best I could, hoping to help him out of a depression that I hoped was temporary.

But what about that depression? Did it have a name? It wasn't new because he'd felt it coming. Where did it come from? How did it manifest itself?

"What's wrong Gilbert, what's the matter? Unless you tell me I can't understand, I can't help you."

All at once he straightened up, pushed me away, grabbed his bag of dope, his papers and his rolling machine and left the table, practically knocking it over.

"Enough people in my life have tried to help me, I'm fucked-up enough to know it can't be done. I'm incurable, Céline, and even what happens between you and me can't change a thing! This morning proves it. Even with the best intentions in the world you'll go away. Like the others. I shouldn't have let it happen. Though I knew. But I was weak … "

He was leaving the kitchen. I ran after him.

"Give it a try at least, Gilbert. Try to explain. Gilbert, you can't leave me ignorant like this! I've got a right to know! After last night I have a right to know! If you don't think of me as a one night stand, you're going to tell me!"

He leaned against the door frame. He didn't turn around to speak to me right away. He started telling me with his back turned. His voice was as unrecognizable as his face, it was broken, nearly toneless. Not until a few minutes later, when he'd made a good start on his story, when he'd assumed his confession, did he come back and sit beside me at the table.

"It's called *la folie circulaire*, circular madness … "

Second Insert

# Beginning of the Story of Gilbert, the Circular Madman

The mother had made her confession to a transvestite who went by a man's name; the son made his to a sympathetic midget who wanted to love him. And who, as fate would have it, turned out to be a roommate of the same transvestite. Several years later. Long after the mother had died and the son had become an adult with problems.

Throughout his childhood, Gilbert Forget had been shunted between school and the Main; between instilled knowledge—education—and acquired knowledge—the experience of the street; between an overly loving grandmother and some overly permissive drag queens. What resulted was a pre-teen who was agitated and precocious, with the self-confidence of a spoiled brat, the inability to concentrate seriously and a kind of unruly knowledge. He had a barnyard vocabulary and a talent for witticisms surprising for his age, but if a teacher asked him a simple question, he froze. He blithely started fights in the schoolyard, but burst into sobs like the worst coward if he was called to the principal's office. He turned out to be hypersensitive when the hookers in the red-light district were slapped around by Maurice's hit men—he rose up, cried foul, occasionally even hurled at them whatever he could get his hands on—and was amazingly indifferent to the wonders of the French language or the ins and outs of Canadian history. He knew lots of things the other children didn't, but lacked the basic knowledge of a normal education.

As for his crazy mother with whom he sometimes spent the whole day wandering the neighbouring streets in the red-light district with outstretched hand and runny nose, he thought she was a beggar, that's all, and he was ashamed. He was proud of his father who'd died in the war, yes, he was a hero, they'd even received a shiny new medal which he'd been quick to show to his classmates. If anyone mentioned his mother though, he would clam up and change the subject. After all, he couldn't admit that she was a lunatic in rags who had to beg for her food, reciting woes that couldn't always be verified to passers-by who often weren't respectable.

He recalled, but it was vague and long ago, the first time she'd dragged him to one of those dimly-lit bars where children weren't allowed, where she put on weird outfits before turning him over to another lady who resembled her, just long enough, she said, to go onstage and earn their livelihood. He thought that she got up on the stage disguised as a gypsy or Scheherazade to beg for money and he wondered why she had to change her personality and her clothes when she went begging at night.

He realized that certain men were crazy about her but did not really understand why. He would see them in her dressing room after the show, goggle-eyed, holding bouquets of flowers, and he thought they were grotesque with their bows and their over-the-top compliments. Sure, she was beautiful, but did they realize how crazy she was when she got lost in the ramblings of a weeping widow and even more, in the long bouts of alcoholic drinking that made her unbearable so much of the time? But maybe that was what excited them. Maybe they were as crazy as she was.

She would throw her head back, come out with the throaty laugh that he hated so much, and he knew that he'd have to wait for hours before she deigned to remember that he existed. Because she was busy elsewhere. Begging again? Earning their livelihood with incoherent stories that had less and less to do with the truth, getting tangled up in absurd tales featuring herself as innocent victim and the rest of the world as torturers who held a grudge against her because she had met her true love, and were making her pay an exorbitant price?

The arrival of Greta in his life—she didn't call herself Greta-la-Vieille until Greta-la-Jeune arrived in Montreal—was a blessing for

Gilbert. He loved the strange woman with the peculiar voice in a way that he could never love his mother—with total abandon and unalloyed passion: besides gladly taking the place of Madame Veuve in whom he found it harder and harder to recognize the kind woman who had brought him up, she let him do whatever he wanted!

She protected him during the dog-days of summer when, left to his own devices and crazy with boredom, he would whine at the girls on the Main to buy him an ice-cream—if an impatient hand came up to whomp him one for being a pain in the neck, Greta would appear out of nowhere and come to his defence—she would mother him for hours when Madame Veuve, towards the end, would disappear for a long time with just about anybody so she could bring home a few bills that she'd crumple up like used Kleenex. Sometimes she actually threw them in Gilbert's face as if everything—her collapse, their poverty, their begging—were his fault.

Greta would break off work at the risk of displeasing the couriers of Maurice-la-Piasse—whose idea of compassion was nebulous at best and who saw to it with imperturbable seriousness that their girls were always on the job—she would take him by the hand and go to Ben Ash for a smoked meat even if it was too late and the spicy meat would probably sit heavily in their stomachs for part of the night. Or to the Montreal Pool Room for a steamed hotdog, accompanied of course by limp and greasy fries. She kept him busy, told him what little she remembered of her own childhood fairytales. She confused Perrault's tales with Aunt Lucille's, introduced Québécois characters into medieval Europe, she mimed witches, imitated dragons, swore like a lumberjack—all while pouring vinegar onto her fries or spreading mustard on her smoked meat.

He, despite his youth, concentrated more on her odour than her stories. He'd never met anyone who smelled so good, not even his mother, though she never skimped on perfume. He would rub his nose on Greta's skin or clothes at the slightest opportunity, rest his head on her bosom which was generous though rather hard compared with his mother's, and take big gulps of that intoxicating aroma—a mixture of sweat, especially in summer, and skin cream that an Avon lady delivered once a month to the hookers in the red-light district and that smelled different on her than on the others. On them, it was cheap perfume from a travelling saleslady; on her, it became the fragrance of motherly love, a balm that entered through the nose and made you want to go on living.

Because Gilbert was already thinking about death. Not suicide, no, he did not yet know that it existed, but his grandmother had often talked about the place where every good little boy would go after he died, a safe place for the desperate, ultimate reward for a lifetime of sacrifice and self-denial, and Gilbert began to dream about going there right away, because he suspected, most likely on account of his mother, that life wasn't always a bed of roses and, in any case, sacrifice and self-denial didn't turn him on. So why not get the reward now? Before any suffering. Before any big disappointments. But his grandmother explained that it didn't work that way, that the good Lord—Gilbert pictured a kind of strict and serious Santa Claus in a white nightgown, lying on a cloud—expected more before rewarding us, that we had to prove that we *deserved* the great gift, the great shelter, with its choirs of angels and its eternal feast to be savoured in the presence of everything respectable and Catholic that the world had ever known.

"You get nothing for nothing, kiddo!"

It was a leitmotif that he heard every day, several times, and learned very young to deny. If it turned out to be possible, he would arrange to get *everything* for nothing!

Death had continued to haunt him then, but more as a flight into the unknown, a consolation without much personality, than as a reward to be earned through sacrifice.

And now that smell, though synthetic, of too many different flowers combined haphazardly to make money and sold for too high a price in the form of perfume to some poor creatures who didn't know better, had restored his own desire to go on living. So that he could inhale the scent of the woman who for his benefit had donned the mantle of motherly love that he needed so badly. Greta became the first great passion in his life.

Fairly early he had detected a significant and peculiar difference between the two kinds of ladies who plied St. Lawrence Boulevard every night, "waiting for the bus." Some were massive, with broken voices and a not always elegant gait, and they were by far the nicest. They were crazy about him, thought he was funny, practically egged him on in his pranks and went into raptures over how quickly the sense of repartee he'd learned from them had developed. The others, with more delicate builds and voices like his mother's, grew impatient with him, were less tolerant of tantrums and for some reason or other would often tell him that the Main was no place for a child. One night when he asked Greta about it, she had told him it was because some of them had one or more children and were probably right to want to keep them away from the red-light district. After all, it wasn't normal for a little monkey like him to walk around a neighbourhood like this without supervision. You never know what will happen. In the end though, being the son of Madame Veuve may have protected him from meeting up with the wrong kind of people. The fact, as well, that all the ladies who waited for the bus, especially the sturdiest ones, would have gladly eviscerated anyone who dared lay a finger on him.

The ladies who rebuffed him were real mommas, she'd told him, but he hadn't understood what she meant. He had levelled his gaze at her—the gaze of a child who was bright but still knew hardly anything about life—and asked very candidly, but shrugging as if it weren't all that important, "Is it just the small little ladies that have children? What about you big ones—have you?"

Greta's laugh, famous all over the neighbourhood, had risen up in the sticky July night, disappearing somewhere in the darkness of the sky. Somewhat insulted, he asked why she was laughing. She stopped. To her slender neck, like a chicken's that hadn't reached maturity, she brought her hand, fragrant with Avon cream, and became serious again.

"You don't know, do you? You don't see a thing, right?"

Gilbert, who prided himself on understanding everything before other children did, froze at this question, which was to say the least enigmatic. What was she talking about? What was he was supposed to see? Had he missed some detail that was staring him in the face? Humiliated now, he sulked for the rest of the evening, and only a club sandwich at Ben Ash, served by Thérèse, his favourite waitress, could cheer him up. But even while he was wolfing down the three-decker sandwich, he went on thinking. And couldn't come up with an answer to the question he was pondering, about the ladies who were waiting for the bus, the ones who were mothers and the ones who weren't, the small little ones and the big ones.

That night, Thérèse and Greta had a whispered conversation near the cash, one of those exchanges between adults that Gilbert hated so much because he was always left out, and their bursts of laughter—they pointed to him now and then, so it was obvious they were talking about him—made him furious. Over his butterscotch sundae he suffered one of the first real episodes in his life, which the two women thought was the rage of a spoiled brat refusing to be defied. They overdid their complicity then, presumably to teach him a lesson, but without meaning to they had just opened a Pandora's box that would never close again. They also missed an obvious fact: what was smouldering inside Gilbert was more than the whim of a badly brought-up child, it was a genuine sickness.

Just before they left the restaurant—Madame Veuve's last show was ending and Greta had promised that once again, she would bring Gilbert back safe and sound—Thérèse had leaned across the little boy and stroked his neck. She smelled stronger than Greta, but it was far from unpleasant.

"Didn't you ever notice that your friend Greta's got an Adam's apple?"

Greta pointed her finger at the waitress's nose.

"Don't start putting things in his head!"

Gilbert was already on tiptoe, his nose level with Greta's neck.

"I know that. So what?"

Thérèse had answered before Greta could order her to shut up.

"Look ... I haven't got one."

His gaze had moved from Greta's throat to the softer, more tender one of the beautiful Thérèse.

"That's right. What does it mean?"

The two women had exchanged a strange look. Was this another detail that he didn't see, or that he did see but didn't understand? The answer was far from clear. Thérèse had shrugged, saying that one of these days he was going to get a shock, while Greta merely told him in a confidential tone of voice, "When you do find out, try not to be too mad at me ... "

Find out what? Be mad at her why? There was no way he'd be mad at her for anything, he loved her too much! He told her that and watched her melt with emotion at the corner of the Main and St. Catherine Street.

He fell asleep very late that night and his slumber was haunted by the throats of ladies being offered to him, not by abandoning themselves, like when you're expecting a kiss on your neck, but aggressively. He woke up recalling a detail that he'd learned at school and then forgotten. Yes, it was something very simple, having to do with the body, with the throat of a human being, that escaped him ... because he didn't want to see it! The shock was terrible: all at once he was positive he didn't want to see something that was very obvious, because on the day he understood what it was about, his life would be changed forever.

From then on, he started to look closely at every person he met, both at school and in the red-light district, to see who had an Adam's apple and who didn't. It wasn't obvious because not everyone who had one showed it off like a trophy or a proof of good looks. At school, their shirts were supposed to be buttoned up to the neck, so he would sometimes undo his classmates' shirt collars or so he could poke his nose in their necks, which gave him an even stranger reputation, when people already thought he was weird. They started calling him "Forget the Queer" and he was of course humiliated, even though he had only a vague idea of what it meant to be *queer*.

Meanwhile, he checked and saw that his grandmother didn't have an Adam's apple, and neither did his mother. But his classmates did. And his teachers. And the Brother Principal. The ladies who waited for the bus were half-and-half with or without. Strange. Tooth Pick, Maurice's right-hand man, had a huge one, nearly as big and pointy as the impressive one on a friend, a girlfriend really, of Greta, Jean-le-Décollé, who scared him because she had a man's name but wore women's clothes.

Too many questions, not one answer. And still the impression that what he was trying to find out had something to do with the Adam's apple.

His denial was shattered all at once, much later, during a conversation with his dear friend Greta whom he so admired and whose scent he'd have liked to inhale for the rest of his life.

The girls' dressing room at the Coconut Inn—separate from the tiny one of the house star—was always full of costumes that were never put away, of trinkets in every colour, props for the strippers' acts or useless baubles bought on a whim and never worn; there were wigs, too, often blonde because the clients of the club were partial to anything that reminded them of the new Hollywood idol, Marilyn Monroe. They liked to think that it was the star herself in person who'd stepped out of *Niagara* or *Gentlemen Prefer Blondes*, who had just titillated them on the Main, in the heart of Montreal, practically at the end of the world, while they were polishing off a tepid beer or a glass of hard liquor that the barman, with no compunction, cut with water. As for her French counterpart, Brigitte Bardot, she wasn't sexy enough for them. As Willy Ouellette, official mouth-organist of the French Casino, who'd been asked, at the end of one of the biggest binges of his life, which one he would take to a desert island, he'd responded so elegantly, "Brigitte Bardot? She's the lukewarm soup before the meatball stew! Marilyn Monroe though, she's the whole meal! That you can eat without bread or butter … And for sure you don't need pepper!"

The girls at the Coconut Inn, unlike the strippers at the other clubs on St. Lawrence Boulevard, didn't have assigned places in front of the big mirror lit by dozens of electric light bulbs and in front of which had been pushed an old refectory table that Tooth Pick had unearthed at the Salvation Army. Which had led Maurice to say, "Generations of nuns ate at that table for hundreds of years, in some convent that never even knew the Main existed. And now hookers are gonna paint their kissers and tell dirty stories that'll make the hair stand up on your head! First the good Lord, then curses! Now that's a table with a history!"

Each stripper sat in whatever place was free, borrowing the others' makeup, grabbing Kleenexes from pretty well everybody, cursing if the available lipstick was the wrong colour, howling if she messed up a false eyelash and yelling that she was going to rip out the eyes of the goddamn cow who'd ripped off her best brush again.

Gilbert loved the sense of anything goes that it gave off. And as a lover of perfume, he could boast that he was well-served. What floated permanently in the dressing room was very different from what Greta's body gave off, or his mother's, or the much less interesting lap of his grandmother who apparently didn't believe in the virtues of Avon skin creams and was content with plain old Barsalou soap. When he pushed open the door to the room that was too small for so many women who took up so much space, a mass of odours sprang out at him, a dense wall of all kinds of emotions, and he felt as if he were entering a huge flask filled with everything on the market that smells strong: an apotheosis, indivisible yet made up of hundreds of notes too different to go together, flooded his nostrils, and occasionally he sneezed, three times, like when he moved too quickly from the shade to the sun in summer. Nowhere else had he found that powerful smell of bodies overheated by the spotlights, combined with the heady fragrance of everything on the market by way of cheap toilet water, all the way from Dupuis Frères to Ogilvy's, from L.N. Messier on Mont-Royal Street to the five-and-dime on St. Catherine Street. An endless symphony made up of a single note that would never stop. It was unique, and every time, as he'd been telling himself since he was very young, it stank pretty.

That night, his mother had once again entrusted him to the ladies who were waiting for the bus, in particular to Greta, his official guardian, whom he adored, especially because his mother had had a rough day and had started drinking earlier than usual. She looked the way she looked on her bad nights and Gilbert didn't want to be around when everything blew up.

Just before leaving the Coconut Inn to dart into the traffic on St. Catherine Street, Gilbert had heard the other girls complain about Madame Veuve's lack of professionalism, saying they thought she was going too far ... Now she was having trouble getting to the end of her acts, she was hiding bottles of Bols gin under the lighting system, insulting clients who dared to talk out loud instead of watch her strip ... He called them all terrible names, then took off before any well-aimed slaps and stiletto heels could land on him.

He'd recounted it all to Greta, who'd told him not to get upset, not to listen to the other girls, every single one of them was jealous of his mother, who they thought was too beautiful despite her many woes and, more important, too popular with the clientele of the Coconut Inn, who were known to be picky. Despite the fact that he was so young and hadn't finished growing, Gilbert was well aware that Greta was lying, that the girls weren't jealous of his mother at all, they looked down on her without hiding it, and that the Coconut Inn clientele weren't in the least picky. Because how can you be picky when you barely know where you are and you're too drunk to see clearly what's happening onstage? And for the pittance they had to spend, they had to be satisfied with a weeping widow, beautiful though she may have been, instead of Marilyn Monroe, the sexiest woman in the world. You take what you're offered and you shut your mouth. Above all, you don't show yourself to be picky.

He took revenge by stealing a package of Thrills chewing gum and walked out of the Montreal Pool Room without paying for his daily hotdog, knowing that Greta would cover it when she dropped in at the end of her watch, which would go on for many more hours. He'd been in a bad mood all night. Suddenly, nothing interested him. Neither the comings and goings, exciting though they were, of the bystanders in the red-light district, nor the neon lights that made his skin turn incredible colours, nor the ladies who for once were waiting in vain for the bus because there were more of them than usual, since public transportation, you would swear, arrived so seldom.

He heard Jean-le-Décollé, who he thought was so scary, (and why on earth did she go by a man's name?) vilify the goddamn whores from Toronto who came here and stole their johns, but he didn't understand what she was talking about and simply made a face as he walked past her.

Jean-le-Décollé had grabbed him by the scruff of the neck and shaken him a little.

"You're a bit too full of yourself, little boy ... Just because people feel sorry for your mother, it doesn't mean that you can get away with murder!"

Greta had appeared quite suddenly, as usual, but this time she lit into him, "Don't get on my nerves, Gilbert, this isn't the time!"

"What do you mean, get on your nerves?"

"You know perfectly well what I mean!"

"I haven't got anything to do, I'm bored!"

"Go across the street to a movie."

"I'm not old enough!"

"Don't be a smart aleck! Roméo at the Midway lets you in at least twice a week, do you think I don't know? Go see Mylène Demongeot at the Français, you might learn something ... "

"I don't feel like it!"

"Then just keep still!"

"I don't want to keep still!"

"Go eat a hotdog!"

"I already did!"

"How did you pay for it?"

"I told Gordon you'd drop in ... "

She couldn't take any more and gave him a little slap upside his head.

"And then you get me into debt! Who do you think you are? My pimp?"

Immediately, he started to wail. The girls who'd approached had applauded Greta's move—he'd been getting on all their nerves, the little brat, he deserved it!—and the whole thing nearly ended in tragedy. Greta sent him to the Coconut Inn, claiming that his mother's act was nearly over. But he hung around with her until the end of her shift.

And it was on that night—Out of exasperation? Because she was fed up with his ignorance? To get revenge for his rudeness?—that something happened that would change Gilbert's life forever and bring their wonderful relationship to an end.

Greta never knew why she'd done what she did—though it needed explaining, she had to know that—or why she had revealed her true identity to Gilbert without preparing him, on a sudden impulse, she who bragged so often that she was level-headed and thoughtful. She did it in good faith, she'd always been convinced of that, no doubt to put an end to a misunderstanding that had gone on for too long, for the education of this child who was smart for his age though fundamentally very naïve, but she would regret it for the rest of her life and often said to clients, if she thought they were understanding, or when depression struck, that she had lost a child sometime in the 1950s because she'd said too much.

As if it were intentional, the show wasn't over when Greta and Gilbert went into the Coconut Inn late that night. The doorman—a simple-minded hulk who didn't match his name, which was Gaspard Petit—told them that Madame Veuve was in good shape that night and that she'd decided to double the pleasure by encoring every number she performed, in their *complete* version, police surveillance or not. He had emphasized the word *complete* with a huge wink whose significance only Greta understood.

Greta had to be sure that Gilbert didn't see his mother naked on the stage of the Coconut Inn, so she'd decided to go in and see where she was in her act before she crossed the club in the company of such a young child who was bound to attract the attention of the drinkers crushed by alcohol fumes and cigarette smoke. Or of the policeman on duty—no doubt bought by Maurice—who might forbid them to come in, out of bravado, to show Maurice that he still had a bit of independence even though, like several of his colleagues, he was on his payroll.

Madame Veuve, as if suddenly struck by nostalgia, had brought out all her old acts, though she'd renounced them for so long, and at that moment was in the middle of "Paris, reine du monde," but minus the hoop-skirts or the powdered wig. Greta frowned. So she was doing her whole repertoire in her widow's weeds? And when she'd finished undressing, the stripper left the stage, put on her black two-piece suit, her hat, her veil, her gloves and began again, changing nothing but the musical accompaniment—scratched old records she'd been dragging around forever? And the audience wasn't complaining? After all, though, it was not so much the costume that mattered, in the end it was the stark naked woman, in spite of and because of the prohibitions, the forbidden fruit in all its glory, the fantasy never realized and always renewed, that made hearts beat and brought the blood up to the head, and it hardly mattered what had come before. Naked, Madame Veuve, formerly Peach Blossom, was the same no matter what costume she'd just taken off, and the men in the Coconut Inn didn't give a damn that she'd stripped off her widow's weeds instead of the elegant garb of a Marie-Antoinette. It was what they saw for some too brief seconds—the most beautiful thing in the world, the most exciting, the most inaccessible too—that mattered. They gazed at the large pink smudge that was moving on the stage, the darker triangle in particular, and every time, they were struck by their own insignificance. Never would they possess a beauty like her, that they knew, and they drowned their dejection in the alcohol that cost the least but hit the hardest. To forget their own helplessness.

And so Greta brought the child in before the crucial moment. Gilbert waved to his mother, who couldn't see him. He craned his neck a little to look at all these men who'd come to see his mother beg them for money. He could see her though. It was strange to note how different she was when she was onstage. On the street with her hand held out and an insult ready to let fly she was an uncontrollable demon; there, with the pink spotlights, she transformed herself into an angel covered in diaphanous tulle whom you wanted to hold against your heart. His real mother, the one in his dreams, was that one, the beggar woman in an improved version. But the one who was going to join them in the wings later on, who swept into the dressing room, in search of a cigarette or a bottle of Bols as usual, would be very different: without the miracle of the flattering lights, she was once again the weeping widow to whom he had to be subjected every day for such a long time and who weighed on him more and more heavily.

There was no one in the dressing room. As Madame Veuve's was the last act of the night—what was called on the poster in English *the special feature* and in French *la vedette principale*—the other girls had slipped away as soon as their acts were done to party somewhere else, with friends from the neighbourhood or clients of the Coconut Inn who'd noticed them, considered them, then hefted them like merchandise to be had for the lowest price possible. Strictly for want of anything else to do—she was afraid the evening would drag on forever—Greta sat at the other girls' makeup table instead of in Madame Veuve's cramped dressing room and started fiddling with everything on it—lipsticks, jars of cream, tubes of foundation, tweezers and toilet water in bottles of every shape and every colour. She sprayed herself with Jean Patou's *Moment Suprême*, which took her back to her early days in the red-light district, during World War II, when Montreal Mayor Camilien Houde had been thrown into jail because he dared to publicly oppose conscription. When Greta arrived, the city had just been emptied of its men who'd gone to war in the old countries. Everything the hookers, male or female, could expect by way of customers—and this had been the case for years—was soldiers on leave or priests ashamed sometimes to the point of impotence and life, already, had shown itself to be a bitch and not easy.

Even today, when she tells this story, holding a beer and smiling sadly, she maintains that it was Gilbert who'd started everything, that it was his fault, ultimately, if she'd committed an act that she swore was not premeditated but that sprang from exasperation stretched out over too long a period of time, not from a will to instruct a child who was ignorant of the facts of life.

While she was perfuming herself, she'd seen her reflection in the mirror through the cloud of rice powder she'd just stirred up with a candy-pink powder-puff that made her want to sneeze.

Gilbert had brought his hand to his throat and said very softly, as if he were talking to himself, "I've got an Adam's apple too."

Then, with eyebrows in circumflex accents and furrowed brow, he looked at her. She understood that he had called for help and without giving it a moment's thought, she'd given him a silent demonstration, probably for fear that she would lack the words for explaining clearly to him the difference between those with an Adam's apple and those without, and consequently, what she was.

She said just one thing before she started. She was looking at him in the mirror where, she still remembers, there was a crack because one night one of the girls in a fury had flung a prop or a bottle of perfume, and she'd murmured, "Take a good look at this, Gilbert, later on you'll understand ... "

And as the child looked on with alarm, she had removed every trace of the woman that for years, she'd been playing like a role in the theatre, to earn her living, yes, but also because she needed it and because she liked the mask that she painted onto her face every day in the hope of forgetting the man she didn't want to be: first, she pulled off the false eyelashes, then she removed most of the makeup with a cream that smelled like cucumbers, after that the eye shadow, the glue that hid her real eyebrows and the lipstick that extended onto her cheeks. She rubbed quickly, like someone used to doing it. Her forehead was longer, her cheeks rounder, her mouth practically non-existent, her chin flabby and drooping. Something between a man who doesn't take good enough care of himself and a woman who has given up any hope of being beautiful.

She no longer looked like herself. Not at all. Already she was not the Greta Gilbert loved so much and his eyes were wide with surprise. Alarmed, almost. He'd often seen his mother without makeup, but never a transvestite—in fact he didn't even know that they existed, though he'd been hanging out with a bunch of them for years. Without her makeup, his mother was less beautiful but still the same; Greta though had been transformed into something he'd never seen and wished he hadn't now. Another person. He didn't want her to be a different person from the one he knew. He didn't want there to be two of her. He just wanted Greta. His second mother. His chosen mother.

She had looked him in the eyes for a long moment, though, before administering the coup de grâce, shaken by doubt, by the sudden thought that it might all be pointless. And that she was going to lose him forever.

Then, hesitantly, hands trembling, she took off her wig and the nylon stocking with which she tied back her own hair.

She turned towards him, bent over, held out her arm to stroke his cheek.

Still, he didn't understand.

Greta's eyes filled with uncontrollable tears. Tears of regret. Already.

"Gilbert … You must have learned about it in school but maybe you've forgotten … Women don't have an Adam's apple. Men do. And I've got one so I'm a man. Like you. D'you understand?"

Gilbert didn't answer, he was frozen in a grimace that could mean various things: fear, disgust, terror. But still not fully understanding.

"My name is Roger, Gilbert. Roger Beausoleil. That's my real name. It's just here that I'm Greta, when I'm working … No, that's not true. It's never Roger any more. It's time you knew that and that you learned to accept it. You're big enough. You're old enough. Tell me you're big enough and old enough and that you understand … "

And the words came. With disconcerting ease. The right words, the most effective, the clearest, put in the right places and used with a mastery she didn't know she had. She explained everything:

hookers, drag queens, what they were doing when Gilbert thought they were waiting for the bus, why they did it but not how because after all, it was too soon for those details. She'd taken long minutes to explain everything, hands on the child's knees or stroking his cheek while she rubbed his forehead with the tip of her thumb. And he'd listened all the way through, without flinching.

Was she telling him things he already knew but had never wanted to see, or was he totally taken aback? She couldn't read it on his face and was already cursing herself for being the one to tell him, the one who'd burst his balloon now that he knew and could never again pretend not to. All at once, she would have preferred to erase everything so that the time she'd spent on those damn explanations would have never existed, to put on her false face again, and her wig, make a funny face and tell Gilbert, Come on, sweetheart, we're going to treat ourselves to the biggest hotdog on the Main! And take off with him while promising herself to keep him ignorant as long as possible.

Too late.

When Madame Veuve came back she saw them facing each other, motionless and silent. She knew right away that something irremediable had just happened and without even bothering to go to her dressing room to change, she grabbed Gilbert by his shirt collar and took him out of the Coconut Inn.

He never talked to Greta again.

By choice.

Betrayal. All those years they'd lied to him. About everything. They'd made fun of him. Some men dressed like women to earn their living and as funny as aunties, for the pleasure of deceiving him, had made him think all kinds of things about themselves, about their work, their lives, and he'd believed them. He had opened up to them, he'd loved them—Greta, the biggest liar, most of all. He refused to think of Greta as a woman now, the most dangerous woman, the one he'd adopted as his second mother, to whom he'd poured out his heart, with whom he'd had so many laughs and eaten so many steamed hotdogs and smoked meat sandwiches, in whose company he'd spent whole summers watching him walk the sidewalks of St. Lawrence Boulevard but never knowing who he was dealing with, never suspecting the conspiracy. Why hadn't he seen anything? Now that he knew, it was obvious: they'd all united against him to keep him in childhood, in the ignorance of childhood. He'd thought he was smart but in the end he'd been nothing but an average baby who'd let himself be led up the garden path by a bunch of male bitches who wanted to keep him with them—he was so naïve, such an easy victim—to laugh at him. A defenceless toy.

He'd been fooled. Those women weren't like the others: they had Adam's apples when he knew perfectly well that women don't, he'd learned that in grade one! When he saw them again in his mind— tall, square-shouldered, with hoarse voices and movements that were often abrupt, he called himself an idiot and he wanted to die of shame.

And all that time he could have been talking to real women ... He'd tried, in fact, but they'd pushed him away. Greta had told him it was because those ladies had enough with their own children, they didn't want to look after someone else's. So they had betrayed him too. By not warning him. About the fake women. Who knows, maybe they'd all been in on it together.

All of them. All of them had betrayed him.

A hole was being dug, a pit of resentment where there used to be so much love. Resentment of the fake women. Of the real ones. How they had laughed at him behind their backs. Even his mother, who never thought twice about leaving him in the care of a professional liar to go and beg for the crumbs that would allow them to survive.

So it was shame more than pain that had him confined to his bed for weeks, feverish, spiteful, howling with anger and swearing revenge. Absolutely delirious, he constructed deadly traps, senseless plans, he destroyed one by one everyone who'd laughed at him, including his mother and, even more, Greta, then resurrected them so he could kill them again; he imagined other ways to make them suffer and to humiliate them before he killed them once again ... He felt the excitement of imagined reprisals and the relief of endless insults.

Emerging from his torpor, exhausted and melancholy, he refused to go back to the Main with his mother and took refuge with his grandmother, the only person he had left, who he knew would never betray him. And he allowed himself to sink into that clinging love, knowing he was totally dependent on her but unable to fight. For years. In school, he was the solitary child no one dared to confront because everyone was afraid of his rages, which were sudden and devastating; at home, his refuge was the brand-new television set, perfect sanctuary for those like him who'd been voluntarily abandoned. In his teens, he began to suffer from incomprehensible, brutal and always short-lived episodes of overexcitement—he was Nero and set fire to Montreal while singing a comic opera aria—and from increasingly frequent and prolonged fits of depression; no one is unhappier than me, I'll show them what a tragic character is. He swung from one mood to the other, sometimes without transition, without warning, and he revelled in it. His circular madness was starting to build the nest for its poisoned eggs.

When his mother died, the most beautiful death there ever was—an angel without wings takes flight on a winter's night and crashes onto a pure white snowbank!—he closed all the doors and retreated into a constant pain that made him almost happy. He would have stayed there, deep in his hole, constantly tacking between highs that were too high and lows that were too low, had music and drugs and sex not intervened in his life at the very moment when he was becoming an adult.

But that's another story ...

To start writing the story of the circular madman she'd used two sources: first, the detailed account Gilbert himself had given her that morning in the kitchen when she'd found a man very different from the one she'd loved during part of the night, then the bits of information she'd dug up here and there from drag queens old enough to remember events from nearly fifteen years before, including the Duchess, Jean-le-Décollé and some others. She hadn't dared to question Greta-la-Vieille herself though. Out of tact, for fear of opening old wounds, of bringing to the surface pain, resentment or frustrations that would have taken time to heal.

The Duchess in particular had been very helpful in her research: still close to Greta-la Vieille and to Greta-la-Jeune after the Boudoir was shut down, she was in a good position to report on what the old hooker had been talking about during her more and more frequent and prolonged binges. And not surprisingly, Gilbert occupies an important place in her rambling at the end of nights awash in too much booze.

She's quite happy with what she has written. She has devoted an entire week to it. From honesty towards Gilbert. She doesn't want her blue notebook to give too dark an image of him, she refuses to turn him into a heartless son-of-a-bitch when he makes others suffer without really being aware of it because his own suffering is so intense that he doesn't see the pain he causes. Gilbert doesn't see the pain that he has caused her with his love so all-consuming that it makes her head spin, and his uncontrollable mood swings that make him switch from being a good, too-charming boy with excessively good moods to a pathetic wet rag, unable to struggle, it's the doctors who say so, against an imbalance of something or other in his brain whose name he hasn't retained. The few medications he has tried knock him out until he can't function, so he has stopped taking them. And he swears that he had decided to stay *on his own for a good long while just before meeting her, who is, he swears, the love of his life.*

*He gave her his heart, she accepted it. Even though she suspected that it was a poisoned offering.*

*Time to go to work. The dull routine of everyday life awaits her. She'll have to be patient for another few hours before she takes shelter once again in the version of the story she has created by writing it. Her own routine revised and corrected. For two years now she has been giving herself a point of view that she hopes is objective over what is going on in her life. But maybe she's deluding herself... Is it possible that she is creating illusions for herself and that when all's said and done, what she is living and even more, what she is doing with it in her notebooks, is and will remain appallingly trite?*

*She pushes the blue notebook under the lamp. The last pages are covered with strike-outs, cross-references, ink stains. She has crossed out corrections scribbled all over the margins because she preferred her first version. If anyone ever gets his hand on her notebooks, particularly this one on which she has done the most work, there'll still be puzzles impossible to solve, which is all for the best. She writes for herself, she doesn't want anyone to read it.*

*The following night, when she comes home from the Sélect, or the next morning, she'll make a start on her own descent into Gilbert's world. She makes no claim to understand everything—especially not his experiences—but what she has been close to for months now fills her at once with horror and with admiration for Gilbert.*

## Part Three

*... si tu ne m'aimes pas je t'aime ...*

It came out all lopsided, in big formless bubbles, sometimes murmured, sometimes spat out like a frog in the throat you have trouble getting rid of, the story of his life mixed in with the effects of his illness, his missing Greta which had never subsided, along with the unchanging and unshakeable impression that he had been betrayed and could not forgive, his unbearable fits of depression followed by overexcitement that was just as hard to live with, the helplessness of doctors in the face of an illness, because there were no remedies that worked.

Between hiccups, he had explained that he was constantly being promised a miracle drug, a panacea that had been in preparation for years, apparently, in the deepest recesses of the pharmaceutical labs, but he was still waiting and had to be content with the existing antidepressants which became less and less effective from overuse. Though the dose was increased, hopes were generally vain—whence his inability the night before to curb his dizzying descent into the dark and pitiful state that he'd hoped to spare me. Over time his circular madness became more pronounced, more devastating, and he didn't know where it would lead. Incarceration in a mental hospital awaited him maybe, sooner or later, even though he was neither genuinely crazy nor dangerous, and he lived in dread.

"This damn illness is like a toboggan ride. When I'm down it's as if I'm going down a steep, icy hill on a toboggan and I know I won't be able to stop till I get to the bottom. And when I feel a high coming, I'm on an elevator! The fastest one in the world, that goes up the highest. Everything's possible! The sky's the limit! At those times, I'm not sick, I'm Superman! Circular—that means something turns, but I always feel as if I'm in perpetual motion, going up or coming down, and I know there's no end to that vicious circle of mine that isn't even a circle but a straight line! And that straight line, there's no getting around it, leads to a little padded cell with a so-called circular madman inside it."

What could I say to such a deeply moving confession? Generalities, silly things and it angered me but I couldn't do otherwise. I reacted to his heartbreaking confidences with one of the most idiotic statements I've ever made.

"You don't take care of yourself. And all those drugs over the years haven't helped."

He gave me a look as if he thought I hadn't been listening for more than an hour while he tried to explain his ordeal. Or that I hadn't understood a word about his suffering.

"Drugs come in handy, Céline. At least they numb you."

I could have kicked myself. I apologized for being so insensitive. He told me he understood and that he put it down to surprise at something unexpected that was already threatening our relationship.

He swore to me—had he detected the beginning of concern in my eyes?—that he was only dangerous to himself, that he'd never been violent to anyone, that he always stopped in time; true, he sometimes waved his fist, but he'd throw himself out the window rather than hit anybody.

Especially me.

He must have sensed my growing hesitation while he was telling his story, even if my affection for him, my compassion, too, was ten times stronger, and he wanted to reassure me. It was both touching and pathetic. And absolutely correct.

At first I doubted that such a handsome guy could love me, then I nearly believed him, and now this new and totally unexpected situation changed everything. Were my suspicions well-founded? Maybe in the end he needed not a lover but a sympathetic soul, an understanding sister, a devoted mother ... a second Greta. I didn't want to become a second Greta for him, I wanted to be loved like the first time, in the apartment on Place Jacques-Cartier, like last night, I wanted to howl with pleasure and happiness without having to ask myself questions! I refused to be forced to suspect behind this relationship, which was so unexpected for me, reasons other than passion, the urge to drop everything for a night of bliss, the irrepressible need to find him again, with his odours, his moods, his body crucified in the sheets by a brutal joy or experimenting with all its possibilities, with the goal of the ultimate sublime pleasure; to turn the clock back, to feel once again the doubt that has always pierced me, that undermines everything I take on; to be the midget people feel sorry for! I wanted to be Céline, someone who would be loved for herself!

His crisis seemed to die down. Had the account that he'd just given me been enough to wipe it out or at least to diminish it? Probably not. It had more to do with the substance in his brain that was out of whack, I realized that now, than with a clear explanation or an impassioned debate. The relief that he might feel was temporary—we'd gone back to his bedroom, I'd put my arms around him and was rocking him in the sheets that had been soiled and rumpled by our love; we formed a strange Pietà, with a midget as mother and a tall beatnik as son—and it was so new for me that I was nearly trembling with fear; I knew that at any minute I might see him, suddenly, before my eyes, transformed into someone I didn't know.

"Don't be like the others, Céline, don't go away. Don't walk out on me."

I was fiddling with his curly hair that many of the women I knew would have envied, women of both sexes: the drag queens from the Main and the waitresses at the Sélect. The colour as much as the shine. It was thick and silky, but unlike the previous night, the smell it gave off now wasn't pleasant, far from it. It smelled of sickness and fever.

"I didn't say anything about leaving."

"I can hear you think … "

"That's paranoid."

"No it isn't. Every time I've confided in someone, Céline, every time, that person has walked out on me when the conversation was over. Even before, sometimes. Especially my girlfriends. Thanks a lot, so long, bye-bye. You're handsome, you're nice, but I don't want to get involved—too complicated."

"I don't want to get involved either, Gilbert. It really is too complicated. For me, for everybody ... but I don't intend to leave. Not because of that, anyway."

"See, you want to leave!"

"That's not what I said!"

"You said 'not because of that' ... Because of what, then? You didn't enjoy the night we just spent together?"

"There are other things in life than sex, Gilbert."

He sat up in bed, wrapped himself in the sheet.

"If you want to talk about feelings, be my guest, it doesn't scare me ... My episode's nearly over, I can handle it."

"What if it's me that has trouble talking about feelings?"

He smiled faintly, but it was a smile so beautiful, so forthright that I could have sworn love and loyalty till the end of my days. I was ready to do anything to see that smile as often as possible, to feed on it, to take it with me and get through everything, the best, the worst, and all that came in between. But I also knew I had to be wary of that smile, I had to be sure that the relationship just beginning, with its good aspects and its unexpected complications, wasn't concealing a hidden agenda that could blow up in my face any time. In the end, I was the paranoid one, I was well aware of it. And had been since the start of our relationship.

He took my face in his hands. My head may be big but I always feel as if it's very small in his fingers, that he could easily crush it, like a ripe fruit, if he wanted. One of those wonderful June strawberries, so red and juicy. I like to think of myself as a ripe fruit ready to burst in his hands.

"If I told you I'm falling in love with you, Céline, what would you say?"

"It's too soon to be talking about love, Gilbert, we've only seen each other three times."

He chased after me in the bed. It was almost funny. A tall, gangling young man wrapped in a dirty sheet in an unmade bed chasing a very small woman who's on the chunky side, but agile.

He pinned me to the bed, holding down both my hands. His eyes were so blue I could have eaten them. Strawberries, then blueberries? I felt totally ridiculous.

"You're scared, aren't you?"

"Scared of what?"

"Of talking about love."

I gave him a good long look before replying. Long enough to think to myself, God he's gorgeous, why is he so gorgeous, why doesn't he look more like me ... it would be so much easier.

"I've never talked about love with anybody, Gilbert."

He loosened his embrace, got rid of the sheet, and sat in the middle of the bed in the lotus position.

"I didn't take your virginity though; I'd have noticed!"

I couldn't help laughing despite the seriousness of the situation. So the macho fixation with being first still existed, despite looser morals and free love!

"I didn't say I've never had sex, Gilbert, I told you I've never been in love."

"And I suppose you're going to tell me you can't?"

This time I could have hit him. I'd have gladly given him a good whack that would turn his left cheek red for part of the day.

"Do I look like somebody who isn't capable of loving? Actually I'm more the type that can't imagine anyone loving me!"

"Why?"

What was most surprising was that the question sounded sincere. And it hit me like a punch in the solar plexus.

I stood up in the bed and spread my arms.

"Look ... Take a good look at me ... "

He ran his hands over my body—I had on one of his old T-shirts which I'd put on in a hurry when I got out of bed—he kissed my stomach, which was a little too pudgy for my liking.

"I don't see anything I don't like, Céline."

I melted. I liquefied. I flowed out of the bed and disappeared between the boards of the hardwood floor. Mostly I was silent as his kisses became more and more precise.

Then the idiotic question, "Why?"

He raised his head.

"Why what?"

"What ... I don't know how to put it ... what is it about me that you like? I've got nothing to appeal to a guy like you ... "

He brought his arms down and sat on his heels as if he wanted to stop everything.

"I'm the one having a crisis and you need reassuring?"

He bent over me.

"The crisis you just witnessed was nothing next to the ones I have now and then ... So I'm the last one to reassure you ... I made a declaration of love to you, Céline, take it for what it is ... I can't explain it, what I love about you is things I can't put into words, things you can't say ... because there aren't any words to describe it ... Ask me any time you want me to show you, but don't ask me to put it into words! I don't think I could ever do that!"

I took shelter in his arms, I wanted to stay there forever but I was not reassured! *I was not reassured!*

"I'm scared ... "

"So am I, I'm scared, too, Céline ... "

"No, that's not what I mean ... I'm scared that all you need is company, Gilbert ... I refuse to be a new Greta for you ... if that's what you want ... "

His shoulders were hunched, he lowered his head, I saw with horror the moment coming when he would tell me I was right, that he just needed company, and I thought to myself, That's it, I've just ruined everything with one remark, but still it's better to know the truth right away than when it's too late. It won't be as painful now as it would be later.

I was also afraid that another crisis would come, worse than before, and strike him down before my eyes, in the middle of the bed.

He wrapped himself again in the big sheet soiled by our lovemaking and got out of the bed.

"If it's impossible to convince you, Céline, there's nothing I can do. If your self-esteem is as low as mine, we'll never be able to convince each other of anything. I don't want to have to explain myself all the time, it's a waste of energy and spit. If you don't believe me now, you won't believe me after the most complicated or most detailed explanations. It's not that you don't believe me, Céline, you don't believe in yourself."

He went to the bathroom, head hanging, a white Buddhist monk who withdraws after delivering a sermon he's not proud of.

"I'm going to take a shower. The crisis is definitely over, I think. Thanks for listening."

He was dismissing me—politely, it's true, but it was still a dismissal—and I deserved it. As I was getting dressed I wouldn't let myself think about what had just been said; I wanted to wait till I was home, in my own surroundings, with my own things, in my own bed, before castigating myself and sentencing myself to eternal celibacy because I wasn't able to accept a declaration of love, no doubt honest, that I'd dreamed of for so long.

"You damn fool! You'll never change."

Leaving Gilbert's place—it was April in all its magnificence, with singing birds, melting snow, a slate-blue sky that looked scrubbed clean—I was positive I'd never have another boyfriend and sure that it was my own fault.

Of course I spent the afternoon brooding over it, looking for—and finding—a meaning that it didn't have, interpreting what had been said to his advantage and to my own detriment. He was right about everything and I was wrong. I was on my own once again and once again it was my fault. As it always is. Like the last time. Like the next time. I'd been unable to give myself over body and soul to his beautiful declaration. I had resisted the seductive traps and dangers of love, probably using Gilbert's illness as a pretext for slipping away ...

Luckily I was alone in the house, my three roommates were out, doing errands or enjoying the beautiful spring day, so I was able to cry as much as I wanted, and I must admit I took good advantage of it. Without disturbing a soul.

I was pretty well positive that I'd never see Gilbert again when I went to work that night.

It must have been to taunt me that the weather was glorious again. Suddenly it was no longer April, it was already May, and I wouldn't have been surprised, when I turned the corner, to smell the first lily-of-the-valley. I knew it was impossible, in Montreal lily-of-the-valley comes out in early June and sometimes even later, but there's no charge for dreaming. I wished I could skip the next few weeks and find myself with no transition in the time of lily-of-the-valley or the lilacs that scent the air of Montreal for two short weeks and give back the will to live when you've lost it. I knew that the weeks to come would be filled with criticisms and regrets that I could have got along without. Meanwhile I breathed in the air of this beautiful late afternoon that was filled with hope for everyone but me. I was on the lookout for leaf buds on the trees and was thrilled when I saw even a tiny one.

There are days when chance creates moments that are unique, or sometimes nearly absurd, that will stay engraved in your memory for your whole life, privileged encounters or weird events that leave you astonished and unable to explain to yourself what set them off. Or what they mean.

Which was the impression I had that night at the Sélect.

The supper hour was spent racing back and forth to the kitchen, arms full of food that made me feel sick to my stomach, not salivate, just then. I could barely see my customers, they were vague shadows, faceless and lacking personality, to whom I still had to talk and who gave answers that I understood because no one complained about the service. So I plunged into my work, trying to put my feelings on hold, and I nearly succeeded.

The heart of the evening was boring in the extreme. No one to serve, Janine deep in a head cold and a Harlequin romance, which in my opinion is pretty much the same thing, Nick and Lucien, who for once weren't in the mood to chat, the cashier shut away inside her cubicle. I folded enough paper napkins for at least the rest of the spring, I drank countless cups of tea, I tried, in vain, to take an interest in what the day's papers had to say. I was hoping to see my old friends from the Boudoir come in, chattering gaily, having come miraculously to pull me out of the first signs of depression with their silly gags and empty gossip. To laugh at the Duchess's warmed-over jokes or discuss the new spring colours with Babalu—anything but sit on my backside, and stare into space.

Of course I thought about Gilbert, about his kind of depression, the hell that was liable to keep him prisoner his whole life, between two equally intolerable poles unless a remedy was found. I thought about my own selfishness, too, which was keeping me from getting involved, at the dawn of the first love of my life, for fear of suffering. I knew very well though that Gilbert was worth some occasional suffering, no matter how acute, and I was aware of my interest in him, which kept growing, but the need to protect myself against adversity that I'd developed over the years was more powerful than anything else and I had to trust my instincts.

To the detriment of happiness?

What happiness?

The two nights Gilbert and I had spent together had been amazingly wonderful, more than that even, perfect, but the wakening after the second one, what I'd lived through that morning, had been too abrupt for me, I wasn't ready to face such a responsibility. Because it was one—and then some. To take care of someone with clinical depression, to keep an eye open for every one of his mood swings and every kind of behaviour, to back him up in everything he did was beyond me and I refused to do it, in spite of everything exciting and thrilling that Gilbert had made me experience.

But oh, God, his kindness, his sensitivity, his body, his eyes, his odour—how could I live without them? I poured my anger and helplessness into the repetitive and ludicrous task of folding the paper napkins, piling them up and stuffing them into a cupboard that was already overflowing.

Around ten o'clock, the restaurant door opened to let in two young men, one in his twenties, the other in his early thirties. I recognized the older one, Yvan, who often drops in for a quick bite to eat. He's a theatre director and actor, one of the ones Janine can tolerate because they're quiet and not as wild as the others, and she's willing to serve them. He comes sometimes with his wife, who's an actress, sometimes on his own, wolfs down his club sandwich or hamburger platter in silence, or kidding around with us in a friendly way, then he leaves without our knowing much more about him, whereas some of the other theatrical types act as if they've come to the Sélect just to give us the latest news about their flourishing careers. About which, need I add, we couldn't care less.

The other one I'd never seen before. He had a friendly face and was quite obviously shy. I thought to myself he's probably an actor—it's strange, but fairly often actors are timid—one Yvan was working with, and I gave them menus because they'd sat in my section.

The two greeted me, then they ordered a beer and plunged into their menus. Like all the regular customers of the Sélect, Yvan knew the menu by heart, so I was surprised to see him turn the pages and look through it as if it were the first time. He told me before I had to ask, "You must be wondering why I haven't ordered the same as usual, Céline … It's because we're celebrating … "

He stopped in mid-sentence.

"Actually, excuse me, both of you, I haven't introduced you. Céline, this is Réjean Ducharme. He's a writer. I'm mounting two of his plays for my theatre in the Laurentians and I think those two shows will be … without bragging too much … let's say … at a conservative estimate … absolutely fabulous … The reason I say that is because the scripts are magnificent."

The other man turned red merely at the uttering of his name. He even brought his hand to his heart as if Yvan had just betrayed a highly important secret. But he seemed thrilled at what the director had said about his plays.

As for me, I was bowled over. Everyone had been praising the writer lately, talking about his genius and his originality; because he stayed in the shadows and never gave interviews, some people had even claimed that he didn't exist, that his name was the pseudonym of a well-known person who wanted anonymity.

"You really exist! I'm so glad! So many things are going badly, at last some good news! Your beer is on me!"

They both looked at me, a little surprised.

"I haven't read *L'avalée des avalés* yet because I haven't had time, I've been waiting for my summer holidays … "

Which wasn't altogether true. The novel had been on my bedside table for months and I'd been waiting for the right moment to start it, probably when I've finished the Rougon-Macquart.

To celebrate, they wanted to order the most expensive thing on the menu, but I suggested they stick to the simplest because that was what Nick and Lucien did best and it was the basis of what makes the reputation of so-called *continental* restaurants like ours.

"There's a reason why we have specialties. That's what you should choose or you don't know what you're letting yourself in for."

They thanked me. Yvan praised the hamburger platter and the writer let himself be tempted. I was going to serve a hamburger platter to Réjean Ducharme! But I had no one to share this unexpected thrill with.

I was coming out of the kitchen a few minutes later, carrying my plates, when a new threesome came in. It was the young director with whom I'd nearly worked two years earlier, who was starting to get a serious reputation in Montreal's theatre world; he was with his actress friend, Rita, who'd played Andromache in the production of *The Trojan Women* at the Théâtre des Saltimbanques, and a pal of theirs, a young playwright with too much beard and too much hair for my taste, who worked in a print shop nearby and often came for his half-hour lunch break. (Need I add that I'd never seen a human being eat so fast in my entire life!) All three seemed excited, maybe they were coming from a show at the Comédie-Canadienne or the Gesù. Or at the Théâtre du Nouveau Monde ...

They sat far from my other two customers but still in my section. Janine looked up from her Harlequin romance, seemed relieved that she wouldn't have to look after them, and went back to her book. When I came for the menus I suggested, smiling ironically, "You can have them if you want, Janine. I've already got two customers, it's your turn ... "

She didn't even deign to look up from her book as she said, "Those creeps? Be my guest! You can handle them, I can't. They're rude, they're foul-mouthed, they think the sun rises and sets on them, and they haven't got two cents to rub together!"

I was laughing when I brought the menus to my three new customers, though I already knew what they'd order. The two men anyway. Some customers are like clockwork: they always come at the same time, they always order the same thing, and they always leave the same tip when they depart. The young director and his printer friend were like that. Quick to order, quick to eat, quick to pay. All interspersed with comments about everything they'd seen or read since their last visit (sometimes the day before). I had the impression that they devoured everything cultural that Montreal had to offer, and to me they were artists at the beginning of their career, ready to sacrifice everything to buy a book or a theatre ticket. The actress I didn't know so well, I couldn't have said exactly what she would order and I felt obliged to make the same suggestion to her as to the other two earlier, when she seemed to be interested in the filet mignon which was no doubt beyond her means. Okay, one more hamburger. The one for the director had something special about it, I knew that, and there was no need to remind me: three gravies, no coleslaw.

I found out right away why they were so excited, all three were so happy they couldn't restrain themselves: they had just signed their first contract with a professional theatre, the director was going to mount the bearded one's first play at the Rideau-Vert and Rita would be acting in it. None of them drank, so I couldn't offer them a beer, but I brought Cokes and they thanked me effusively. The young director had just spotted Yvan and waved at him. I didn't dare tell them who he was with, I didn't want to give away the other writer's secret. But it was hard.

Two playwrights celebrating almost the same thing on the same night in the same restaurant, that was something else!

Anyway, the young director—his name is André Brassard, I ought to start calling him by name—André was heading for Yvon and Réjean's table so the question was going to be settled. But I never found out if the introductions had been made, I was already back in the kitchen where Nick had started preparing the food for the new arrivals.

"Nick, what would you do if they'd ordered something else?"

With an expert hand, he lifted the basket of fries out of its boiling oil and with a flip of his wrist, emptied it onto two plates.

"Won't happen!"

"But if they're celebrating something?"

"They'll celebrate with what they know, otherwise they'd be somewhere else."

When I came back from the kitchen—there was a whole series of repetitions that night—a wind of madness took over the Sélect: the wild bunch of young people who were working on the show at the Quat'Sous, who included Gilbert, had taken over the Sélect in a matter of seconds and was spreading through the restaurant with songs and laughter. They seemed excited about something. Also. They must have had a successful rehearsal. There were more of them than usual—the guys had brought their girlfriends—and a lot noisier. Nick had already stuck his head out the kitchen door to count them, while Janine was behaving as if she weren't there. It must have been the most fascinating Harlequin romance of all time.

Some of them knew André by sight, Yvan, too, because they'd worked with him, so greetings were being shouted. Louise, the singer of the group, embraced Rita, everyone was congratulating those who'd just signed their first professional contract, the young playwright was flushed with happiness. I saw Yvan and Réjean exchange a few words, get up and try to disappear, then leave the restaurant in the midst of the outpourings, the laughter and the cries of joy.

As for me, I'd joined Janine in the corner reserved for the waitresses.

"I hope you aren't going to leave me all alone on the floor, Janine!"

"Why not? You like them, look after them!"

"There's over a dozen of them!"

"You've seen worse."

"Sure, at rush time, but it's the end of the evening now, try to have some heart, I'm dead on my feet too!"

"You'll make more money."

"You know perfectly well it's not about money ... Oh, never mind, stay with your blonde princesses and your superheroes. Go on dreaming instead of earning your living!"

What I'd just said didn't seem to bother her and she happily dived back into her syrupy prose. I could have complained to Nick who probably would have forced her to serve some of the new arrivals, but it would have meant a week of hell so I decided to go it alone.

Around the middle of the meal—everything was fine, no one complained about the service, the drinks had been drunk, a little quickly, amid the general euphoria, the soups were served hot and each of the numerous main dishes delivered to the right person—

Nick came out of the kitchen to make a scene, discreet but obvious enough that everyone was aware of it, directed at Janine who still hadn't taken her nose out of her book and was acting as if she were in a reading room at the municipal library. No one could hear what he said, not even me, though I had to walk past them several times to take the dirty plates to the kitchen, but from the look on Janine's face it can't have been very enjoyable. He could have called her into the kitchen to tell her off but he'd obviously preferred to do it in front of everybody in order to drive home the message, thereby departing from one of the basic rules that every good boss has to observe: never chew off an employee in front of customers.

Sometimes Nick is over-protective of me but he's never unfair, at least I hope not, and the other staff of the Sélect, even if they're really fond of me, don't like it. This time, though, Janine had gone too far, and Nick was right to light into her—there's an unspoken rule that you don't leave a waitress all alone on the floor if you can help her, a tacit agreement that every waitress in the world follows and never questions—but not in front of everybody.

Then, all of a sudden as I was taking away Louise's half-eaten club sandwich while she crooned a silly song about someone called Dolores, the reason why, all night, Janine had been behaving with me the way she did became blindingly clear and I realized once again that it was my fault: I hadn't told her what had happened last evening and even more, what had happened that night, and she was mad at me.

She couldn't know, poor dear, what I'd gone through after I got up that morning and she had expected a description in intimate detail of my lovemaking with Gilbert, my excitement, his, how long it had lasted and the chance of a repetition any time soon. She'd decided to make me pay for my excessive discretion by sulking like a child. Maybe she hadn't read a word of her stupid novel!

In the restaurant meanwhile, the party was still going on. A guitar had been taken out of its leather case—so Gilbert wasn't the only guitarist in the show—and we were treated to an avant-première of what awaited the audience at the Théâtre de Quat'Sous the following month. The songs, rhythmical, swinging, colourful, would no doubt appeal to the young audience who were more attracted to the Beatles than to Gilles Vigneault. I'd have cut the blasphemy though—I'd heard Louise come out with *une chute, une Christ de chute en parachute* that had made me jump. It was probably the very first time a curse had appeared in a song written in Quebec and not everybody would like it. But I imagine that if I mentioned it, they'd say their aim was not to please but to provoke.

For one brief moment I envied them—again. They were using their talent to express what they felt about life and its turpitudes. And if that was translated as une chute, *une Christ de chute en parachute*, why not? Then I thought about my own way of escaping, my two notebooks, the black one that's so sad, the red one that's so festive, into which I'd poured everything that had been in my soul for two years, and I felt closer to them. The only difference between us, when you get down to it, was that I insisted that my notebooks stay a secret, that my own *Christ de chute en parachute* be imprisoned in the pages of a journal rather than feel the need to shout it out on stage in front of everybody.

If I were to go and see the young playwright at the other table, if I told him that I too put on paper things that I'd never dare to tell my friends and acquaintances, everything that caused me pain and everything that gave me pleasure, how would he react? Turn up his nose? Refuse to believe, out of snobbery, out of crass ignorance, that a humble waitress like me could express herself in a clear way and with a certain aptness, simply because she's not a product of the prestigious schools where they *show* you how to write? Was there a wall, a genuine wall, between the people I served and myself just because I was serving them and people who serve, it's inevitable, have no right to be in the arts?

I didn't have much time to develop my thinking because all eyes suddenly turned to the restaurant entrance.

In a sorry state, hunched over, face as white as a sheet and clothes badly rumpled, Gilbert could barely stand up in the doorway. He was trying to shape his lips into something like a smile but his attempt was pitiful and all he could produce was a sad grin that made him look ugly. He aroused pity—yes, pity, even though I hate the word—and if I hadn't held back, I would have thrown myself into his arms to give him some comfort. I didn't budge though, because I knew that he'd come to the Sélect to see not me, but his friends from work.

Yvon, the oldest of the group from the Quat'Sous, got up right away and went to meet him. He didn't appear to be in a good mood and Gilbert hunched his back ever more when he saw him approach.

"Where the hell were you all day? We were expecting you … "

"I was sick."

"You could've called and let us know."

"I was too sick."

"We phoned about twenty times and you never answered! Are you sure you were at home?"

"Yes, yes. I had a migraine. A really terrible migraine … "

He looked in my direction. I was the only one who knew the truth.

Yvon went on, "A headache kept you from phoning to say you're going to miss an important rehearsal?"

Gilbert leaned against the cashier's cage and Françoise jumped as if Typhoid Mary had dared to touch her precious cash-register.

"If you knew what kind of migraine I had, you'd understand … "

"Is it liable to come back when we're performing?"

"Not if I don't drink. I promise I won't drink till the end of the run."

"We know about the promises of a drunk, Gilbert."

"It isn't a drunk's promise … I don't want to be sick, Yvon … I don't want to be sick … "

I knew he was telling the truth but unfortunately it was also true that Gilbert had no control over his illness, which was a lot more serious and devastating than a mere migraine.

Yvon coughed into his fist.

"Are you okay now?"

"It's not as bad as this morning ... I just wanted ... I just wanted you to know that I absolutely intend to stay with you and that I'll do whatever I have to, everything in my power so it won't happen again."

"Are you going to eat with us?"

"No, I'm not up to it ... I'll be a lot better tomorrow, I'll come to rehearsal ... I promise ... "

After glancing around at the others—I sensed right away that they'd already discussed Gilbert's problem and that he'd come very close to being kicked out of the group—Yvon put one hand on his shoulder.

"One chance. We're giving you one more chance. One."

And went back to his place amid a weighty silence.

Instead of going out, Gilbert walked the length of the restaurant to join me at the waitresses' table, where Janine had finally put down her book. For good reason. Something juicy was about to surface, she must have been quivering with expectation.

He planted himself in front of me, as upright as possible, but his attempt was pathetic, you could make out the pain in every fibre of his body.

"I love you, Céline Poulin, and I'm begging you, help me!"

How could I resist?

Just before he left the restaurant, André turned to the gang from the Quat'Sous and asked, "Have you got a name for your show yet?"

And the others replied, in chorus and quite obviously frustrated, "Nope! Not yet!"

A night of love without physical love is possible and may even turn out to be extremely satisfying, as I found out that night. We didn't have sex but it was as if we had: his confidences overwhelmed me, mine seemed to delight him, it was our words that made love. What we exchanged was ideas, essential ideas. We'd both put our cards on the table once and for all, sometimes laughing uproariously, sometimes with tears in our eyes, our touching was without ulterior motives, our kisses simple proof of affection. When we rolled around in his bed it was to change position, and if a cry slipped out it was because of surprise at something the other had said or friendly teasing at a somewhat shameful confession. I had decided to lay aside my doubts and try to believe everything he said. It worked. I drank in his words, his declarations, his promises, I turned them into poultices for my bruised and wounded heart. It felt so good that I forgot any qualms. I knew it and, for once, I didn't care. I wasn't even going to wonder if there would be a price to pay.

I recounted my whole life in detail—my difficult childhood with all its hang-ups, my alcoholic mother, my first attempt at independence—the Sélect—and then the Boudoir, Expo 67 and my return to the restaurant. In a few minutes I summed up what had taken me two years to write. And finally, his arrival in my life, which had been more of a curse than a blessing. He didn't appreciate the word *curse*, but he seemed to understand what I meant.

I melted in his arms, it was as if it had always been my place: my entire person fit in between his head and his torso, his arms rocked me the way a child rocks its teddy bear—and suddenly I didn't mind being someone's teddy bear. Or even looking the part. My own arms, too short, could only wrap around his neck, my fingers got lost in the hair that fell to his nape, I played in the dampness of his scalp. And rubbed my cheek against the stubble on his, which prickled my skin.

Hours went by but we weren't aware of it. I actually think that we were happy.

Of his illness, his episodes, of what they might lead to between us in the future, not a word. Not now. We were there to enjoy the present moment, the present moment was wonderful and we took advantage of it with no second thoughts. The rest would come soon enough.

A chilly wind blew in through the wide-open window, I could have sworn that it smelled of bursting buds but maybe it was just that my mind wanted it to be May. If it got too cold, we covered ourselves with the sheet that Gilbert hadn't washed yet—he who was so clean—and if it got hot, we kicked it off. When I'd seen that the bed was in the same state as when I'd left it in the morning, I offered to change it but he told me that he only had one set of sheets which he washed now and then in the laundromat at the corner of Ontario Street. Everything was obsessively clean in his house but he slept in dirty sheets? He shared an amazing confidence: he liked the smell of his body and actually liked going to bed at night in his own smell from the night before.

"The house is so clean that when I go to bed at night I like to remind myself of the weirdo I'm supposed to be ... I make my bed every morning but I don't often wash my sheets."

"You didn't make your bed today."

"I wasn't myself today, Céline, I was so incredibly down and making my bed wasn't a priority."

This man was full of surprises! I told him, though, that if he wanted to see me back in his bed he'd have to buy some more sheets and keep his bed as immaculate as the rest of his apartment. First loud laughter of the evening. But no promise. Was I at my age going to learn to sleep in dirty sheets? Then again, why not, if they smelled of Gilbert Forget!

Especially because the depressed and defeated Gilbert Forget I'd known the night before had made way once again for the sweet, considerate, affectionate one who'd been with me until his first episode. As he'd been the summer before on St. Catherine Street. Or when I'd seen him at the Sélect a few weeks earlier. I was used to changing personalities, after all the times I'd seen my mother turn into a monster in the space of a few hours, but I'd always known the cause: the bottles she hid all over the house which we pretended not to see and which made her crazy. Gilbert, though, carried his illness in his head; he was a time-bomb that could explode at any moment and I couldn't behave as I did with my mother, as if it didn't exist. No, better not to think about it, concentrate on what he was saying, about his love for me which he claimed, with a laugh, was worthy of the world's great love stories— Romeo and Juliet, Tristan and Isolde, our very own Donalda Laloge and Alexis Labranche. When I pointed out that all those love stories had a tragic ending, he silenced me with a long kiss that nearly led us into something we wanted to avoid and I pushed him away with protests that were rather feeble but that he was gentleman enough to respect.

Eyes glued to the window where a square of sky was just beginning to fade, I thought to myself, Someone is talking about love to me, Céline Poulin, and I shuddered with pleasure. If Gilbert asked why I was trembling, I would tell him I felt chilly, and the teddy bear I'd always refused to be would snuggle against his neck which smelled like his sheets.

We watched the sky turn pale, then blue, saw the sun rise, become blinding. A scene that is always the same but constantly renewed according to lovers of every colour and every background, something that I hoped to experience and verify as often as possible.

Gilbert had recently had a shower installed in the dilapidated bathroom which until then only had a traditional claw foot tub and he threw himself into it with obvious pleasure around seven a.m. Stretched out on my back with my left leg crossed over the right, I was given a free concert: the nearly complete show that was in preparation at the Théâtre de Quat'Sous. But murdered by a voice hoarse from lack of sleep and a flagrant lack of singing talent, the songs, new though they were and maybe for that very reason, lost a lot of their charm, and I wondered again how they would be received.

He emerged from the shower clean, freshly shaven, sexier than ever in his shameless nakedness and I allowed myself to bring up again the matter of his disgusting sheets. He shrugged, laughing, and dropped a quick kiss on my nose that smelled of Colgate toothpaste and powerful mouthwash.

"Gotta run. Rehearsal's at ten ... Did you hear what they said last night? I have to toe the line ... Stay as long as you want. You can even wash the sheets if you like!"

He left the bedroom with a mocking smile on his lips and a guitar over his shoulder. The young Félix Leclerc in his photos from Paris. I realized that the guitar had spent the night in one corner of the room, like an indulgent chaperone with an eye open for trouble while protecting the lovers. Who'd have thought that one day I would be watched over by an old guitar that belonged to a bohemian afflicted with a kind of insanity that no one understood and that had a poetic name for want of a genuine patronym?

Opening the door on his way out, Gilbert shouted, "I love you, Céline Poulin!"

And as my mother would have put it, They must have heard him seven houses away.

But I didn't reply.

Not once had I told him I loved him.

And was that not the crux of the matter?

Just like at the restaurant and in my parents' house when I was a child, a small bench had been placed in front of the bathroom sink in the apartment on Place Jacques-Cartier to make it easier for me to have access to running water, the mirror and the medicine chest. My roommates curse when I inadvertently leave it there and they stumble over it, but most of the time I remember to stow it in a corner or push it under the sink to avoid accidents. When you share an apartment with three drag queens who are drunk or high more often than they should be, who're coping with a hangover most mornings and take refuge in the bathroom, hiding their eyes melodramatically because daylight hurts and reality kills, it's best to take precautions.

When I got home that morning—it was too early for even a semblance of life in the house—I went straight to the bathroom, I pushed my little bench into position, climbed up on it, holding onto the sink with both hands, and looked myself straight in the eyes. It's something I've always done in times of crisis, when I wanted to get back in touch with myself. At my parents' home, at the restaurant, here in the apartment on Place Jacques- Cartier. It seems to me that you can't lie when you look at yourself in a mirror.

For years I'd dreamed about what was going on right now, never daring to think that it would, but there it was, real and tangible: Gilbert's looks went way beyond my wildest hopes and it was all happening to me, who'd always felt unworthy of being loved. But something was blocked inside me as if one final key to one final lock were missing, or one door in my heart was stubbornly refusing to open. I knew it was pointless to chalk it up to Gilbert's illness: love, the real thing, at least what I thought of as true love, wasn't concerned about this kind of detail, it struck with no concern for its victims or the price they'd have to pay. It wasn't caution then that was holding me back.

So what was it?

It was one of two things: either I was incapable of letting myself go, of abandoning myself to love regardless of the consequences, or else—and this was much more serious—I was incapable of loving. Had I got my fingers burnt in childhood, frustrated when I sought my family's love and the love of people who would have been my friends but who'd quickly turned into torturers until my heart was closed forever to any form of true love, to anything that went beyond friendship and demanded that I let myself go without hesitation? If I could find the key to letting myself go somewhere deep inside my heart, if I let myself go and used it, would my life be completely transformed? Would I be driven mad by love, ready to drop everything for a guitar player with an uncertain future?

And deep in my own eyes I read—I could swear that it was a voice I didn't hear but *read deep* in my eyes—a tiny little voice, a green little voice with gold sequins, that was saying to me, Poor fool, you're two steps away from doing it, let yourself go for once, make the leap, stop analyzing everything or you'll end up all alone in your corner, like a rat, because you'll never have known what it meant to let yourself go.

I would have liked to listen to that voice in colour, throw myself head over heels into irrational passion, run to the Théâtre de Quat'Sous and proclaim in front of everyone, "I love you, too, Gilbert Forget!" But to my great despair I couldn't do it. The key could not be found and the door in my heart remained shut.

And yet, and yet, deep down, if I really, really looked, I knew that I loved Gilbert. Not just because he was gorgeous or because of his good points, which were many, that was too easy, too obvious, it was the very basis of love and anyone can succumb to it, it was also for his weaknesses and his vulnerability. I'd seen Gilbert capable of doing everything, thinking he was invincible, I'd seen him weak enough to break at any moment, I'd also guessed at the touching child who'd never recovered from an immense sorrow that he saw as a betrayal, and he had bowled me over so much that I wanted to do something good for him, become some kind of relief to his manifold pain. If he loved me as he said he did, for once I was going to let myself be loved!

And in the end, it may have been at that moment that my plan began to germinate in my head.

The least one can say is that the early days of May were up and down. Gilbert and I were rather cautious about our relationship, except in bed where everything was permitted, attempted and often succeeded. Our nights sometimes made up for what we'd made a mess of during the day.

For my part, I tried to predict his crises, to guess from his behaviour or his words the detail that would precede an extreme high or down so I could prepare for it, but it was more subtle than I'd thought at first and his mood swings, which were quick and devastating, generally turned out to be impossible to anticipate or if I did manage, it was too late to dodge them, the harm had already been done: in a matter of minutes, an omnipotent giant was born before my eyes, or a wreck of a man fell into my arms, screaming in pain. He came back from rehearsals either filled with enthusiasm or depressed, telling me that he was an excellent musician or a total asshole. When he was somewhere in between, when he was what I supposed was the real Gilbert Forget, he was adorable, attentive, it was as if his two extremes didn't exist and we spent some amazing moments together.

The staff at the Sélect, though, continued to look at him suspiciously. Janine didn't care who heard her when she called him a creep in front of me, wrinkling her nose. Nick gave him the cold shoulder and even seemed to refuse to believe that we were really lovers. As for Madeleine, who didn't see much of him because she worked days, she shook her head whenever she spotted him, maybe because he looked too much like her oldest son, her *bête noire* and the despair of her life—a self-styled musician, too, and around the same age as Gilbert. Françoise, the cashier, seemed for some unknown reason to be afraid of him. And Lucien made fun of him behind his back, miming a guitar player. For once I had a boyfriend but it was far from a triumph. I stood up to them though, even going so far as to claim that I was happier than I really was, just to prove they were wrong and to silence them.

One night around closing time a delegation from the Main—my three roommates plus the Duchess herself in person—came to visit me. I thought they were going to back me against the wall, tell me things I didn't want to know about Gilbert—other women, other vices, other failings—try to prove to me once and for all that he wasn't worth the trouble, that he would make me suffer, that I'd regret it for the rest of my life, and I wanted to run away. Why were they coming to see me at the Sélect? Why hadn't they organized it for home, over a strong coffee or a monster joint? To make it more official? To frighten me even more? Because I was more vulnerable at the restaurant than in the apartment on Place Jacques-Cartier? Whatever the reasons, I was in no mood to see them if they were intending to put me on trial, and I let them know it.

With a grand dramatic gesture, the Duchess took from her reticule—a tiny purse for such a large person—a handkerchief perfumed so strongly, I thought the Sélect would smell of Tulipe Noire for a week.

"I always forget how much it reeks of grease here."

Such humourless hostility worthy of a snob surprised me coming from someone who'd always made it a point of honour to be incisive in criticism and amusing in any kind of situation. It was the first time I'd caught fat Édouard being not funny and it must have shown on my face because he immediately shut up and returned the handkerchief to his purse. And I realized how true it was that he had aged since he came back from Acapulco. His fat face was wrinkled because he'd lost too much weight too quickly, his double chin drooped right onto his glass-bead necklace, the bags under his eyes weren't really hidden by a coat of excessively brown makeup that created no illusion in his pathetic attempt to suggest a tan brought home from Mexico. It was said that he'd been the victim of a certain Peter—down South, that is—that he couldn't get over him, that he'd aged all at once and that his brain was going soft at an astonishing speed.

Jean-le-Décollé spoke first. He seemed hesitant, uncomfortable, as if this meeting with me wasn't his idea and he'd given in with bad grace. I was sure he knew about my resentment and that he shared it: this lightning visit was pointless and would lead nowhere. And what came out of his mouth was so hackneyed that I nearly laughed in his face.

"We never see you any more, Céline ... "

We were sitting in a big booth for six at the back of the restaurant, purses in implausible colours had been plunked down next to cups of coffee that no one was drinking, the ashtray was filling up at lightning speed. A strange nervousness hovered over everything too, as if the meeting had been poorly prepared and everyone felt a little ashamed.

"Is that all? Is that all you've got to tell me? You came as a delegation from the heart of the Main to tell me we don't see much of each other when you could've told me when you wake up tomorrow afternoon over a coffee I'd have made myself?"

They exchanged a look as if to give each other some courage before they took the leap.

The minutes that followed are hard to describe: a four-voice choir, improvised and with no organization or structure; a wall of criticisms, advice, of contradictory opinions that clumped and scattered like a shower of confetti; hands that squeezed my arm hard enough to turn it red, or were placed on hearts to prove the sincerity of what was proposed; cigarettes mashed in one quick-tempered move but that continued to stink up the atmosphere with their sickening grey swirls; phony laughter when they aimed at irony; forefingers pointed at my nose and a few tears too, all genuine, because this was about my well-being and my happiness, which I seemed unaware of and everyone was worried about my recklessness. It was magnificently, absolutely sincere and I listened as if it were a piece of modern music composed just for me and performed for me alone in the privacy of the restaurant which was about to close for the night. I picked up sentence fragments, some words spoken louder than others, I could imagine the rest, I reconstituted the mental puzzle that was coming apart in front of me by telling myself that, in any case, I was lucky to have such good friends. The only one missing was Fine Dumas in a lilac or lemon-yellow outfit. She would have shut them up, though, she'd have taken the floor without asking permission and what she told me would have been clear, controlled and effective. I'd have had no choice but to listen and think about it. But with no leader to hold onto them and guide them, my friends went back to being long-winded drag queens you couldn't take seriously because they set their sights pretty well anywhere, and what I took in from them was nothing more than a shower of formless words that were highly ineffective, though very beautiful, and that would have no influence over what I thought or what I did.

At the heart of it all of course was not so much my absence from their lives for the past while but the presence in mine of Gilbert, whom they'd been so fond of fifteen years before, but now fled like the plague because of what they called his ingratitude. They knew his story better than I did, the Duchess even talked about how devoted he'd been during what she thought was his wonderful love affair with Greta-la-Vieille, which she placed among the most beautiful and most moving stories of all time. Their sympathy was for me though, and they practically demanded that I swear on the spot to abandon Gilbert to his fate, his music, his illness. Their warnings were unconditional, they played Cassandra on the eve of the fall of Troy, but there'd been too much at the same time and they didn't realize it, but they cancelled each other out.

When they'd finished their delightful number, when peace and quiet had fallen over the Sélect, I took a deep breath and without thinking, I delivered the coup de grâce.

I started of course by thanking them for their friendship, for their concern about me, even for their unexpected visit. But I quickly added that instead of persuading me to drop Gilbert, they had on the contrary backed me up in a plan I'd had simmering for some time. Right away, they sensed that something unpleasant was about to pounce on them and all four shrank back in the fake leather booth. The Duchess plucked a yellow pill from a small bottle she'd taken from her purse and swallowed it with the dregs of a cup of coffee, grimacing.

"If you were a nice girl, Céline, you'd wait till my Valium kicks in before you said anything. It takes around twenty minutes, but I know you're in too big a hurry to knock us out. So, go ahead, fire away, point blank."

That was when I told them about my plan to reunite and if possible to reconcile Greta-la-Vieille and Gilbert Forget.

They didn't shriek as I'd expected. Too stunned, I imagine.

The Duchess took out another pill and swallowed it dry.

"They'll kill each other!"

I laid my hand over hers. It was hard and cold, as if the Duchess had died during their high-wire act and *rigor mortis* had already started to set in.

"You're freezing cold, Duchess!"

She produced a hint of a smile, the saddest one I'd seen in a long time, and a sigh that went on forever.

"All my extremities are cold, little girl. My head, my feet, my hands. My honorary member too! It's as if my blood can't get there any more! I'm on the way out through the extremities, Céline, don't kill me before it's time!"

I crossed my hands on the Arborite table. I was kneeling on the banquette so that I'd be more or less level with their faces.

"They won't kill each other. Sure they've got lots to deal with, but they won't kill each other. I thought we could do it at home, in the apartment on Place Jacques-Cartier. With no advance warning of course, because they'd probably both refuse if we said anything ahead of time. I think it's important. For both of them. They've never had a chance to explain ... "

Jean-le-Décollé pounded the table with his fist.

"It's his fault. He took off like a coward!"

"He felt he'd been betrayed, Jean, and he's never had a chance to tell Greta."

The Duchess was fiddling with her too-numerous necklaces so much, I was afraid that she'd break them.

"Why are you getting mixed up in it, Céline?"

It came out without my realizing and I think I actually blushed like I've never blushed in my life.

"Because I love Gilbert Forget. Because he deserves to have us look after him. Because it would be a good thing for him."

Jean-le-Décollé reached out for my hand.

"What about Greta-la-Vieille, do you think it would do her good too?"

I looked him squarely in the eyes. And I could see that however much he liked me, his allegiance would always be towards his comrades, that Greta, the old drag queen, would always be more important to him than Céline the Midget. And my admiration was reinforced.

"Have you ever given a child to his mother after a separation of fifteen years, Jean? Eh? You haven't? Me neither! True, we don't know what might happen but we can certainly try! And hope!"

For one whole week I tried to persuade them. They resisted all my arguments, claiming that she'd drop dead on the spot or that he would kill her, arguing that it was too late, the harm had been done so long ago that it was pointless to try to make amends, it could even be disastrous for both of them. In fact they were telling me mainly and in other words to mind my own business. And in a sense they were right.

But I loved Greta-la-Vieille, with whom I'd worked at the Boudoir for over a year, she was like a kind auntie you'd spent some time with and now you miss her. As for Gilbert, his place in my life was becoming more and more important, the place of the lover whom you more than love, whom you respect and to whom you want to give unassailable proof of your affection. And what had happened between them went straight to my heart. I wanted to save them, maybe even despite themselves, I felt that I could do it and I was rather proud of my idea.

I was sure I was right: as a very young child, Gilbert had been deprived of the crazy mother he hadn't chosen and of the one he *had* chosen, so restoring one of them could do no harm! And I was sure, because I knew her so well, that Greta-la-Vieille wanted nothing so much as to hold him in her arms after their long separation. They were themselves sentimental clichés—everything people say about prostitutes with a heart of gold is true—in the end it was the cliché that got the better of my friends. First, of the Duchess, who I suppose was already picturing a kind of Épinal image, a *tableau vivant*, a fresco for the ages, entitled quite simply *The Return of the Prodigal Child Surrounded by His Muses and His Favourite Midget*. She must be seeing herself in the foreground, at the exact centre of the picture, a venerable and dignified duenna, barely hidden by a black lace mantilla and very obviously the person behind this charming encounter. A major work to be hung in the pantheon of the Main.

And so she took on the task of persuading the other three, succeeding after several rather stormy sessions during which words about me that were worse than nasty were exchanged. But I thought to myself that the guaranteed success of my plan would show that I was right, redeem me in their eyes. I was waiting very impatiently for the moment when I would finally reunite—for good—Greta-la-Vieille and Gilbert Forget.

We agreed to have Greta and Gilbert come to the apartment on Place Jacques-Cartier for a friendly supper one night when I wasn't working at the Sélect. But there was a major problem: what to do with Greta-la-Jeune, heir apparent, devoted apostle and inseparable companion of the other, whom we didn't want to involve in our plan because she was liable to screw it up out of sheer jealousy or fear of losing her predominant place in the heart of Greta-la-Vieille? After some lengthy discussions we decided that Greta-la-Jeune was unavoidable; we couldn't send her away without making Greta-la-Vieille suspicious, we had to accept her being there. The Duchess had even offered to get her drunk as soon as she arrived so she wouldn't realize what was going on. Greta-la-Jeune liked martinis a little too much and the Duchess could whip up doubles and triples that would do the trick—as I'd found out more than once to my cost.

It was even more complicated to persuade Gilbert to come to the house for supper with my friends. He claimed he'd already told me what he thinks about drag queens, I told him he was wrong, that he was full of prejudices, of misplaced resentment, and that if he loved me—I felt like a liar, a manipulative hypocrite, but I told myself it was for his own good—he owed it to himself to give them a chance; they were dear friends of mine, individuals close to my heart, he couldn't pretend for as long as our relationship lasted that they didn't exist. He finally gave in, but he gave me a funny look. Did he sense something, did he suspect some hidden meaning behind my words that he didn't understand and mistrusted? Whatever the answer, I felt a pang of remorse and anguish when I invited him to the house on the fateful day.

The great night arrived then, my chicken with olives and lemon had been simmering in its juice for hours—my grandmother Poulin's secret: a 200-degree oven all afternoon—the air in the apartment was filled with rosemary and the scents of the south of France and five nervous people were waiting for the arrival of three guests who didn't know that they were going to meet.

We had invited them at half-hour intervals. First, the two Gretas, so there'd be time to get the younger one drunk, then— Surprise! Surprise!—Gilbert himself, innocent victim of his girlfriend's machinations.

The night before, we'd made love as we never had before. Did I want to be forgiven in advance if my plan didn't work? Whatever it was, this time I was more expert, more excited, and Gilbert didn't resist, he let himself go and his pleasure was mixed with amazement. I was a veritable tornado, all at once my caresses, involved and professional, turned out to be so skillful, so complicated that they were new to me, I was everywhere at once, I moved with no transition from succubus to incubus, I nourished myself with the squeals like a piglet's and the gasping of the man-object Gilbert had become in my hands, and thanks to him I'd been acquiring experience and it was all to my teacher's advantage. Our lovemaking, repeated several times, was rewarded by our feasting on a huge bowl of cereal, puffy with humidity because the box hadn't been closed properly, followed by a session of tickling that took us both to the verge of hysteria.

Greta-la-Jeune made things easier for us by turning up already tipsy. Her drinking problems were already making tongues wag when the Boudoir closed and her inevitable return to the street in recent months had been a disaster. I saw her every now and then, she came to the restaurant for an order of fries or a fish and chips when she was able to escape the vigilance of Greta-la-Vieille, who kept a nearly maniacal eye on both their weights and every time, her obvious, gradual, unavoidable decline broke my heart.

(The two younger "girls" of Fine Dumas had been the most affected when her establishment closed the year before: Greta-la-Jeune who, despite the care and the angelic patience of Greta-la-Vieille, was sinking into alcohol and junk food to numb her despair, and Babalu, already depressive and fragile, who was foundering without resistance into a kind of permanent, debilitating neurasthenia. She paced her strip of sidewalk, nose to the ground, hands in her pockets, absent from everything and barely present to her clients. Threats by Maurice's henchmen, though numerous and explicit, had no effect: of our own Brigitte Bardot, with her freshness, her mischievous little face and her astounding naïveté, all that was left was the pitiful little scarf knotted under her chin which hadn't fooled anyone for ages, and she was becoming the laughing stock of the Main. But Babalu still brought in enough money so that everyone left her alone and Maurice's emissaries were content to laugh in her face when they went to collect their due.

Greta-la-Jeune was getting fat before our eyes, steeped in alcohol, pickled, though it didn't interfere with her work because certain wealthy clients were keen about her ample pink flesh, while Babalu melted like an anorexic teenager and neither one, we feared, could be rehabilitated.)

I don't think I need to add that Greta-la-Vieille was not in a very good mood when they arrived ... She kept glaring at her companion. In any other circumstances, those looks would have nailed Greta-la-Jeune on the spot, but this time they just seemed to amuse her because she mocked them openly. I felt that our plan for her would be easy, we just had to give her a little more to drink, she probably wouldn't even realize what was going on; it wouldn't work with Greta-la-Vieille though, she was bristling and preoccupied by the appalling condition of her friend, who might refuse to fall into the trap I was setting. And would hate me for it till the end of my days, I was positive, and I began to curse myself for being too lenient.

My four partners in crime already saw the situation as desperate, I could sense it, and I was the only one in the big parlour with its garish colours who showed a little sparkle and a bit of *joie de vivre*, even if it was fake. Shattered, my three roommates were standing like fence-posts, drinks glued to their hands and, for once, silent. While the Duchess kept looking at the front door until even Greta-la-Vieille exclaimed, between two offensive remarks intended for the other Greta, "What's up, Duchess, looking for a prospect? You can't take your eyes off the door! Are we here for your engagement announcement? Did your Mexican Peter come here to join you?"

Greta-la-Jeune raised her glass and bleated idiotically, "I'll drink to that!"

Exasperated, Greta-la-Vieille said, shrugging, "You don't have to tell us! You'd drink to anything!"

And poor Greta-la-Jeune had to fan the flames by coming back immediately with, "Sure, especially to your funeral!"

It took all our diplomatic skills—which we weren't renowned for—and the Duchess's comic expertise to restore some life, if not peace, to the room. Greta-la-Vieille, draped in her wounded pride, wanted to leave right away before the other Greta did something irreparably stupid, Greta-la-Jeune collapsed heavily onto the forties-era sofa and kept threatening to vomit in the lap of her protectress, while my three roommates were content to shift the bowls of chips and other nibblies on the big coffee table while looking daggers at me. As for me, I was starting to pray that Gilbert wouldn't show up. Our attempts at reconciliation were going unheeded, our attempts at conversation were dead ends, when the Duchess, suddenly inspired, had the brilliant idea of putting on Mae East's old turntable Greta-la-Jeune's favourite piece of music, Glenn Miller's "In the Mood," and launched into her own personal version of the jitterbug which was so silly that it always made us laugh. But I think it was not so much her clowning that restored the good mood to the room as the grotesqueness of the situation: regardless of what you have to say about them, drag queens have a sense of the ridiculous as sharp as a knife, and seeing the big whale of a Duchess flinging herself around like a lunatic on the fake and threadbare Persian carpet to save a young evening that was beyond a shadow of a doubt doomed to failure was enough to tickle their sense of humour. Towards the middle of the piece, everyone but Greta-la-Jeune, who was still slouched on the rough, worn velour of the sofa, was dancing, arms flailing and voices blaring. There was something desperate and hysterical about this forced dance being performed by six individuals who quite obviously had no desire to, but felt obliged to, follow her as they tried to redeem a situation that was already lost.

And it was just as the Duchess was threatening to move the needle back to the beginning of the piece that the doorbell rang.

Five persons stood motionless in the parlour, turned to stone, while a sixth, under the reproachful gaze of the seventh and last, began to shout while brandishing a bottle of Beefeater, "Duchess! Duchess! Your prospect!"

I wanted to be anywhere else, at the other end of the world, on another planet, in a different, forever inaccessible solar system. Or at the Sélect, serving hamburger platters to faceless nobodies.

But Greta-la-Vieille, while ignoring him, saved the day by grabbing Greta-la-Jeune bodily and saying to her, "Whoever it is, he mustn't see you like this, you're a disgrace! Come on, we'll go to the bathroom and try to make you look human ... As human as possible ... "

I went to answer the door.

Gilbert was greeted by silence as heavy as a wet winter overcoat. You'd have said that someone had cut the sound so as to study just the body language of the people in the parlour. Jean-le-Décollé, Mae East and Nicole Odeon, with a coldness that was strange in them, merely nodded when he came in, while the Duchess, who only knew him by reputation, inspected him like some vulgar piece of goods, from head to toe, from toe to head, stopping, but barely, on the parts that seemed to interest her, appearing more stunned than seduced. I could have killed them! They could have pushed themselves a little, helped me out, at least put an end to the stupid silence that had us all in knots! I knew that they didn't hold him in high esteem, but all the same a little decorum wouldn't have hurt anybody! I heard myself asking, hesitantly, if anyone wanted a drink. Someone, probably Gilbert, asked for a beer. The others turned down my offer, pointing to the drinks they'd just refreshed before they launched into the mad dance prompted by the Glenn Miller music.

Gilbert seem to be having one of his good days. No sign of nervousness on his face, no sign of depression either. There was always that, but with him you never knew ... All day long I'd tried to convince myself that he would react well to the surprise I'd arranged, but now that he was there, even in good shape, and no one seemed willing to help me, I wasn't sure of anything and I felt like cancelling, like getting rid of Gilbert before Greta-la-Vieille left the bathroom, and hiding under my warmest blankets, intending to stay there till autumn.

While I was serving his drink—before the guests arrived I'd put a few beers in a champagne bucket because I knew it was practically the only thing Gilbert drank—we heard noise from the back of the apartment—slamming doors, loud, furious voices, a broken glass— and I thought I made out a few words: disgrace, goddamn drunk, never again ... My three roommates gawked and didn't try to cover the racket. The Duchess actually seemed to be enjoying it. Gilbert asked me if there were any other guests when I'd assured him there would only be six of us. The Duchess of course couldn't stop herself from saying, "Yes, your surprise!"

Gilbert half-rose, frowning.

"Surprise? What surprise?"

The disappointed look he gave me then was already tinged with blame.

"Do I smell a trap, Céline?"

I stayed silent, with my glass raised and a guilty smile on my lips.

"Tell me right now, Céline, or I'm getting the hell out … "

I didn't need to answer, Greta-la-Vieille was emerging from the kitchen, wiping her hands on a tea towel.

"If she isn't asleep in ten minutes I'll knock her out myself."

Silence is a rare commodity among drag queens and when Greta-la-Vieille realized that no mischievous retort or ironic remark was coming in response to what she'd just said, she felt right away that something was wrong and she leaned against the old record-player, bringing her hand to her heart.

"For God's sake, girls, did Marlon Brando die while I was in the loo?"

No one laughed. Or seemed to have heard her. It was as if the parlour had been poured into a plastic mold the way animals are at the new taxidermists who don't bother empting their victims before mounting them on a metal stand, but plunge them into blocks of transparent acrylic, carefully cut and perfectly symmetrical, that you can exhibit anywhere in the house, claiming they're works of art and not ordinary animals stuffed in a more up-to-date way. One of these days, who knows, some filthy rich lunatic might buy our fossilized parlour—with the title *Five Drag Queens and a Midget Cruise a Beatnik*, a relic of the decadence that characterized the second half of the twentieth century.

The stillness that had settled into the parlour on the arrival of Greta-la-Vieille was all the more surprising because usually it was buzzing with pointless activity since its inhabitants were as wary of peace and quiet as of the bubonic plague.

So the only movement in the paralyzed room came when Gilbert turned to see who'd just come in. Had he recognized her voice? Then, during the quarter of a second that it took for him to turn his head, the world as I'd known it collapsed. The floor opened up beneath my feet, a gaping hole that revealed the bowels of the Earth, and the seething of Hell was hollowed out where a moment earlier a fake Persian carpet had been, the parlour and everything in it slid into it unbearably slowly and I thought to myself that if that was where my life was leading me, to this resounding flop—I no longer had any doubt about it—then it was my own fault because I'd been the sole instigator and it really wasn't worth bothering to live.

They didn't even take a thousandth of a second to recognize one another.

And the shock was terrible.

You see it in the movies sometimes, people reunited suddenly, by chance, and depending on whether it's a comedy or a tragedy, you laugh or cry because you've been manipulated by the filmmaker, the actors, the background music that does its share as well; but in real life, at home on the Place Jacques-Cartier, in your own parlour, in the company of friends who aren't acting and with no background music to guide your reaction, you stand there, stupefied, you feel superfluous, a voyeur, guilty, you want to disappear into oblivion and never come back, especially if you're behind this event and no one knows where it will lead—to horrible tragedy or boundless joy. And it all takes place on the smoking ruins of the world as you've known it.

I say that the shock was terrible, but I guessed that more than I saw it.

Because they didn't move. They both turned white and wide-eyed, incalculably powerful energy exploded between them, lighting up the parlour and its occupants like a camera flash, but they didn't move.

And if I hadn't stepped in I think they'd still be there, dumbfounded, speechless, until someone came to take them home. After a fairly long moment, and seeing that nothing was going to happen unless I did something, I found the courage to put my hands on his shoulders. He didn't make a move to free himself, he didn't push my hands away, and I thought to myself that maybe all was not lost after all.

I turned towards the other four witnesses, still glued to their seats, and gestured to them to leave us alone. I was afraid that the Duchess, with her absolute lack of subtlety, would make some stupid crack, pointless and uncalled-for, but for once she seemed to understand the gravity of the situation and she merely exited the parlour like a great actress after a successful scene.

Alone with me now, Greta-la-Vieille and Gilbert did not make a single move towards one another, did not exchange a word. They only looked at one another for long minutes, transfixed, mesmerized, and they cried. In silence. Scalding tears ran down their faces, sobs shook their bodies, they were bent double when pain, or happiness, or both, was too powerful, they blew their noses noisily and cleared their throats to stifle the cries that wanted to get out. They couldn't take their eyes off one another but they couldn't speak either. They drank each other in with their eyes but couldn't express in words what they were feeling.

Greta-la-Vieille had stayed leaning against the old record-player and gesturing broadly. She could have been a French singer from the 1930s, about to open her repertoire of songs about sailors' girls, about shop girls abandoned by the man who'd seduced them, who have been rendered mute by emotion. As for Gilbert, he was bent over as if he wanted to leap out of his armchair and run into his adoptive mother's arms, but something, modesty, shame, shyness, kept him from doing so and he sat there, overcome by a sluggishness against which he was helpless, that immobilized him. And like her, he was crying. In silence. They looked at one another and all they could do was cry. As if they'd felt a need to drain themselves of excess emotion before starting again from square one. Or leave one another forever without exchanging a single word.

As for me, I hoped I'd be forgotten. But I suspected that they weren't even aware of my presence anyway, that I did not exist, that nothing mattered to them but the other person's appearance in their life after a separation of so many years. But why didn't they get up, why didn't they embrace, even if it meant hurling insults or blows afterwards if they felt the need, why this immobility when it seemed to me there should have been wild cries, hysterical music, riotous and uninhibited dancing, the Duchess's impersonations or the snappy retorts of Jean-le-Décollé to celebrate it? To celebrate what exactly? It couldn't be called a reunion, reunions weren't those endless sobs, those gulps of pain, those silent looks; reunions were shouts of joy, slapping thighs, impossible promises—and they were celebrations! Would they be content with a long, silent scene before they turned their backs again once and for all? Without a reconciliation? Without even a curse? Had I brought them together so that nothing would happen? Deep down, I knew very well that millions of things were happening, were being expressed, shouted, at the heart of this silence—confessions, declarations of which I'd been merely the project manager without the right to test them and that until the very end my job would be to play the thankless role of silent witness and accomplice.

Then, from two exchanges I heard, brief but filled with meaning, I realized when the silly shyness finally dropped away and the flood of words gushed out, that the atmosphere would lend itself more to murmured confidences, to confessions exchanged *sotto voce*, than to outpourings and bursts of laughter. I had been naïve enough to organize a party when a simple, informal meeting would have done, idiot that I was, and I found that I was in the way, unwanted in my own overly complicated scenario.

After blowing their noses and dabbing at their eyes, from all appearances exhausted by the inarticulate violence of what had just gone on between them, Gilbert looked at Greta-la-Vieille and told her in a husky voice I'd never heard before, "All those years, I was spying on you … "

With the faintest and the saddest smile I'd ever seen, she answered him, "I knew."

And during the long, intertwining account they both gave of the past fifteen years, I imagined the evening's other four guests relegated to the kitchen, useless and knowing it, ears pricked for any bits of conversation, cursing because they'd left their drinks in the parlour and were condemned for the rest of the evening to tea, Seven-Up and Pepsi.

Third Insert

*Final Episode in the Story of Gilbert,
the Circular Madman: The Spy*

After an adolescence of no interest—teenage acne like every boy his age, ill at ease wherever he went, practically an outsider in his slender body with limbs that were too long and growing too fast, pathologically shy around girls—Gilbert came into his own at eighteen when, without warning, he turned into a magnificent young man who without being forward—that would come later, with experience—had all at once progressed from the belated child he'd been for so long and become an independent and fairly resourceful being.

He had abandoned his studies after high school, intending, or so he claimed, to give back to his grandmother a little of what she'd done for him since the death of Madame Veuve, but actually because he was bored to death at school where he didn't learn a thing because he didn't listen. He worked here and there, accepted jobettes that he thought were unworthy of him but that allowed him to put a little bread on the table plus some butter on the bread. He learned the fundamentals of seduction in the arms of married women to whom he delivered groceries and the rudiments of theft in his bosses' cash registers. Little by little he turned into a likeable bum of whom you weren't really suspicious: you knew that deep down he wasn't dangerous, you closed your eyes to his escapades because he was handsome. Or funny. He learned how to be funny when he realized that it could pay.

When his grandmother tried to talk about his future, which was, to say the least, tenuous given how little importance he attached to it, he would answer with a joke or change the subject. At times he would even tell her, with a big sardonic grin, that he was going to devote his future to being carefree and idle. She would give him a slap upside the head as she used to do when he was little and threaten to send him to his room. He would grab her around the waist, difficult because of her corpulence, sweep her into a minute waltz danced around the dining room, and all was forgotten to the accompaniment of laughter and hugs. She wasn't fooled, but acted as if she was because she loved him.

The point is, Gilbert was afraid of the future. For the simple reason that as he came into his twenties, nothing interested him enough to give him an urge to devote his whole existence to it. Passions, all unattainable because they would have taken years of study that he couldn't afford and a kind of intelligence that he did not possess, would fascinate him for a while—nuclear medicine, astronomy, microbiology—impossible dreams, very likely chosen because they were inaccessible—but soon enough he resumed his slide into laziness which was not a character trait but a shelter against his helplessness and his indecision in the face of life.

When the first real episodes of his illness occurred—he'd always had a penchant for gloominess and melancholy which he attributed to his overly idle life and wasn't too concerned—he was terrified and tried to hide them from his grandmother because he didn't want her to worry. But they recurred more and more often, sometimes with such violence, especially during the downs, that afterwards he had no memory of what had happened, or just a vague one. He would wake up as if from a bad dream, glimpse a few images, fleeting and disagreeable, and ask himself what he'd done, where he'd gone and in particular, how it had ended. Drinking helped a little, soft drugs sometimes a lot—a joint shared with passing friends, for instance, could ease his plunges into depression and his climbs towards summits that were too lofty—but did not prevent actual crises from fermenting inside him and waiting to explode like fountains of poison or dreams of grandeur, and when they did occur, unavoidable, and more powerful than ever, he wanted to die.

That was when the messed-up childhood he'd lived around the Main in the company of his insane mother and, more important, the enveloping and reassuring presence of Greta, his adoptive, loving mother, would come back to him, along with his nostalgia for another time, though he'd chosen to forget it and bury it deep in the folds of his memory, would worm its way into him and he would take off on a sudden impulse, to divert the course of his ever-darker thoughts, in search of his past. A search for a consolation he could take from it for the illness that was making a nightmare of his life and that he didn't understand at all. During all that time, in the beginning at least, Greta was thinking about him too. Every day. She knew, someone had told her, that he refused to see her again, that he had seen her sin of omission—though it was very naïve, after all she'd only wanted him to consider her as his second mother, not as a man dressed like a woman—as an unforgiveable betrayal, and anyone she asked about him, especially after the death of Madame Veuve, would tell her that he was growing into a troublemaker tied to his grandmother's apron strings and that probably, like all children who are spoiled rotten, he would do nothing good with his life. When she found out that he'd left school she had been sad, but when the Duchess told her that he was going to take care of his grandmother, to spoil a little during her old age the woman who had sacrificed herself for so long, she'd run all over the Main to tell anyone who would listen that she'd been right, and make no mistake: Gilbert was a good person. If people laughed at her a little, it was with a certain affection because they knew how much she loved Gilbert, the child who had not been born to her, whom she'd partly brought up in conditions that were, to say the least, distinctive, and who had left, cursing her.

Greta used her need to play unappeased mother to look for a second Gilbert. Not to replace him, she knew that no one could do that, but to while away her idle time and to pour her overflowing affection onto someone other than her passing clients. (Jean-le-Décollé, who had trained a good number of the Main's drag queens, often said that the day when hookers started to have feelings for their clients, it would mean that something was wrong … ). Children dragged around the streets of the red-light district by an insane mother who used them as hostages while she begged for her daily bread were rather rare however, and Greta's attempts to find a semblance of a successor to the son of Madame Veuve, for whom she had been at first merely the chaperone before she grew too attached to him, were in vain.

Until the day when one Michel Nadeau turned up on St. Catherine Street, having landed the day before from some remote little village which turned out to be Greta's birthplace as well, a beautiful youth quite obviously terrified by what he'd seen in the Metropolis, which proved to be very different from what he'd imagined. He needed someone to protect him, helpless as the naïve youth was before the traps that would soon be set for him by Maurice's men if he didn't watch out.

He'd already been trained, he even wore dresses and wigs with a certain style, but he was a little green and Greta's pride had been flattered when he admired her right away. And a further quality, he'd soon begun to copy her. She hadn't stopped him, just as a person lets an overly adoring puppy follow him around to keep him from whining.

And that was how the second Greta was born, by mimicry, by osmosis: the young Marilyn Monroe—*Niagara* or *All About Eve*—when the more mature Greta no longer had any hope of resembling the American idol at the end of her career—*The Misfits* or *Some Like It Hot*—Shirley Temple when her elder dressed up for a Halloween party as Bette Davis in *Whatever Happened to Baby Jane?* which amounted to pretty well the same thing and always got laughs because the two had made twin costumes and worked out an amusing choreography. Shirley-la-Vieille, Shirley-la-Jeune. They'd become inseparable, ate together at Ben Ash or the Sélect, often did johns *à deux*, shared an apartment on Sanguinet which was the envy of the other drag queens because it was tastefully decorated and always smelled good.

Their names had come on their own, as if self-evident, and the two had accepted them without protesting. Greta was now called "la vieille" and Michel became her young twin. For a long time, there were whispers that they were a couple, but it wasn't true; they were more attracted to hairy longshoremen and muscular truck drivers than to someone who resembled them.

And so Gilbert had gradually been erased from the memory of Greta-la-Vieille and as the years passed, became a pleasant but vague memory, a passing weakness, like a great, youthful love that is finally healed and stops causing you pain. She still thought about him often, every day sometimes, but the boy's face had gradually been erased and, in any case, she thought to herself, he must have changed after all this time, she probably wouldn't recognize him if he ever showed up on the Main: he was an adult now, and the child who'd been so dear to her had disappeared long ago. And from what was said about him, she doubted that the adult he'd become was worthy of the bright, open, resourceful child she had brought up for someone else and perhaps loved too much.

She was wrong.

Gilbert had found Greta-la-Vieille again in a few minutes and recognized her immediately. It was so easy. He had forgotten how much the Main, which he'd been avoiding for years, was never far away, located as it was at the very heart of the city; it was a dull knife that cut Montreal in two, a wound that never healed, and he learned when he ventured there again that it was unchanging too. He discovered that it was identical to itself, just as he had left it years before: the same hookers, plus some new ones of course, the stock had to be refreshed now and then, even drag queens, with a few additions here and there, like Greta-la-Jeune and Babalu, the same pretentious pimps, the same clients hugging the walls. The nightclubs hadn't changed and still advertised their eternal novelty acts and their strippers with evocative names—Bosoms or Mama Mia or Lady Lollipop. The places still smelled of stale alcohol, especially beer, steamed hotdogs and fried potatoes—basic foodstuffs of society's rejects who hung out there. He thought he recognized some corrupt policemen who had plied the streets when he was a child, in the fifties; others, honest ones, who had aged faster because they had to watch out for what was going on behind them if they didn't want to end up stuffed in a garbage can with a bullet in their foreheads or a knife between their shoulderblades. A gift from Maurice-la-Piasse. Or from their less scrupulous colleagues.

And when Greta showed up at her post, always the same stretch of sidewalk across from the Coconut Inn, accompanied by a kind of fake twin who followed her like a pitiful shadow, the shock was so violent that he thought he would never recover. If the Main was unchangeable, the same was alas not true of its creatures. Greta had not only aged, she'd come undone, she seemed to have shrunk, to have been tamped down, though in the past she'd been so regal, nearly haughty with her clients and always peremptory when expressing her opinions. She had traded her role of healthy, happy little doll, friendly and motherly, for that of an old woman with loose morals who no longer has any illusions and has long since given up on the mere thought of wanting to please. To Gilbert's great surprise, however, she still had a lot of clients—he thought he recognized some faces, old now too, from the time when he thought the girls were waiting for the bus—and every week, had to turn over a small fortune to Maurice, who was more arrogant and more prosperous than ever when he deigned to grace the sidewalks of the Main with his presence, strolling down St. Lawrence Boulevard with his henchmen.

With time, Gilbert had no doubt simultaneously idealized Greta and darkened her reputation, recalling, as selective memory requires, only her maternal side, her kindness, exaggerating her beauty, her goodness, the better to be affected by the hole created by her inexplicable betrayal, and the better to hate her. The pathetic, shattered creature he'd discovered had nothing to do with the Greta he had known and he'd nearly left the Main for the second time, never to return. But a gesture of hers, a way of lifting a lock of hair that had fallen over her eye, a sad smile directed at her young twin who was trying to make her laugh and who resembled her more than she resembled herself, the way she brought her hand to her heart too, as if she'd just seen a ghost, reawakened for a brief moment the woman he had loved so dearly and he wanted to cross the street and embrace her. But he couldn't. He saw that this broken woman could now offer him no consolation and he decided to stay hidden and watch her live just as he'd done when he was a child.

He started to spy on her, without really knowing why. He would turn up several times a week in front of the Coconut Inn, conceal himself in the doorway of a drygoods store that closed at six o'clock, smoke a joint to ward off loneliness, drink a beer or two, and watch her live her life. People had got used to his being there, the two Gretas waved to him now and then, he assumed that they thought he was some gentle hobo who'd taken up residence at the heart of the Main. Which was nearly true. To kill time he bought a guitar and gradually began to play on his own a few chords that he'd learned during his beatnik period, at El Cortijo on Clark Street in the late 1950s along with Tex Lecor, the house star, or a passing singer-songwriter like the famous *chansonnier* François Villeneuve. When he sensed a crisis coming on he would go away for a few days, stay inside at his grandmother's and suffer his hell before going back to watch his former adoptive mother cruise for johns.

The years passed, made up of days that were all the same. He continued to earn a living for himself and his grandmother, as delivery boy or messenger, packing books in a print shop, one winter he even became a short-order cook in a small restaurant on Rachel Street. And when evening came, he watched his adoptive mother earning hers. He loved her but never approached her, and at the height of the evening he played serenades for her that she probably didn't hear. At times, when he'd drunk too much or his joint was of superior quality, he would stand in his doorway and watch her walk her stretch of sidewalk. He imagined her when she was younger, imagined himself when he was younger, and he dreamed that no time had passed, that she was going to bring him back to his mother at the Coconut Inn, after taking him to Ben Ash for a smoked meat sandwich. He recalled her odour, that of a woman who's been working hard, her relieved laugh after so many clients, each one more nondescript than the others, and his cheeks were often wet with tears. Never though did he have the courage to cross St. Lawrence Boulevard, not even simply to say hello without revealing who he was. Or, rather, who he had been.

Only once was he close to her. When he got to his post in front of the drygoods store one night, thinking she was with a client, he'd gone into the Montreal Pool Room, next door to the Monument-National, for a hamburger. There was just one seat empty at the counter, next to Greta who was absentmindedly tucking into a grilled cheese sandwich and a Coke. Without the other Greta, who was probably getting it on with a client for real. Gilbert had hesitated, then decided to take the small, round stool next to Greta's, hunching his back and lowering his head. His heart was pounding, he wanted to throw his arms around her and kiss her, after all that was why he'd come back to the Main, wasn't it? But he'd just muttered his order and waited in silence, cursing himself, hands crossed on the Arborite, head turned towards the front window through which scrolls of grease seemed to be trying to escape. When his burger arrived, he realized that Greta was looking at him very seriously in the mirror that covered the wall opposite the counter, as if wondering where she'd seen him before. He had gripped the handle of his guitar which was beside him and right away she had understood, so he thought anyway, that this was who'd been serenading her and that she was seeing him up close for the first time. She smiled at him, a timid little smile that seemed to be looking for something, he smiled back. Greta's face had frozen briefly, as if she'd just seen a ghost and he thought he even saw a tear form in her left eye. But it hadn't lasted. She had shaken her shoulders, paid her bill, told the waiter so long and nodded at Gilbert as she left.

During the eighteen months that Fine Dumas's establishment had lasted, not once had Gilbert dared to go inside the Boudoir, which was too expensive for him. At first he did the same thing he'd done for the stretch of sidewalk: positioned himself across from the bar, holding his guitar and craned his neck whenever the door opened, trying to see if a costume he glimpsed might belong to Greta. He knew he was being silly, childish even, but he went back night after night. Like all the denizens of the Main, he couldn't afford to pay the prohibitive price demanded to watch Greta and the other drag queens murder the French and American repertoires, but eventually, reassured about the fate of his adoptive mother who now at least was sheltered from bad weather, and convinced that any contact with her was impossible, he gradually fled the Main where finally he'd found no consolation, on the contrary, to devote a large part of his time to his new friends from Expo 67—musicians who seemed to think he wasn't a bad guitar player and who dreamed of producing a show that would be revolutionary in the history of Quebec songs. And that was how he abandoned Greta for the second time, thinking that a second time was final.

What he didn't know, however, was that she had recognized him too. Right away. The first time he'd appeared on St. Lawrence Boulevard after such a long absence. And that she was waiting for him to decide to approach her. She couldn't have said how or why—his gait, maybe, his curly hair, his face which was longer but not so different as to be unrecognizable, his eyes, so beautiful, that looked at her in the same way they had in the past, his unique smile—but she'd known right away that it was him, and if she hadn't run across the street to throw herself in his arms, it was because in her opinion it was up to him to make the first move. He was the one who had taken off, showing no gratitude, who'd refused to see her again, and now he was coming back after so much time had passed, no doubt to ask for forgiveness. She would grant it, and willingly—when he left, it had nearly killed her and she'd thought about him every day since—but he had to make the first move. It was a matter of pride. And her pride was greater than anything.

The night when Gilbert had sat beside her at the Montreal Pool Room, Greta-la-Vieille had thought that the long-awaited moment had finally come, that the reconciliation was going to happen, that forgiveness would be possible. The ceremony would take place there, with the smell of burnt cooking fat, at a stained and sticky counter. She'd imagined herself kissing him on the forehead, playing with his luxuriant hair, indescribably happy to be with him again and to offer him forever love, compassion, warmth. But she'd quickly realized that only a coincidence had brought them together and she'd had to be content to watch him devour his hamburger without interceding. It would have taken just one small move by Gilbert, an outstretched hand, a word, and all would have been forgotten. Instead, nothing had happened and everything had gone on as before.

A silent debate had been going on between them, a cruel game consisting of pride but also of shame, uneasiness, hesitation and a misplaced sense of propriety. That had gone on for years. When Greta went for too long without seeing Gilbert, she imagined the worst and was positive that she'd never see him again, that he had abandoned her yet again, and she was sorry she'd resisted him. When he serenaded her—she knew that it was for her that he played the guitar—her heart melted and the evenings spent pacing the sidewalk seemed not so long. For his part, when Gilbert saw Greta leave with a john who looked sinister or too devious for his liking, he worried about her, every time, and he sighed with relief when she came back, intact yet a little more soiled. He dreamed of saving her of course, of freeing her from the claws of the Main, as the Errol Flynn of the seedy part of town or the John Wayne of the poor, he saw her moving in with his grandmother—even bringing Greta-la-Jeune if necessary—he saw them all living together, himself as a great musician who'd made a fortune from his compositions ... But then he would wake up in the doorway of the drygoods store, his hands too cold to play in winter, slippery with sweat in summer, a poor helpless circular madman who never knew when the next episode would strike. When he felt one coming on he would take off like a thief, go into hiding, wait for it to pass and then resume his position, a pathetic soldier of deception and failure.

So they spied on one another surreptitiously, each too bound up in his own pride to feel the need, though it was so powerful, so urgent, for the other: consolation for one, forgiveness for the other.

And when they were together again for real in the home of the midget who'd decided to reunite and reconcile them, each dropped his guard, the barriers of pride collapsed, until what was left was two broken individuals, face to face, who had sewn their own unhappiness and wasted precious time for hollow reasons.

It was not too late for confidences, which came, but it was too late for a genuine reconciliation. Which didn't happen.

No promises were made, no appointments either, while they exchanged stories in my presence, she still standing next to the old record-player, he slumped in an armchair, both looking exhausted. They went on and on, each describing to the other the years that had passed, the miseries, the pain, but I was not convinced that they were listening to what the other had to say; it was as if they weren't ready to listen to each other, only to confide. Or to justify themselves.

The quest on which they had both set out with passion so long before had perhaps not been intended to reach a conclusion after all. I understood that too late: inaccessible, it remained perfect, complete, they could idealize it, make it the centre of their life, its ultimate goal, they could dream about it while persuading themselves that they would accomplish it one day; if that were true though it would lose its mythical aspect and hence its importance, it would become almost anecdotal, an ordinary story experienced by ordinary people, and they must have been sorry not to have had time to prepare themselves after a fifteen-year wait. Because they themselves had chosen neither the occasion nor the moment for it, because I had deprived them of the excitement found in large-scale preparations, the stage fright at imagining they wouldn't be ready in time, that they would miss their chance, that everything would have to be done again. Separate, they were still heroes in their own eyes, fantastic individuals who'd been chosen to experience something unique and overwhelming; together, they were of no interest because they would now be called on to mimic friendship, when they knew very well that too much had happened in their lives for them to turn back and become again the adoptive mother and the ordinary child.

Their stories told, they'd stopped looking at each other. Gilbert had his hands on his knees like a good little boy, Greta-la-Vieille had started rummaging in her purse for a cigarette which she lit, trembling, with a plastic lighter. So that was the accomplishment of a quest that had gone on for years? Silence that reclaimed its rights? And that was all?

This time I should have intervened, I sensed it, but my guilt at thinking I had done the wrong thing in bringing them together left me at a loss. I'd been too well-intentioned, all I'd managed to do was to throw two unhappy people into a new problem for which they weren't prepared, for which they may not even have been meant. On my own I had pushed two heroes off their pedestals and I would never forgive myself. I wouldn't even have been surprised if Gilbert had got out of his chair to tell me that he wanted nothing more to do with me.

Greta-la-Vieille was the first to break the silence.

She said, without looking at us, as if she were speaking to herself, "I'll go and wake up Greta."

She left the parlour. There was something final about that departure, as if the empty space she left behind her next to the record-player was now impossible to fill, as if no one would ever be able to fill it with any presence. When someone walked past the spot where she had stood that night, they would disappear briefly, swallowed up by an abyss that her departure had created. A vacuum. A maelstrom. A black hole.

I imagined her trying to persuade Greta-la-Jeune to get up, then wait, smoking, for the apartment to empty before she came out of my room along with a person who would never replace Gilbert.

He, meanwhile, seemed not furious, only demoralized. I would have preferred insults, reproaches, to this eloquent silence. But nothing came. After a long moment he finally extricated himself from his daze. Leaning on the armrests of his chair, he struggled to his feet. An old man. He who was so handsome, so haughty when he wanted to be was now unrecognizable. With his drawn face, his bent back, he gave the impression of someone who had gone beyond exhaustion and now wanted to die all alone because the rest of his existence was not worth living.

I thought he was going to leave me without saying a word. That he was going to choose to lose me too. And I considered that I'd brought it on myself. I wasn't angry with him, I would cry for him the way he'd cried for Greta. Gilbert, his magnificent body, his odour which drove me crazy, his soul to which I had just barely started to open up, I would mourn, pathetically, deservedly. And I would keep an astonished memory of the man who had made me discover love.

He crossed the parlour as if he had forgotten where he was and then, just before leaving the apartment, he turned in my direction.

"Don't get mixed up in those things again, Céline. Ever. Don't talk about them either. You've caused enough damage as it is."

When I turned around to take a seat on the sofa, my three roommates and the Duchess were all crammed into the parlour doorway.

# Part Four

## *... et si je t'aime, prends garde à toi!*

We went on seeing each other despite the obvious rift that my faux pas had created. In fact we only talked about it once, the day after the rough and unsettling incident. At the Sélect, over banana splits, like teenagers with a serious problem to solve.

Gilbert proved to be understanding, he actually thanked me for my good intentions and generosity—all of this while pointing out, with a sensitivity close to that which he showed when we made love, that I'd got mixed up in something that was none of my business and he didn't want it to happen again. I reassured him: I'd learned a lesson, never again would I venture onto the avenues of his life where I did not feel welcome, from now on I would respect his secret gardens, act as if he no longer existed when he disappeared from my field of vision. He thought my images were entertaining and shook his head, saying that he'd finally found someone with a more tragic view of life than his. "There are other reasons why I want to keep you in my life, Céline Poulin, you know what they are, but that one, I confess, is one of the most important. You're a bigger drama queen than I am, but you at least find solutions to your problems."

I pointed out that the one I'd tried to implement the night before was far from the right one and he deigned to smile. A dinky little sad smile.

"Please, Céline, let's not talk abut it again. Ever. And go on wanting to solve your own problems, not other people's."

I didn't dare ask if he intended to see Greta again or if he'd accept another invitation from me; I knew the answer. Consequently, in future I would keep the two parts of my life separate, impervious: on one side, my work, my customers, my apartment, its inhabitants; on the other side, Gilbert and his extreme pleasures.

And his many problems. I didn't want to lose him and I thought that the price to pay for keeping him—secrecy, discretion—was not too high. For now. If things got complicated though, because of his illness or for any other reason, I would reconsider my options, as they say, and I would make the right decision. I didn't want to be alone and I loved Gilbert very much, but I wanted to avoid undue suffering. Be concerned about him, about his health, help him during his bad patches, yes, certainly, but let love turn me into the slave of a sick man, of his episodes, his moods—no way. For a while I would have to negotiate a tightrope, watch where I set my feet, curb my emotions. As usual, for that matter. But differently. This time, with a love as well as my own small person to protect.

I had really put my foot in it when I tried to do a favour, it had nearly cost me an exorbitant amount, now I had to play the card of caution.

When we were together it was still as wonderful, with colourful conversations, endless, passionate nights of love, but I sometimes caught in Gilbert's eyes not doubt, I don't think he doubted my feelings for him, but a kind of hesitation, as if a tiny shred of his confidence in my judgment had taken off on that ill-fated night in May when I'd tried to reunite him and Greta and now he was wondering if once again and despite my promise not to, I was going to get mixed up in something that was none of my business and end up making some blunder that couldn't be undone. I didn't dare reassure him. I behaved more lovingly, something I had no trouble doing, I tried to make him laugh when I felt a wave of depression crash onto him, or bring him down from him his high when his delusions of grandeur overcame him and he thought he was stronger than anything.

It was much easier for me to get around his episodes, to be discreet when necessary, and present if I sensed that he needed me. I was no longer afraid of the excessive states in which his illness plunged him, while he continued to warn me, as he'd done on that second morning when he felt swamped by irresistibly powerful anguish.

The fall was all the more painful then because I hadn't seen it coming. No, I had seen it coming, but I couldn't interpret it quickly enough to avoid it.

It happened in two moments, two incidents around the show that Gilbert was rehearsing at the Théâtre de Quat'Sous.

*That's it. The time has come for her to talk about the escalation that led to her break-up with Gilbert.*

*For the first time since she started writing her blue notebook, she hesitates. So far, everything has gone well, everything has flowed from her pen according to her will, it followed naturally and at an astonishing speed, she placed her characters in real-life situations, she described all the events that led up to those two fateful days, she's sure that she has captured Gilbert's personality and her own impressions in the face of what he represented when he came into her life. Several times she felt the relief that writing has brought her for two years now, the illuminating moment when she grasps the significance of what has happened because she's been able to dissect it, explain it to herself. Or so she thinks. But a discomfort she has never felt before when writing has just seized her by the throat and she sits there, paralyzed, in front of the blank page.*

*She has read a lot on the subject, she's heard writers, real ones, talk about it on the radio or television, more or less seriously, some joking to minimize its importance, others with terror audible in their voices: fear in their bellies, a heart that no longer beats with the same regularity, dry throat and anxiety, so stressful, when facing the blank void of the paper. Writer's block, the worst nightmare. It's not that she doesn't know what to write, she knows, and precisely, so she doesn't lack inspiration, what she feels is anxiety that she won't be sufficiently precise, that she will express badly what she has lived through and how she lived it. And above all, yes, above all, because it would be a grave error, the fear that she won't be able to avoid showing Gilbert as a monster when he isn't, she is still sure of that in spite of everything that happened.*

*She gets up. Goes to the kitchen and pours herself a glass of milk though she never drinks milk. A slice of chocolate cake is drying out on the top shelf, she eats it without appetite, thinking about other things. She gulped the milk too quickly, feels vaguely nauseated as she rinses her glass, her plate, her fork. She thinks she's being ridiculous. She has never been afraid of writing until now; on the contrary, she has found in it the strength and the courage to go on making her own choices instead of letting herself be tossed about by the ups and downs of life. So why right now? Because of the sensitivity of the subject? She has brought up equally difficult ones without asking herself any questions. That may even be the problem: at first she wrote strictly from a need to express herself and nothing else … What then? Is she starting to think of herself as a writer? Perched on the little plastic stool that she'd pushed in front of the sink, she leans across the chipped porcelain. For a brief moment, after laughing at herself for a few seconds, she thinks that she's going to vomit, then all it once it passes—both her bogus nausea and her genuine fear. And her ironic laughter. She couldn't say why or how, but it's all over before she is even aware of it, maybe because she has understood that she mustn't take herself too seriously, that the blue notebook is to serve the same purpose as the two others, that's all. She finds herself, without knowing how she has come back to it, in front of her open manuscript on her work table.*

*Outside, the weather is horrible. She had to close the window a while ago to keep the rain off her writing. The forecast is for a week of violent storms and she thinks to herself it will be perfect for what she has to describe. She'll take every day this week if she has to, but she will go on writing her story to the very end.*

*She picks up her pen, wonders briefly where to start, then throws herself into the heart of her subject by tackling the first of the two disastrous evenings. And forgets that she is writing.*

I knew that it wouldn't be an evening like any other.

It was the supper hour, we were three waitresses on the floor—Madeleine would leave as soon as the evening rush was over—and we could barely seat our clients, who were more unruly and harder to please than usual. Whether it was this mild end of May that was exciting the senses and getting people worked up or the pale green spring that was bursting everywhere, they were as boisterous as children on the eve of a school holiday, so much so that all three of us wondered if they were getting on our nerves deliberately, out of spite.

They all seemed to know one another too: they went from table to table, crowded the aisles, talked from one end of the restaurant to the other, telling dirty jokes, proposing ridiculous toasts, eating their supper cold because they let the food congeal on their plates. Janine had finally asked Lucien, quite seriously, if he'd put some voodoo powder in the shepherd's pie to make them so weird.

"Voodoo comes from Haiti, right?"

For a while now Janine had been surprisingly intolerant of Lucien, looking down on him as if he were there to serve her rather than as Nick's assistant in the kitchen. She claimed, and I knew it was false, that customers complained about certain dishes which they thought were too spicy and she told anyone who would listen that she thought he was slow and lazy; I'd even heard her call him a goddamn nigger between her teeth when his back was turned. Later on, I found out that she'd tried to get her brother the job of assistant cook, but it hadn't worked because everyone adored Lucien, loved the spicy and exotic variations he'd brought to the usual fare of the Sélect, and even more because Nick didn't want a second Janine on his back. She tried to take revenge on Lucien with her usual lack of tact and intelligence. She always distorts what goes on at the Sélect and she's going to lose her job one of these days. She'll end up all alone and she'll probably blame other people.

Lucien, hunched over half a dozen hamburgers sizzling in their grease, hadn't even bothered straightening up to answer her. His voice under the hood from where the heat was trying unsuccessfully to escape, had taken on a new, deep resonance, a darker colour.

"I was born right here in Montreal just like you, Janine, I know as much as you do about voodoo."

She merely shrugged.

"Your father's from Haiti. Voodoo gets passed on."

"Like a disease?"

"Exactly. Like a disease. Voodoo's something you catch! Anyway, give me my hamburger platters, I've got two starving customers. But skip the magic powder."

"Let me tell you something. If I had anything like magic powder it wouldn't go in the customers' food!"

She let out some shrieks, pointing at him.

"Did you hear that? I've got witnesses! Two witnesses—Céline and Nick! He just threatened to poison me! If you ever find me on the floor, stiff as a board and foaming at the mouth, don't look any farther, it'll be him! Him and his voodoo powder!"

Nick had put an end to the row by yelling that dozens of customers were waiting for their goddamn food on the other side of the door, voodoo powder or not, and that was more important than our family squabbles.

"You can deal with your problems when the rush is over. Meanwhile, swallow your gum and get busy!"

When I was back in the restaurant two of the people I least wanted to see had just made their entrance. Janine pointed to them with a nasty laugh, "Take a look, Céline, your *real* prospect just came in!"

The person Janine calls my real prospect, pronouncing the word *real* as if it were in italics, is a midget who comes to the Sélect now and then, a painter who always smells of oil and turpentine, whose name is Carmen—as if Carmen could be a man's name. He's always flanked by his best friend, a big, lazy lunk called François Villeneuve, handsome as a god who's going downhill after a brief but very dazzling career as a singer-songwriter a few years ago and who has never recovered from a fall that was as spectacular as it was fast, caused by the confession in several of his songs that he was homosexual. It's said that his record is a kind of cursed masterpiece that you can't find any more and that those who own a copy, the Duchess for instance, guard it as if it were a priceless viaticum. It is also said at Radio-Canada where he works as a radio producer that he's impossible—arrogant, unfair and worst of all, pretentious.

They're both homosexual and don't hide it. By that I don't mean that they're screaming queens like some customers who come to the Sélect on weekends and act out the frustration that comes from life in the closet with shrill voices and effeminate gestures, but they talk about it openly, pride themselves on it as much as any drag queen, even laugh about it while telling us—telling me at any rate—about their amazing escapades, their sometimes absurd crushes and their misadventures which usually are unbelievable and comical.

I have nothing against midgets, or against homosexuals either, I live with three of them, but a homosexual midget was not exactly what I needed in my life at that moment, especially since Gilbert's arrival. Though I explained it to Janine, she played the idiot, acting as if she didn't understand, shrugging at everything that was beyond her and laughing uproariously, saying that Carmen and I made such a handsome couple, proving yet again that nastiness is always stupid. And if ever, God forbid, I were to have a relationship with Carmen I know very well that she'd find flaws in him too. Janine is like that, she always knows what's best for you, but when you achieve it she'll claim that you've made a mistake—forgetting that often your choices originated with her.

The two newcomers were already well on the way to being drunk, I could see it from a distance by the way they were waddling by the cash register, looking for a place to sit. There's no hostess at the Sélect and everyone sits where they want or, depending on circumstances, where they can. There wasn't even one table free so they had to wait next to Françoise, who has always found François Villeneuve to her liking and turns red as a poppy every time he hands her the bill. This time, he stood next to her longer than usual and even though he paid no attention to her, I thought she was going to faint from excitement.

As soon as he spotted me, Carmen waved and approached me in an offhand way that I didn't like, "Do something, Céline, kick somebody out, we're famished!"

He didn't even seem to be joking. I have to say that his pretentiousness is in inverse proportion to his talent—I've seen some of his paintings that he brought to the restaurant to show me one day and I shuddered with horror, without showing it of course, I'm well-mannered—and that he doesn't take himself for goose shit.

Besides, he smelled of stale booze and I wanted to hold my nose in disgust.

Sure, we're both midgets, but that's about all we have in common. We didn't raise pigs together, I'm not his sister or his girlfriend or his servant, and I don't owe him anything. I don't even particularly like him. So I certainly didn't want to play along. I didn't even feel like being polite as a good waitress should be with a customer, regardless of behaviour, gentleman or boor.

"I can't help it, you'll have to wait your turn. There'll be two or three tables free in ten minutes ... "

"Ten minutes! I've never waited for ten minutes to eat at the Sélect and I'm not starting today!"

"If you're in such a hurry, go and have a pepper steak at Géracimo, it's very good."

"I want to eat here!"

"So wait!"

"You're being really mean tonight! You're usually nicer to your regular customers."

I planted myself in front of him. My eyes were level with his, for once I didn't have to twist my neck to talk to someone.

"That's right, I'm mean. Tired and mean. With regular customers and new ones! I can't snap my fingers and make a booth appear, Carmen, I'm not a magician. They're all occupied, you're smart enough to see that, so don't yell at me, it's pointless!"

All around us, people were enjoying the show, not even trying to hide it. Two squabbling midgets, that's a rare bonus, let's crane our necks and listen. But I was in no mood to put up with that kind of humiliation, I had no desire to put on a show, so I moved away with as much dignity as I could, chin high, lips pursed, but the harm had been done, the customers, having decided it was funny, went on laughing. Someone who was too far away to hear Carmen and me even said, as I was walking past the booth where the disgusting remains of the gargantuan meal he and his obese friend had devoured sat on the table, "Lovers' quarrel? You put your boyfriend in his place, eh?"

I replied without slowing down, without even looking at him, "My boyfriend, that? That little thing? I wouldn't want him as a rag to wash my floor! If you could get a look at my boyfriend, kiddo, your jaw would drop into the rest of your gravy!"

It was the first time I'd talked like that about somebody like me and immediately I felt deeply ashamed, as if I'd just betrayed my own race to get a laugh from someone. It was also the first time I'd boasted about having a boyfriend who was surprising for someone who looked like me. I stormed into the kitchen, leaned against the stainless steel counter piled with dirty dishes and cursed for one good minute—I who never curse. I used the whole Québécois repertoire, I stripped altars, insulted the Holy Family, distorting the name of every member, I even paid a brief visit to the English language, taking from it a few expressions that focussed more on sexuality than on religion. It did me a world of good. I felt as if I were spitting out venom,

Nick and Lucien gawked.

"I'm going to kill one! Hold me back or I'll kill one!"

The worst thing was that four plates were waiting for me on the warmer. I had to go back on the floor, appear in front of people I'd just inadvertently entertained, set down food swimming in grease on a table while acting as if nothing had happened.

"Goddamn shitty job!"

Nick leaned across the counter, reached out an arm to lift a lock of hair off my forehead.

"I've never heard you talk like that, Céline!"

"True. And I don't think it, for sure. But let me tell you again, it's such a relief: goddamn shitty job!"

I picked up my plates which were getting cold—tough luck for the customers—and left the kitchen, still cursing.

And the first person I saw, at the other end of the restaurant, was Gilbert, deep in conversation with François Villeneuve and Carmen. Three old pals who haven't seen each other for ages, who meet by chance and fraternize with slaps on the back and drunken, probably incoherent babbling.

Just what I needed.

I nearly flung my plates to the floor and ran away, with the firm intention of never coming back.

When Gilbert saw me arrive with my arms full, he threw his hands up and practically shouted, "At last! The woman I've been waiting for!"

He gave François Villeneuve a slap on the back, then came up to me, grinning from ear to ear.

I knew right away that he'd been drinking to curb the onset of an episode—a high most likely, from the odd look on his face that was so deceptive, that I'd learned to be wary of in recent weeks—and I quickly served my four plates, hoping I'd be able to draw him into the kitchen. We aren't allowed to take anyone in, for any reason, but I didn't want to have to sort things out with him in front of everybody. I'd already given the Sélect's customers plenty to laugh at without having Gilbert Forget deliver a declaration of love dripping with sentimentality that was dictated by an attack of circular madness plus a few too many beers.

"Gilbert, I really haven't got time for you right now, but we can talk in the kitchen for two minutes ... "

As I went past the table of the guy I'd talked back to earlier I wanted to shout, "See how handsome my boyfriend is? Mind you he's a pile of problems too!" Of course I did no such thing. Especially because Gilbert was talking to me while he followed me down the noisy, crowded aisle.

"It won't take long, Céline my love. I've just got a little favour to ask you ... "

It was the first time he'd turned up at the restaurant to ask for a favour and I was immediately alarmed.

"Couldn't it wait till the end of my shift?"

"No. I need you right away or, well, practically right away ... "

"During the suppertime rush?"

"Afterwards if you want, around seven-thirty, eight ... "

Nick folded his arms when he saw us come in.

"Céline, I'm warning you ... "

I cut him off, raising my arms in a sign of peace. One argument was enough for the time being.

"Two minutes, Nick, I think it's important ... "

He went back to his grill, muttering something in his mother tongue, Greek, the translation of which I wouldn't want to know.

Gilbert was more and more agitated, the effect of the alcohol must have dissipated faster than he'd reckoned.

"You'll have to come with me ... "

"You want me to leave my work in the middle of supper?"

"No, no, not right away, I told you ... Look, it's very simple ... "

"No, it isn't simple at all. Leaving your work in the middle of your shift isn't simple, Gilbert, it's complicated!"

"You don't understand ... "

"You're right, I don't understand ... and I'm not sure I want to."

He knelt down in front of me. The anguish I could see in his darkly circled eyes, absolute and uncontrollable, took my breath away. And at that moment I knew that no matter how absurd what he was about to ask, I would do it, even if it was just to see the disappearance of what I sensed was his panic, to relieve for a while, no matter what it might cost me, the unbearable hell where he found himself because of that damn illness. Yes, I was at that point. Distraught because I realized that he could make me do almost anything, but prepared to take on anything to help him.

"I'd like you to come to the rehearsal at the Quat'Sous with me tonight."

I nearly burst out laughing. In amazement.

"Gilbert! Why on earth do you want that?"

He put his hand over my mouth so gently that my eyes filled with tears. Instead of hitting me to make me listen as someone else might have done, he caressed my mouth.

"Please! Listen to me! Stop interrupting!"

I let him know that I wouldn't interrupt anymore and he took his hand away.

"I didn't go to the last rehearsals ... I was ... I wasn't well. And I get the impression I'm about to be kicked out ... But I know all the scores by heart, that's not a problem, I'm not endangering the show ... I know you think it's ridiculous but ... The guys have been bringing their girlfriends to rehearsal for a while now ... To test the material, see how people will react ... You've never gone, though, even when I invited you ... And since they all like you a lot ... I don't know ... See, I think it's silly too when I'm explaining it to you ... But if you're there, Céline, to explain, I think they'll listen to you ... they'll believe you! They won't believe me, they think I'm a slacker! Ask somebody to fill in for you, just for one night, and come with me! I know it's a lot to ask but it's the last time, I swear!"

The promises of a drunk I'd heard all through my childhood and I've known for a long time how to flush them out, how to know that I am being manipulated before it even happens, and I learned from my mother's alcoholism how to resist them. Now though, facing Gilbert's woes, his helplessness, his undeniable sincerity—because I was convinced that he was unaware of the true meaning, of the outrageousness of what he was asking me, I admit that I was at a loss.

Without replying, I went to ask Madeleine if she could fill in for the rest of the evening. Janine, who'd heard me, frowned. No doubt she sensed that a big fat problem was about to appear on the horizon and she was already licking her lips.

Gilbert went to sit with François and Carmen, who'd found a very good table, and had supper with them. He'd met them in the late 1950s at El Cortijo, where François Villeneuve had sung for a few months, and he was clearly happy to have found them. The beginning of his manic phase made him talkative, he gladly made them laugh with his never-ending drunken tales. He cruised them both shamelessly, behaving as if he didn't realize it. Now and then he checked his watch, then looked in my direction. Around a quarter to eight the place suddenly emptied and Madeleine came to tell me I could leave.

"Are you sure you know what you're doing?"

"What I'm doing, no—but I know why!"

Janine snorted one of her cynical laughs that every time make my hair stand on end, they're so spiteful.

"I hope it's worth it!"

With François and Carmen gone after lengthy hugs and vague promises to get together again, Gilbert, who'd paid the bill like a great lord though of course he couldn't afford it, joined me at the waitresses' table. None of my co-workers said a word to him. There too he acted as if he didn't see it and was quite charming with them, despite his impatience to go.

Just as we were going out the door, I said to him, "Didn't you tell me, Gilbert, to never get mixed up in things that are none of my business?"

"It's different this time, I'm the one who asked you!"

Floating in the air around him was the universal smell of alcohol being digested, of old beer fermenting, that was so familiar to me. It did not augur well for the events to come. I followed him, sighing.

Going back up St. Denis towards Pine Avenue where the Quat'Sous is located—and with an agitated and talkative Gilbert keeping the conversation going—I thought rather incredulously about the absurdity of what I was doing—in my opinion, the equivalent of a mother writing a note to the principal of her little boy's school to apologize for his playing hooky. I was agreeing to be Gilbert's alibi, his screen, the person he could hide behind to exonerate himself of all his mistakes. But I couldn't turn him down. Refusing to do this favour would be tantamount to breaking up, to erasing him from my life, because I knew that I wouldn't be able to go on seeing him without helping him. And I loved him, I imagine, precisely because of the way he needed me. Greta-la-Vieille had never been able to replace Gilbert, but Gilbert may have been in the process of finding himself a second Greta-la-Vieille.

He took my hand while we were going up the Sherbrooke hill and I pictured with dread a papa who is dragging along his little girl, when what was happening was the very opposite.

The Théâtre de Quat'Sous is located in a former synagogue at the corner of Pine Avenue and Coloniale Street, in the heart of a residential neighbourhood where you wouldn't expect to see one. It doesn't look like a theatre, unlike the Comédie-Canadienne or the Rideau-Vert, where the lights of a marquee proclaim the title of the play being performed and posters are pasted all over; it's a simple and beautiful square house, painted all white, with an attractive wrought-iron balcony just above the entrance and old windows of finely-worked wood that had been bricked-up without disfiguring them.

There was just one poster on the front of the theatre, a fairly big one, on which was written the title of the show, which I didn't understand till I'd read it aloud in my head: *Osstidcho*. I smiled. They'd come up with a title that translated their exasperation when they were trying to find it. But did it give a good idea of the contents? I might be able to judge that in the next few minutes and I started to feel excited.

I'd never been inside the Quat'Sous and I was surprised that I had to go down some stone steps to reach the entrance, which was in a semi-basement, a massive door painted red.

The rehearsal was in full swing, you could catch the vibrations all the way to the sidewalk on Pine Avenue. If someone was singing you couldn't hear a voice, just the rhythm of the bass and the pounding of the drums. The immediate neighbours, if there were any, couldn't be very happy. About the theatre, yes, it's fairly reserved and discreet, but rock music ...

Once we were through the basement door the noise was deafening. What must it be like in the house? This time I could hear a man's voice drifting above the music. The song rocked, irresistible, it made you want to swing your rear. It seemed to be about some girl called Dolores.

At the back of the small dark lobby, on the right, was a carved wooden staircase—so the actual house wasn't in the basement—and Gilbert went to it right away.

"Hurry up, they started without me! They were supposed to start the run-through at show time! But it's just started … "

I climbed the stairs behind him as fast as I could, then ran down a kind of corridor parallel to the stairs which led to the house.

Our sudden appearance at the very start of the show was not what you'd call discreet: the old wooden stairs and the battered floor must have made a commotion to usher us in.

As soon as they saw Gilbert, the musicians stopped playing, Robert, the singer, broke off his song, and a silence as deafening as the music fell over the theatre.

They were all wearing white, miniskirts on the girls, well-cut pants on the guys. It was probably one of the first times they'd tried them on because they didn't seem comfortable yet. Or it was the "neat and tidy" aspect that bothered them. It was as if they'd all had a memory lapse at the same time, brought on by our arrival, and they stood there frozen at their microphones. The musicians behaved as if they weren't even there and stared vacantly at their instruments.

Yvon gestured to Gilbert to stay where he was and stepped down, careful not to soil his brand new costume.

"C'mon backstage, we have to talk."

Any more words were unnecessary: Gilbert and I had understood very well what would happen during the next few minutes and I saw Gilbert stiffen, then clench his fists. In a pitiful attempt to relax the atmosphere, to postpone the disastrous moment, he shrugged and tried to produce a laugh that sounded instead like an drinker's hiccup.

"We can't talk now, Yvon, we have to play! We start pretty soon … "

No one, of course, laughed. Those on the stage looked down, uncomfortable. As for me, I wanted the floor to swallow me so I could disappear, as I was obviously useless: there wasn't another girlfriend in the house. So Gilbert had lied to me—I hoped it was the first time—to lead me into this trap that was worthy of a fifteen-year-old, a final attempt I suppose to save his skin in the face of the inevitable conclusion to this ill-fated adventure. Unrealistic solution for an incorrigible dreamer.

Yvon was joined by another thin young man I'd seen a few times on television, a producer whose first name—Guy—was all I could remember. They flanked Gilbert, showing him a very small door cut into the wall on the right-hand side of the house.

"Come on backstage, Paul's expecting us."

Yvon looked at me, with a big smile that broke your heart.

"Hi, Céline ... We won't be long."

I sank into a seat at the back of the orchestra. So I was going to witness, helplessly, my boyfriend being fired, excluded from society for the umpteenth time, dismissed for good from the show he thought would finally prove to the world that he was good at something. I foresaw a disastrous outcome, permanent after-effects on both his health and his pride and self-confidence. His self-respect was already very low, now he was going to be thrust into unfathomable depths and it would be impossible to remove him. They were going to turn my already fragile lover into someone who was permanently, irreparably broken, and I was afraid I'd never be able to do anything for him again. By excluding him, by frustrating him forever, they were unfairly taking away the small amount of influence I had over him, and I wanted to scream, beg them to give him one last chance; I was even prepared to write a goddamn absentee note and get it signed by a doctor I'd have to pay through the nose!

Voices rose from backstage, mainly the easily recognized booming voice of Paul Buissonneau, the director of the Théâtre de Quat'Sous, who was obviously exasperated; bits of remarks came to me, reproaches, final words, charged with meaning, that I'd have preferred not to hear: " ... goddamn pigheaded ... " " ... how many times did we ... " " ... too late now ... " "May 28, Gilbert, it's just around the corner ... " "can't trust you ... " " ... you fucking idiot!"

Gilbert's protests, if there were any, didn't reach me. I could picture him, shattered, head hanging, incredulous despite the obvious, unable to react despite his manic state, already prepared to take refuge in dreams or allow himself to sink into his illness for good. With his private nurse beside him to hold his hand. Once again I was going to inherit a human wreck, like the one and maybe worse than what I'd found in the kitchen the day after our second encounter.

And the Gilbert who walked through the little wooden door a few minutes later was in fact unrecognizable. White as a sheet, bent, aged, his face impenetrable, he was holding his guitar against his chest. Not once did he look in the direction of the stage and he walked past me without seeing me. Had the high he'd been on just minutes before been transformed already into a destructive depression?

The three men followed him, heads hanging as well, sad—you could see it on their faces—at having had to fire an artist. But they had no choice, I understood that only too well. Gilbert had been warned repeatedly and the show was starting in a few days, they couldn't risk his not showing up.

Just before he left, though, Gilbert regained a semblance of courage. He turned towards the stage, raised his head as he placed his guitar on his shoulder and declared with great assurance (it would be the last time for a good while), "You'll hear about me one of these days!"

His pride was intact but not his honour.

Going down the wooden staircase was slower but just as noisy.

Once I was back in the lobby I heard the music start up again. "Dolorès, ô toi, ma douloureuse … " Gilbert had already been forgotten. The show must go on. So it seems.

The first thing Gilbert did when he left the theatre was to demolish his guitar on the wrought iron fence that lines the sidewalk on Pine Avenue. A few seconds of violence, three blows dealt with unusual force against the black metal fence pickets that glistened in the dark, and the guitar no longer existed. His dream. All that remained of it were some shapeless pieces of wood. The neck of the instrument, broken, was still attached to the disembowelled body by the few strings that had held out. It could have been the debris from a mobile that hadn't worked. Gilbert looked at what he'd just done as if he weren't aware of the seconds that had just gone by. A passer-by on the other side of the street seemed ready to intervene if things became toxic. I gestured to him to stay where he was, that things were under control.

Gilbert ran his hand over his face.

"I had to do it, Céline. Or else I would've done it to myself."

I spoke before I thought.

"Or to me."

At that, he gave me a look that I'll never forget, a mixture of love, adoration and pleading. Of astonishment too, that I'd been able to come out with something so outrageous.

"No. Never. I'd never hit you, Céline. Never. I've told you that already! If I didn't hold back I would totally demolish the Théâtre de Quat'Sous, I feel strong enough, I'd kill them all one by one even though I know they had to do what they did ... but you ... I'd never lay a hand on you."

He'd raised his voice above the music—the rhythm, rather, because we couldn't hear a single voice or recognize any tune—that was coming from the theatre. He held up his fist like the black Americans we're seeing a lot of on TV, but in his case it wasn't a rallying cry, it was an irreversible and definitive curse. He himself was cursed, now he was cursing others so he wouldn't be the only one to fall.

"I've got nothing left! Are you all happy? Nothing! Except for Céline Poulin, waitress at the Sélect, who honours me with her love though I don't deserve it, at least I hope she does, I've got nothing left! You were my last chance! You selfish bastards, leaving me all alone with my mental illness, you can take your *Osstidcho* and shove it! And Yvon's boss and Robert's Dolores too! I hope you'll pay for what you just did! Even if it was the right thing! Even if I'm totally wrong! You and your big fat dream could end up in the hole too, you know! Maybe you'll envy me the day after your première, you'll envy me for not making a fool of myself in front of your invited audience! And your humiliation will be worse than mine because it's public!"

He fell to his knees beside the fence, gripping the fragments of his guitar.

"I'm not even thinking before I speak. But I have to say it!"

I went and stood behind him and put my arms around his neck. We were the same height, as we are when he bends down to talk to me, but this time it was me reassuring him.

"Say what you have to say, Gilbert. Let yourself go. I'm here. If you go too far, I'll hold you back ... I'll sit on the steps of the theatre and keep an eye on you."

Which is what I did.

What happened during the next fifteen minutes was one of the most beautiful but most disturbing things I've ever seen. A poignant scene presented not by an actor doing it to earn his bread and butter, but by a poor shmuck who's been overwhelmed by circumstances he brought on himself and was now trying to exorcise his pain with curses, reproaches, directed at himself as well as others, sobs that he didn't hold back but allowed to gush out. He paced up and down the sidewalk on Pine Avenue like a furious tiger locked inside his cage, he screamed, he muttered, still holding at arms' length or against his heart the remnants of his guitar, the remains of his dream, he laughed, he cried, he went with no transition from elation close to ecstasy to the black depths of depression. The few passers-by thought he was a dangerous lunatic. I reassured them and persuaded them with a gesture to continue on their way and ignore us. Lunatic. Maybe he was, during those fifteen minutes when he let out all his spiteful anger and all his pain. Holding back nothing.

And all that time the music went on as if everything was normal. Could they hear him? Probably not. They thought he'd gone home with his midget, I imagine. Had he told them about his illness, had he tried to explain it? No matter. Whether they knew about his condition or not, they had a show to put on and nothing must interfere.

Exhausted, frenzied, he finally sat beside me on the stone steps.

"That must've been a pretty ugly scene ... "

"Not at all, it was glorious!"

He leaned his head on my shoulder—he was sitting two steps lower—and immediately fell asleep. I think I did too, because I have no memory of the minutes or the hours that followed.

The trip home was horrible. He was indescribably dejected and I felt as if I were walking beside a zombie. As if his sleep had drained him of his entire substance, of all his resistance. He'd stopped protesting, he'd stopped cursing, he didn't even seem to realize where we were and what we were doing. This time again, I was the one who took him by the hand and guided him through the streets of Montreal. I didn't want to take a taxi because I thought the walk would do him good, but I soon regretted it. And when I finally did decide to hail one, of course there wasn't one to be seen. So we walked down St. Denis, which was empty and dead at this time of night, with me dragging him along like a ball and chain, him following like an obedient little boy.

He was very sick. For several days I took care of him, watched over him, consoled him as best I could. Again and again, I shuttled back and forth between my place on Place Jacques-Cartier and his on St. Rose, worried about Gilbert's condition, leaving his bedside to go to work or to change my clothes, the rest of the time bending over his bed or fixing light meals that he pushed away, or forcing him to get up and take a few steps while I freshened up his bed. He had a fever, his skin was as icy as a dead man's, at times I think he was even delirious. He refused to see a doctor, claiming it was just an episode a little more severe than usual and that it would pass. He kept apologizing for the state he was in, for having to impose it on me, but never did he tell me to leave him alone or to go home and rest.

Without daring to tell him though, I thought he was over-reacting. Not that what was happening to him wasn't serious, a dream that's broken always is, but he wasn't fighting, in fact he didn't seem to know how, he was letting himself slide into depression because no one had shown him anything else, or else it was easier than trying to resist, and so he was passive when he should have been fighting. And inevitably, at the same time I felt guilty for judging him. Who was I to judge someone else's unhappiness, or his reactions? The things I'd experienced, even my worst humiliations, were nothing next to the terrible illness that seemed to leave its victims at a loss, no matter how grave or trivial the events that triggered it. I was a fighter, it had saved my life a few times; he wasn't. But I couldn't be mad at him!

Yet I was mad at him. A little. I wished he'd make an effort, tell them all to screw off as he'd done outside the theatre, instead of his long tearful complaints about what they'd done to him; I wished he'd pull himself up, be aggressive and ready for revenge, I wished he'd buy himself another guitar, hold his head up, and throw himself into his work to prove to them that he could do it and that he was a talented musician. That's what I would have done. Which was the problem. The significant and inescapable difference between us. The enormous gulf that was impossible to cross. We were more than different from one another, we were opposites who'd been attracted, yes, but who were now at an impasse. At least I was. The image of a babysitter often came to mind. I saw myself being obliged to look after this big adolescent for months, even years, if our relationship lasted, fully aware of leaving him to his own responsibility, his own unconcern, while I was the voice of forced enthusiasm and boring common sense and it got me down.

I would sometimes watch him sleep and tell myself that it might be time to leave him with his problems and his illness if I wanted to save my own skin. If not I ran the risk of sinking with him. Once again I was faced with a double choice that would determine a good chunk of my own life. I nearly did it a number of times—write a quick note on a scrap of paper, slink away, asking him not to get in touch with me, run and shut myself inside my room or throw myself into work as a way of forgetting him. In the end though, that would be no more satisfying than looking after him: between being cooped up with my own selfishness, beneficial though it might be and throwing myself into a boundless devotion whose outcome I couldn't know, the choice wasn't too hard. Because Gilbert needed me, and because I didn't know what would happen to him if I left him to his fate. It was enough to persuade me to carry on.

And the fact that I loved him.

At first I refused to go with him to the opening of the *Osstidcho*. In fact I told him more than once that I thought it was a bad idea for him to go. It was good of them to invite him, it proved there were no hard feelings, but I was afraid that being at the show on the night of the grand première would open wounds inflicted too recently to be fully healed and throw him back into the depression from which it had been so hard for him to extricate himself. But he said that he felt better, that he was in good shape, that he was sure that seeing the *Osstidcho* would help him come to terms with the whole adventure, to accept the conclusion, to cauterize the wound for good. He had experienced the show from the inside, now he wanted to see what it would be like from the audience, with no remorse or regrets. And then turn his head in another direction.

He was convincing, I admit it. And I was naïve. Either that or I played naïve because I wanted so much for him to be better and hoped that he'd put an end to that chapter and move on to something else. Turn his head in another direction, in his own well-chosen words. I don't accept the notion that I was an idiot to let myself get caught again: it was strictly from a desire to close the book on a deplorable episode that I finally gave in, not from lack of judgment. Once the evening was over, or so I believed, we would finally be able to think about the future instead of concentrating on the recent and painful past. And if I regret it today, it's more because of the unfortunate incident which took place that night than because of the decision I made. For if he had been in a normal state, it is possible that Gilbert could have dealt with it once and for all. Most likely he would still be present in my life and I wouldn't be shut away here at home writing in my blue notebook to lick my wounds.

There was a lot about the show in the papers. On television too, but I was too busy to watch it and simply read the interviews, which were many and detailed, in the *Journal de Montréal* or *Montréal-Matin*. Which I was careful to hide so that Gilbert wouldn't see them. If he found them he said nothing to me about it.

I often thought about them. They were going to put on a show that they'd thought up, invented, produced from square one, mounted with the means available under the aegis of one of the most innovative theatres in town. They were arrogant and likeable, pretentious and touching in their sincerity, and quite obviously as scared as they claimed to be self-confident. I can't say that I envied them. I'd never felt any creative urge before I started, for reasons that were not at all artistic, to write my notebooks, but once again I couldn't help thinking about the twists and turns and mechanisms of fate. Two years earlier I had myself nearly taken part in a show that I left before the rehearsals began, for personal reasons; the year before I had worked in a brothel where every night a "recital" was put on by drag queens, and now my boyfriend being kicked out of a brand-new kind of show a few days before the first performance. Was I destined to constantly brush up against a theatre crowd without ever being part of it, to be the nice waitress whose customers were destined for a future that was fascinating if not glorious? Would all the roads that were presented to me with surprising regularity always lead to the Sélect, to its hamburger platters and shepherd's pie as interpreted by a Haitian assistant cook? Was I also prisoner of a kind of mood swing, a vicious circle that no matter what I did would always bring me to the same place, with an apron around my waist and a starched cap on my head? I was sometimes down; and I sometimes thought how lucky I was that fate had spared me the suffering that Gilbert experienced and that may lie in wait for all creative artists.

If they came to wolf down a club sandwich or a BLT after rehearsal, they would ask about Gilbert and I would tell them, without going into details though, so they wouldn't feel too guilty.

I was always polite and cold. They had hurt someone I loved, I understood why, but I wanted it to be perfectly clear that I would always be on his side. They accepted it without arguing, resumed their desultory conversations which more and more had to do with worries and anxiety. The première was approaching and I didn't dare tell them that I would be there with Gilbert.

The big night arrived and I have to say, I looked quite stunning. The day before I'd gone to St. Catherine Street West to look for something decent to wear and I came across a gorgeous pink silk T-shirt of normal length for any other woman but for me, a very interesting dress. With a black belt, nylons and a big shirt, also black, that I keep for important occasions, it makes for an outfit that's more than suitable and I was quite proud of what I saw in the mirror. No jewellery—that would be too big, too heavy on my small person, it disguises me and I haven't worn any since the Boudoir closed—just a hint of the dark red lipstick that's so flattering, a dusting of powder, a touch of mascara and that would be it.

When Gilbert arrived at the apartment on Place Jacques-Cartier, wound up and holding a bunch of flowers, I should have been on my guard. But I was happy to show myself off in my new finery and I thought he looked fantastic in brand-new jeans, a jacket I hadn't seen before, a white shirt and a narrow tie. Until then, Gilbert Forget in a white shirt and tie was a sight I'd have thought was unthinkable and I couldn't help letting out a little cry of surprise when I opened the door. And a little laugh when I saw the flowers.

"It's not my birthday, Gilbert!"

He merely held out the flowers with his devastating smile that made me melt. After a moment, he added, "With you, every day's a celebration."

It had taken him a while to make that reply, which surprised me: Gilbert's sense of repartee was usually quicker—and more cutting. This unusual slowness, on top of his obvious nervousness—slow and nervous?—should have got me thinking, but I suppose that for once I'd set aside my critical sense to concentrate on the evening that lay ahead. I didn't know what was in store for us, I just hoped it would be a success. I don't know why—that's not true, I know that it's called denial and I was a specialist in it from the days when I tried to excuse all of my mother's bad behaviour—I chose to focus on the flowers instead of on him. Concentrating on a negligible detail and not on what's important is a habit of people who don't want to see. For which they sometimes pay dearly.

"One would have been enough. But a whole bouquet ... "

He kissed me on the neck.

"It's to thank you."

"Thank me? For what?"

"For everything. For still being there in spite of everything. For putting up with me in spite of everything."

He also smelled of a new cologne, a little too strong, sugary, nearly sickening, instead of his inevitable patchouli. It didn't suit him at all, it smelled more like an American out on the town than the Gilbert Forget I loved, but I wasn't going to spoil his evening by pointing it out right now. I would tell him later, or tomorrow, not to use it. Meanwhile, he seemed anxious to leave.

I took the time to put the flowers in a vase. I didn't know of course that the first thing I would do when I came home later would be to throw it on the floor and stamp on the contents. But when I switched off the light I had a kind of foreboding. For a second or two I felt like calling it off, sending Gilbert home, claiming a sudden headache, and taking refuge in my bed, safe from ... From what? When I turned the key in the lock I was convinced that I was heading for disaster. If I'd known it was true would it have changed anything?

Gilbert was waiting for me in front of the house, impatient and agitated.

For years now I've been out of the habit of going out at night. When I see a movie it's in the afternoon, most of the time the first screening. I like to settle in with my bag of chips and my Coke at the empty Loew's, the Saint-Denis or the Palace, lose myself in the darkness in the vast picture box, enter the lives of other people— foreigners, usually, French, Americans, sometimes Italians, and never midgets—which are presented to me readymade, improved, easily understood, colourful and soon forgotten. I suffer with them for two hours or else I laugh like a loon at their unlikely adventures, then go home sated. Nights, I work. On my days off I take care of myself. And my three roommates.

I felt very strange then as I made my way with Gilbert to the Théâtre de Quat'Sous. A real night out. At a real theatre. With a real boyfriend on my arm. It wasn't afternoon, I wasn't alone and, for once, I was going to the theatre and not a movie.

I should have been happy. I was anxious.

The sky, towards what we call the north in Montreal but which is actually west, since the island sits lopsided in the St. Lawrence River, had taken on the nearly violent pink colour that we see after sunset in May. The colour would turn violet before we got to the Quat'Sous, then disappear, forgotten until morning as the sky always is in big cities. No stars therefore, save on streets that are very dark; the moon sometimes, when it's full or almost. It was mild, nearly hot, the people we met looked cheerful, I sensed less mockery or irony in their eyes. Or else my usual paranoia being focussed elsewhere, I didn't see it.

I was keeping an eye on Gilbert, I was afraid that he'd notice and be hurt. Instead of enjoying the present moment, I was analyzing every move he made, every word he said, trying to interpret them, to see if he was over-excited or showing the beginnings of gloom or depression, I was still trying to find a meaning in the bouquet of flowers, in the weird conversation we'd had before leaving my apartment, I was doing everything I could, in fact, to check and see whether he was showing signs of the beginning of an episode.

Talkative and, I have to admit, calmer since we'd turned north onto St. Denis, he was gradually becoming my Gilbert again, thoughtful and funny. All at once he seemed glad to be there, talking about the colours of the sky and how peaceful St. Denis Street was at this time of day, and I decided that I'd try to be like him. As we walked past the Sélect, I waved to Madeleine and Janine, who waved back appreciatively. About how I was dressed of course, not about whom I was with, because they still thought that he didn't deserve me. Feeling even prettier I straightened up proudly in my already high heels and hung onto my boyfriend's arm. Out of pure bravado, but also because I felt like it. It was the first time I'd taken the initiative and Gilbert covered my hand with his to show his gratitude. Who knows, maybe the evening would unfold better than I'd predicted.

A small line had formed outside the theatre, the stone steps leading to the basement were crowded with chic, excited people who were talking loudly and laughing for no reason. Gilbert showed his first signs of impatience.

"I hate waiting in line … I can't stand it … "

"It'll move quickly, Gilbert, there aren't that many people … "

"I don't care, I still hate it … "

He'd stuffed his hands in his pockets and was jingling his change, something I can't bear because it reminds me too much of the men in my family, uncles and cousins who to make themselves look important would shake their change while shamelessly making stupid remarks.

But I didn't mention it for fear of offending him by comparing him with some uncle or other. This was not the time or the place.

By chance, as the Quat'Sous was a small theatre, the wait wasn't long and after a few moments of fidgeting and muttering, Gilbert was able to pick up our tickets.

The lobby was packed, it was hot, there was a strong smell of expensive perfume, and I took a deep breath before wading into it. My head was level with the behinds of most of the crowd and all I could see were well-cut trousers, new designer jeans and the backs of elegant dresses. But there too Gilbert had no intention of taking his place in line and he grabbed my hand and pulled me towards the head of the line.

"Come on, we're going to the front ... "

He elbowed his way, with *excuse me*'s and *sorry*'s under the protests of those who'd been standing in line for a while at the foot of the wooden stairs going up to the theatre.

A red velvet rope blocked the way. The theatre wasn't open yet. Gilbert, more and more nervous, tried to persuade the usher to let us in, I think he even used me as if I were a child who had to be seated right away, but she refused, saying that the theatre wasn't ready to let us in, that the pre-set wasn't finished.

And that was when I saw just how badly disturbed Gilbert was: he'd started to hop up and down like a little boy with an urgent need to pee. Until then I had been hoping that everything would go well, I imagine, I had blinded myself to what must have been perfectly obvious, but I was starting to dread the crisis that had been threatening to explode ever since he'd appeared at my house. It was too late to turn around and go back, a hundred people or so were pushing me from behind, excited and noisy, and with my small size I would have a terrible time clearing a path to the exit.

"I can't wait to see it! I can't wait!"

Gilbert was starting to explain to the usher, talking a little too loudly so that everyone in the small lobby could hear him, that he was supposed to be in the show as guitarist but that his health had made it impossible, when someone at the top of the stairs advised the young usher that the theatre was finally ready to receive the audience.

As soon as the velvet rope was removed, Gilbert raced to the stairs without bothering to finish his sentence. An animal released from his cage.

"Follow me, Céline, I want us to be the first ones in our seats … "

I've explained before that I've always had trouble climbing stairs, which are rarely adapted to my needs, so I wasn't able to follow him. Holding onto the wooden banister with my right hand, I climbed as quickly as I could but people were overtaking me, some of them laughing, thinking that we were part of the show: the impatient spectator who makes a fool of himself and the midget who's with them and tries to hold onto a semblance of dignity under the circumstances. If they'd known what I was living through—what Gilbert was living through as well—no doubt they wouldn't have laughed so hard and would have let me pass. I suppose it was easier for them to think that what they were witnessing wasn't serious: it was the première and, understandably, they didn't feel like witnessing a couple's squabbling or an episode of mental illness.

Once my ticket was torn at the top of the stairs, I raced into the theatre.

Gilbert was standing in the left-hand aisle, arms outstretched, while the other spectators looked for their seats. They were beginning to give him funny looks. They weren't so sure now that they understood what was going on.

"Look at that, Céline, isn't it fantastic! Look how fantastic it is!"

Some women had put their hands on the forearms of their companions, who were doing what they could to reassure them.

I positioned myself behind Gilbert and, as tactfully as I could, pulled on the hem of his new jacket.

"If you don't feel well, Gilbert, we could leave … "

What not to do.

He turned around, obviously stunned at what I'd just said.

"What are you talking about—if I don't feel well! I feel great, Céline, great! Better than ever! I can do anything!"

Before I realized it, he had straddled the space between him and the stage, climbed the little staircase that led up to it and was standing right in the middle of the musical instruments, arms still outstretched.

"This is where I belong, Céline! Right here! Onstage! Not on my ass with people who just want to watch—on my feet in front of them all, with my guitar! Here's where I want to be tonight! And every night to come!"

As my head barely reached the floor of the stage, he crouched down to talk to me.

"Understand, my love?"

I brought my hand up, stroked his face. The worst was that I understood very well. His tremendous suffering in the face of such injustice.

"Yes, I understand. But think about the others. It's their première. Don't spoil it for them, Gilbert. Let's go now."

He pulled himself up.

"They can't even hear me!"

He delivered some kicks to the floor.

"The wings are under the stage! They're probably thinking it's the audience that's noisy! Anyway, they don't give a shit about me! They're too busy focussing on the show they're putting on to think about a poor pathetic guitar player they kicked out because they couldn't count on him."

I could see from his eyes that he wasn't in his right mind. Everything he would say and everything he would do for as long as the episode lasted would be irrational, probably unconscious, and most of all, uncontrollable. I didn't know what to do now to get him off the stage. The theatre was gradually filling up and a few people had started to protest. But not too loudly, in case this painful, zany scene was part of the show and they were being taken for a ride. A fake melodrama while waiting for the real *Osstidcho*. A little provocation before the big one. They were thrown off, didn't know what to do—and they enjoyed it.

A well-built young man came up to me when I was starting up the steps to get Gilbert.

"Do you need help, Mademoiselle? Do you want us to get him down from there?"

Gilbert had heard him. He leaned over, picked me up and held me against his heart.

"I thought you'd understand me, Céline!"

Then he started to shake me up and down like a rag doll.

"I thought that you'd understand me! That you were the only person who could understand me!"

He was shaking me harder and harder, I was having trouble breathing, I could barely hear the clamour coming from the audience.

The young man was climbing onto the stage to help me out when my nose started to bleed. A fountain of blood gushed from my nostrils, onto my dress and Gilbert's new jacket. And all I could think of was that, for once, Gilbert was wearing a white shirt and it was being spattered with indelible blood. I couldn't cry out though, I was too shocked to react.

As soon as he saw the blood, Gilbert froze as if he'd been shot in the forehead. The horror I could see in his eyes was indescribable.

"I didn't want to hurt you! Forgive me! I didn't want to hurt you!"

He held me tightly. I bled onto his neck and his shirt collar.

"You're holding me too tight, Gilbert … You're suffocating me … "

He set me down on the stage, all signs indicating that he was horrified at what he'd just done.

"Forgive me, Céline! For God's sake, forgive me!"

He jumped down into the house and cleared a path for himself, again using his elbows. He knocked over the young man who'd come to my rescue and a few chic ladies who made little cries like frightened birds. A few people were laughing, others protesting, all were on their feet. Some in the balcony were leaning over the guard-rail, those behind them were craning their necks.

I'd taken a Kleenex out of my purse and wiped my nose. I'd never had a nosebleed before, even as a child. And it had to happen in public, on a stage, in front of people who had no idea what was going on. It's stupid but I thought about my mother, who claimed that if you put a key on your neck the bleeding stops right away and I almost asked for one ... Peace was coming back to the theatre but the audience was still looking at me, still undecided about what had just happened before their eyes. Real blood? Stage blood? A legitimate couple, mismatched as it was, that was coming apart in front of them, or excellent actors paid to pass the time while they waited for the show to begin?

To reassure them I made what could be seen as a curtsey and a few people applauded.

Then I climbed down from the stage as best I could, pushing away anyone who tried to help me.

"It's not serious, it's not serious, let me through ... "

Was she still in her role? Had she really bled and was she trying to save face? They would never know. As for me, I just hoped that those responsible for the show that was about to begin didn't know what was going on. I was sure that such an incident couldn't help the stage fright that must be stifling them. No more than two minutes had passed since we'd entered the theatre and I prayed that they'd been spared all of it—Gilbert's crisis, my nosebleed.

Going down a staircase against the traffic is not all that easy, especially if you're a midget with a nosebleed and the rest of the crowd is all worked up because something that's about to happen. Now it was my turn to use my elbows and I must have left bloodstains on a few hands and several dresses as I charged down the stairs.

Gilbert was waiting for me on the sidewalk in front of the theatre, or rather, he had collapsed on the top step of the old stone staircase and was sobbing into his hands. He knew of course that I would leave the theatre, but I'm not convinced that I was the one he was waiting for. His strength had left him as he exited the theatre and he'd collapsed there and waited for someone—me or some other person—to come and pick him up. A few spectators who were no doubt afraid of being late, walked past him, scowling. They must have been wondering who was this hysterical man crying at the door to the Théâtre de Quat'Sous just before showtime. Someone who'd been turned away because he didn't have a ticket? No, surely not … A passing drunk who'd taken refuge on the steps to sleep it off? But he was clean and didn't smell of booze … They didn't have time to see the red patches on his neck or else it was too dark and they walked around him, cursing because he was slowing them down.

I plunked myself in front of him and put my hands on his knees. He wiped his eyes, raised his head, looked at me. He was more than desolate, he was devastated. I wished I were at the other end of the world or in his arms, more nearby, on St. Rose Street, doing things that are said to be forbidden because they're too wonderful, but I was there at the Théâtre de Quat'Sous and I had no choice: the scene that was getting underway was inescapable and it had to unfold right here, right now, an improvised ceremony we hadn't had time to prepare but that had become necessary and that we could throw ourselves into as if into water that was cold and dark and threatening and maybe deadly. I talked to him very gently but also very firmly. Circular madness or not, severe or mild episode, I had to talk now or else I would again wait, stall, repress what I had to say and it would stay forever caught in my throat. And once again I would emerge as the loser. And so I had to think first about myself, about what would be good for me, about my safety.

"I'm very patient, Gilbert. I can take it. For a long time. I'm used to it. But you have to understand, there's one thing I'll never accept. Violence. No, don't say anything, I know what you're going to say. You didn't mean to be violent, you didn't mean to hurt me, I know all that … But if you lost control once, Gilbert, you can lose it again, any time, and that, I refuse, I refuse to play the part of a willing and understanding victim. Too many women before me have put up with that. I'd rather live with self-imposed loneliness than with violence that involves us both but has me as the only target!"

It was my turn to make a scene and it was long, impassioned, lyrical almost, outside the Théâtre de Quat'Sous, and while inside the show was starting—what we could hear was shapeless but highly rhythmical and very happy—I was finally able to express all my doubts, my questions, my hesitations, I freed myself in one go, as he'd done a few days earlier, of something I'd held in for too long that had been suffocating me. He interrupted me now and then to protest, to swear once again that he loved me or to reassure me about one specific point, but I told him to be quiet, to let me have my say, as I'd done in this same spot on the night when he was fired. Now I was the one who was crying. Because I knew that what I was doing was final, that the outcome of this monologue was inevitable and that killed me as much as it did him.

He felt it too because he began to punctuate everything I said with just one reply that he repeated almost non-stop and louder and louder, "You're going to leave me! You're going to leave me! Céline! Please don't do that! Don't leave me all alone!"

I took my time, not to be mean but because I wanted everything to be very clear, my reproaches and rebukes, my anxiety and my helplessness as much as my irrevocable and entirely improvised decision that I was making as I was expressing it, perhaps even to explain to myself what I was doing while I was doing it. Half an hour earlier there'd been no question of breaking up with Gilbert and here I was doing just that, breaking up with the first great love of my life with no preparation and more important, without the slightest wish to do so.

I cried as much as he did, I think I even tried to console him with stroking and kisses that came more from despair at having to leave him than from a need to touch him.

"I'm going up these steps, Gilbert, I'm going to find a taxi and I'm going to disappear from your life ... I don't want to see you any more. I have to save my own skin, do you understand? If you love me the way you say you love me, let me go ... Later on, we'll see ... maybe."

My last image of him is of a man collapsed on a stone staircase, seen from behind. And the last sound is a dagger thrust into my heart, "You're abandoning me too, just like the others!"

Manipulation or desperation? How could I know?

Was the break too abrupt?

Quite possibly.

There's no night when I don't think about him, about the pain I inflicted on him, about the extreme harshness of the decision I'd made so quickly, of the sentence carried out so hastily. But it's not so much the sentence that I regret as having had to impose it on a man I loved so much. And still love, I can't hide it.

Does the first great love always hurt so much?

I know that I made Gilbert suffer a lot. And I know that I suffered a lot too. That I'm still suffering. It's very hard to pretend that you don't have a heart when it's all you have left. Even today I'm still torn between two choices, as usual: he phoned me just now, reason told me to react coldly to his sobs when my entire person, my soul as much as my body, wanted only one thing, to forgive. Actually, I forgave him some time ago, but I refuse with all my might to forget. That's something else I get from my mother: forgive, yes; forget, never.

I must not forget what he would be capable of doing despite how much he loved me, how much I loved him. My three roommates and the Duchess were right on that first night—Gilbert is all the more dangerous because he's adorable. His illness, that madness with the lovely name, makes him vulnerable and touching, but I have to be wary. At least that's what I remind myself every time he phones, every time he rings my doorbell, holding a bunch of flowers, every time I receive a letter overflowing with feelings, promises and resolutions. And every time my imagination takes me to his body, his odour, his humour, his kindness. But that's getting harder and harder. Because instead of sending him away as I had hoped, time has a tendency to erase Gilbert's flaws, to make them seem ordinary, and I'm afraid that it will make them disappear altogether and impose on me a flattering memory of him that will send me into the twists and turns of regret and guilt, a trap that I want to avoid at all costs.

At least until the pain has subsided.

If Gilbert had been hateful my life wouldn't have been so complicated.

My story is over, I am closing my blue notebook with no intention or desire to start another. Maybe some day, if life should take me down some avenues that are interesting, surprising and worthy of being recounted, I may want to rediscover the joy of writing, who knows ... For now, I'm back where I began, the Sélect, with the customers, waitresses, hamburger platters, the comfortable little everyday life that does no harm except in the long run, and I fully intend to hold on for as long as possible.

*She doesn't dare to write the words* The End. *She didn't write them at the end of her other two notebooks and she feels that if she does so now, if she put them at the bottom of the last page of this one, she would be doing something too final, something she still feels unable to accept. Writing has given her a lot over the past two years—relief first of all, then pride at finding out how it was done and how gratifying it could be—Ah! The joy of finding* le mot juste, *the best formulation, the unusual turn of phrase, the pleasure of making others speak and preserving all the flavour!—But she suspects that the life she has chosen to impose on herself for the future, to protect herself, to avoid depending on what she calls the iniquities of fate that have bounced her around and shaken her up so much in recent years, will not be subject to confidences or to long explanations and while she is relieved, she can't help feeling a twinge of regret at the thought of never again bending over a blank page, worried that she cannot express herself clearly or upset by what she has to describe. What will replace these hours of pure joy and huge anxiety? Too much concern about her three roommates who could very well take advantage of her without realizing it? Waitress at the Sélect, waitress in the apartment on Place Jacques-Cartier?*

*Is that how she thinks of herself after all that she has gone through, all that she has learned? Of course not. She knows that she's capable, she knows that she has strengths she knew nothing about in the past; for now though, she feels that she needs a long rest, away from risky encounters, misplaced impulses, questionable choices.*

*To cure herself of Gilbert Forget?*

*To cure herself of Gilbert Forget.*

*Now that she finally accepts that she is worthy of someone's love, she feels that she has to forget him, erase him from her life, though she doesn't have even a shadow of an intention to look elsewhere, to set out to find a Prince Charming. For now, it's Gilbert or nothing.*

*She shuts the blue notebook, brings it to her lips. It smells of paper, of ink, of the polished wood of her worktable too.*

*Outside, it is pitch dark. She heard her three roommates come in earlier; high-heeled shoes were thrown around the parlour helter-skelter, there've been shrieks of boozy laughter, two or three bitchy remarks that she couldn't catch were tossed off like a final bouquet to a night like every other, made up of strenuous cruising and disappointing tricks.*

*Just before dawn broke, at the moment when you despair of the night's ever ending, everything is darker, anxiety more acute, regrets more bitter. If she weren't holding herself back she would be dialling Gilbert's number and in less than half an hour she would be in his arms.*

*Dear God, how sweet it was! The joy of it!*

*She pushes the blue notebook next to the other two. She has moved from the black of ignorance to the red of discovery and then to the blue of fulfillment. But above the fulfillment lurked a circular madness, the inevitable stumbling block cast by fate onto every success, and it's that same illness which she has to fight against or accept if she wants to take her fulfillment to its completion.*

*But not now. Not right away. She's too exhausted.*

*Later on, if she can't shake off the idea of her longing for Gilbert, who knows, maybe she …*

*No. No hopes. No promises. She has to be strong.*

*And it's true that it's all she has left: her strength and her heart.*

In this blue notebook I've invented a narrator, male or female, it doesn't matter, who watched me write, a second writer, the real one, who guided my hand when I ran out of courage, and put some order into my ideas when my uncertainties became too significant. I sensed him, let's say him for simplicity's sake, leaning over my shoulder, following my writing, guiding it, lavishing advice when it was going badly or compliments if I was able to express properly the essence of my thoughts. And allowing himself now and then to make comments. I wasn't writing, he was, even if it was written in the first person. And by me.

I hoped that imagining this notebook being composed by someone else who was dictating it to me would give me a certain distance, provide me with me an objectivity I couldn't achieve otherwise. I treated myself like a character in a novel who is writing what someone else is dictating, and now that my blue notebook is finished, I would like the other person, the true author of the novel—because then it would be a novel—to take my destiny in hand, replace me definitively and suggest or, rather, predict for me how all of it—my existence, its meaning if it has one—will end. What will become of Gilbert and me. And whether some day I will go back to the writing that I love so much. As for me, I don't know. Not him (or her). He could decide that it will end well, or not; suggest either a ray of hope or the bleak ending of a hardboiled novel; he could throw me— and deep down that's what I would like!—back into Gilbert's arms, find a cure for his circular madness, a miracle remedy, a panacea, and give me back my happiness. Give me back my happiness. It's all I ask for.

That's what the narrator of a novel should do, isn't it? Find an ending. A fair one.

I am looking for a fair ending.

*Key West, 19 December 2004–4 May 2005*

Translator's Note:

To understand the significance of the show at the Théâtre de Quat'Sous, *Osstidcho*, you have to know something about cursing in Quebec. While English words of anger and insult usually have to do with bodily functions, as Céline has noted a few pages back, the francophone Quebec equivalents come from religion, from the Roman Catholic church. The most powerful of these is *hostie*, the sacred host, which like the English *fuck* can be, variously, noun or verb or modifier.

In 1968, to use the word publicly was very daring. To call a popular entertainment an *osstidcho* (*hostie de show*) would be like naming one *this fucking show* in English. The show in question, which premiered on 28 May 1968, at the Théâtre de Quat'Sous, was as revolutionary as its creators hoped.

As were a number of the participants and some other individuals, such as the fictional Gilbert Forget, who moved in the same circles. You'll have met some of them in the preceding pages: curly-haired Robert, author of the song about airplanes and airlines, is Robert Charlebois; the song, "Lindbergh," is a Quebec classic and Charlebois himself can now be seen from coast to coast to coast on a postage stamp. Louise is the well-known singer Louise Forestier; Yvon, beloved monologist Yvon Deschamps; Rita, the marvelous actress Rita Lafontaine; the unnamed young theatre director, the famous André Brassard; and the hairy youth whose first play is about to be performed is famous too, as both playwright and novelist—in fact you've just read one of his latest.

The theatre itself, located part-way between the homes of the author and the translator of this book, was torn down some months ago and replaced by a beautiful new version in steel, cement and glass where, who knows, a landmark twenty-first-century theatre piece may well be in rehearsal at this very moment.

Sheila Fischman